By the Author

The Scotty Bradley Adventures

Bourbon Street Blues

Jackson Square Jazz

Mardi Gras Mambo

Vieux Carré Voodoo

Who Dat Whodunnit

Baton Rouge Bingo

Garden District Gothic

The Chanse MacLeod Mysteries

Murder in the Rue Dauphine

Murder in the Rue St. Ann

Murder in the Rue Chartres

Murder in the Rue Ursulines

Murder in the Garden District

Murder in the Irish Channel

Murder in the Arts District

Young Adult

Sleeping Angel

Sara

Lake Thirteen

New Adult

Timothy

The Orion Mask

Dark Tide

Women of the Mean Streets: Lesbian Noir

Men of the Mean Streets: Gay Noir

Night Shadows: Queer Horror
(edited with J. M. Redmann)

Love, Bourbon Street: Reflections on New Orleans
(edited with Paul J. Willis)

GARDEN DISTRICT GOTHIC

by

Greg Herren

A Division of Bold Strokes Books

2016

GARDEN DISTRICT GOTHIC
© 2016 By Greg Herren. All Rights Reserved.

ISBN 13: 978-1-62639-667-8

This Trade Paperback Original Is Published By
Bold Strokes Books, Inc.
P.O. Box 249
Valley Falls, NY 12185

First Edition: September 2016

CREDITS
EDITOR: STACIA SEAMAN
PRODUCTION DESIGN: STACIA SEAMAN
COVER DESIGN BY MELODY POND

Acknowledgments

It's hard to believe this is Scotty's seventh time around the block.

He was originally supposed to be a standalone, which turned into a trilogy, and then somehow just kept going. He is quite literally the ex-stripper who won't go away. So, to begin with, I need to thank everyone at Kensington, especially John Scognamiglio, who first saw something in the slutty go-go dancer and his friends and family and let me write three Lambda Award–nominated books about him; the original Scotty trilogy.

When I thought, you know, there's still some story left in Scotty—mainly because so many people kept asking about him and how he and the gang had fared during and after Katrina—Bold Strokes Books gave him a new home, allowed him to grow up some, and let me keep writing about him. So, thanks to Radclyffe for saying yes the first time, Stacia Seaman for being an amazing editor, Sandy Lowe for her frightening efficiency, and Ruth Sternglantz for about a million other things. Bold Strokes has been, time after time, one of the greatest experiences of my checkered publishing career, and I appreciate all the opportunities you've all given to me—not to mention all the friends. Nell Stark, Trinity Tam, Anne Laughlin, Carsen Taite, Lisa Girolami, Ali Vali, Lynda Sandoval, and so many others have made me laugh until my sides hurt, given me a whole new appreciation for Monty Python, and just made my life better for being a part of it.

You really haven't lived until you've sat next to Ali Vali on a three-and-a-half-hour flight.

My day job: people like Luke LaCava, Morgan Culver, Alex Leigh, Lindsay Peters, Ainsley Bryce, Jesse Campbell, Lauren Gautier, Joey Olsen, and of course, my boss, Allison Vertovec—all of you make my days brighter. Seriously. I mean it. No, REALLY.

So many friends: Al and Harriet Campbell-Young, Michael Carruth and John Angelico, Mark Richards, Stan and Janet Daley Duval (GEAUX TIGERS!), Konstantin Smorodnikov, Jean Redmann and Gillian Rodger, Amie E. Evans, Carol Rosenfeld, Michele Karlsberg, Elaine Viets, Kris Montee, Wendy Corsi Staub, Michael Thomas Ford, Lisa Morton, Rena Mason, Sally Anderson, Dawn LoBaugh, Karen Bengtsen, Valerie Fehr Ruelas, Kara Keegan, Stephen Driscoll and Rob Tocci, Stuart Wamsley, Donna Andrews, Sarah Weinman, Jeffrey Marks, Jeffrey Ricker and Michael "SB" Wallenstein, 'Nathan and Dan Smith, Becky Cochrane, Tom aka Mr. Becky, Timothy J. Lambert, Rob Byrnes, Susan Larson, Michael Ledet and Patricia Brady, Jesse and Laura Ledet, Bede and Melissa Costanza, Victoria Brownworth, Twist Phelan, Erin Mitchell, and so many others I can't think of right now—if I've forgotten you it's not an indication of a lack of importance but rather my aging brain.

Of course, if you can't handle the truth, you can't handle the FLs—even if you're wild about dogs but not crazy about bitches.

And Paul, who made all my dreams come true.

Well, sooner or later, at some point in your life, the thing that you have lived for is lost or abandoned, and then...you die or find something else.

Tennessee Williams, *Sweet Bird of Youth*

Prologue

A New Orleans summer is like a gay man. Ripe, hotly passionate, but fickle, he comes and goes as he pleases, leaving behind damp sheets, sweaty skin, and clothes that are soaked through. He brings the humidity with the heat when he arrives in early May, sometimes not leaving until after Labor Day, sometimes overstaying his welcome and not leaving until mid-October. But when he does finally go, it's sudden; slipping out overnight while you sleep, leaving you to wake up to dry air and lower temperatures, with sunny days with blue skies and no humidity, days so beautiful that locals remember why we are so happy to live here again—something we always forget during those long, hellish days that seem never-ending in July and August. During those months, we wait anxiously for him to leave, as our power bills escalate and our laundry baskets grow ripe. The crowds of tourists start dwindling in mid-July until they are almost nonexistent in August, the hot smelly streets of the Quarter empty and forlorn, the shops and bars and restaurants empty, the ceiling fans overhead spinning crazily in desperate attempts to create a breeze in the soupy, thick air. There used to be an urban legend that the heat created pressure in the sewers beneath the city, the noxious fumes building as the sewage cooked in the heat until it became too much to be contained, blowing manhole covers sky-high with an explosive bang that rattled windows and set off car alarms. It is just a tale, of course, with everyone knowing someone who knows someone who witnessed it happen, and as you mop sweat off your face and your wet socks cling to your feet, it's not too hard to believe that such a thing could be true.

We'd been lulled into a false sense of complacency by a few mild summers in a row—three, to be exact—which also fooled everyone into thinking we'd gotten used to it at long last. So that certain summer when the weather returned to normal was like the nastiest, most unexpected bitch slap. To add insult to injury, it was a record-breaking summer for all three measures: temperature, humidity, *and* the heat index. The heat index hovered around an average of 124 for two consecutive weeks while almost every elective activity in New Orleans came to a screeching halt. Power bills skyrocketed, the air-conditioning in cars couldn't compete, and letting the cold water spigot run from the tap for a half an hour resulted in a flow of slightly less lukewarm water. A power failure at the water processing plant in July rewarded the city with a thirty-six-hour boil water advisory, and those who could afford to escape loaded their cars and fled for hotels outside the reach of the New Orleans Sewerage and Water Board system.

Every time I went outside—which I tried to limit as much as possible—I couldn't help but wonder how life had been possible here before electricity.

Not to mention plumbing.

And they wore a lot more clothing, too.

My name is Scotty Bradley—more precisely, it's Milton Scott Bradley. Yes, my parents named me Milton Bradley. I actually dodged a bullet—they'd been planning on naming me River or after some other geographic feature. My older brother is named Storm and my sister is Rain—although she started calling herself Rhonda when she was in high school, for obvious reasons. Family lore holds that both sides of the family had ganged up on my parents, insisting they not name me River or Lake or whatever it was they had planned. My parents, who have always been the black sheep of their respective families, chose family names—the maiden names of my grandmothers—for me. It's just unfortunate that one of them was Milton. I have stopped pointing out to my parents they could have reversed the names quite easily—why couldn't it have been Scott Milton Bradley?

They always change the subject.

Storm started calling me Scotty when I was a kid because I was getting teased by other kids, and it stuck. He likes to remind me of that whenever he gets on my nerves—which is frequent—by calling me Miltie.

Sigh. He can be such a pain in the ass.

I grew up in the French Quarter of New Orleans, and other than two crappy years in Nashville going to Vanderbilt before I flunked out, I've pretty much lived in the Quarter my whole life. Mom and Dad run a tobacco shop on Royal Street, and I grew up in their apartment over the shop. Mom and Dad are what people used to call hippies. They have been arrested countless times for protesting—they are passionate about their causes, whether it's anti–nuclear energy, environmentalism, civil rights, you name it. Despite their counterculturalism, Storm and Rain turned out to be pretty straitlaced: Storm is a lawyer and Rain married a doctor, becoming a typical Uptown doctor's wife, doing lots of charity work and belonging to the Mardi Gras Krewe of Iris. The joke in the family is that Storm became a lawyer to help Mom and Dad save money on legal fees. He even served a term in the state legislature, but hated it so much he didn't run for reelection.

I'm probably the most like Mom and Dad out of the three of us, really. I flunked out of college, so my grandfathers both ganged up on me and cut me off from my trust funds. I became a go-go boy with a booking agency called the Southern Knights, touring all over the country for several years, shaking my bare ass in gay bars for tips. I also worked as a personal trainer for years. After I quit the Southern Knights, I used to dance at the Pub every once in a while to make extra cash when I was short for the rent or the bills.

Some years ago—never mind how many precisely—having no money in my wallet or my bank account, I decided to accept a last-minute offer to once more put on my thong and dance at the Pub for Southern Decadence. I thought I would just get up on the bar and shake my bare cheeks and make enough money to pay the back rent I owed. Southern Decadence was always my favorite time of the year, but that Southern Decadence, the year I had just turned twenty-nine, was to be fraught with peril and would change the course of my life forever. In the space of less than forty-eight hours a friend was murdered, I was kidnapped and targeted by a hate group, and I wound up working in tandem with the FBI to thwart an evil scheme to destroy New Orleans and kill thousands of gay men.

And they would have gotten away with it, too, were it not for some meddling gays.

I also happened to meet the two men I would fall in love with, and launched my unconventional love life. Yes, I am in a three-way relationship. There have been some ups and downs— to say the least—but for the most part it's been pretty awesome.

I count my blessings every day.

Frank Sobieski was the special agent in charge of the FBI investigation I accidentally stumbled into when someone hid a flash drive in my boot while I was dancing. Frank is...well, what can I say? He's about six foot three, lean and muscled with an amazing body. He trims his torso hair down to a very sexy stubble, his piercing blue eyes and abs so razor sharp you could slice a tomato on them. He also is losing his hair, so as long as I've known him he's shaved his head. Not many people can work that bald head, but Frank is one of the lucky ones. He also has a scar on his right cheek that gives him a real tough look, but he's actually a big sweetheart. He retired from the FBI and moved to New Orleans a few months after we met...and has been working as a professional wrestler for the last few years. He is currently the Gulf States Wrestling Alliance world champion, and he looks pretty damned hot in the gear. The fans love him, and he is amazing in the ring. Frank is older than me and has been making noises about retiring lately...all that pounding is starting to take a toll on his body, he says, and he's started to get tired of all the traveling. I'm not a fan of all the traveling myself—I hate not having him at home with me—but I've never complained because he's living his dream.

And how can you complain about someone living their dream without looking like the most selfish, shittiest person in the world?

The other part of our threesome is Colin Cioni. Colin's— well, Colin is a bit more complicated. I suppose the easiest way to explain it is to say he's a contractor with the Blackledge Agency; that's what we tell people when they ask what he does. They usually let it drop, but if pressed we just say that he's a "troubleshooter" for problems, and that takes him all over the world. We don't say that those who generally contract Blackledge are governments who need some kind of espionage work done when they need plausible deniability. Colin can't discuss his work with us, and we never know where he's going or what he's doing when he takes off for a job; his boss, Angela Blackledge, will call and the next thing you know, he's off somewhere and we will occasionally get a cryptic call from Angela to let us know he's okay. It's unsettling, to say the least, and we try not to think too much about what he's doing. We have occasionally come into contact with people he knows through his work—my favorites are the Ninja Lesbians, a pair of Mossad agents who we've all become close to since meeting them (they swung through my living room windows on ropes that first time; they know how to make an entrance). Colin is shorter than me, about five-six, but he also weighs 220 pounds of solid muscle. He's strong as an ox, smart, and really good-looking, with olive skin usually tanned dark, bright blue eyes, and that amazing bluish black curly hair.

It's really funny, when you think about it. I have two boyfriends, and yet sometimes it seems like I spend more time alone than I did when I was single. Didn't see that one coming, believe you me.

Anyway, that crazy Southern Decadence weekend when we all met wasn't our last experience with dead bodies or conspiracies, either. Frank and I became licensed private eyes after he moved to New Orleans, but we've never had any official, paying clients. I have, as Frank and Colin like to point out, a habit of stumbling over dead bodies or into international conspiracies.

I'm just lucky that way, I guess.

Hey, it's not like I go looking for trouble.

As for me, I'm about five-eight, with sandy blond hair that's starting to recede a bit. I'm getting close to forty, and I've noticed that I need to start paying a bit more attention to what I eat than I ever used to before. I used to joke that I was irresistible because I never had any trouble getting laid…but now I'm a lot more self-conscious than I used to be. It might be because both Frank and Colin are lucky with their bodies. Frank could eat everything in sight and not gain a pound of fat, and Colin is built like a brick shithouse.

Maybe I am overreacting, I don't know.

It also doesn't help that Frank's nephew Taylor, who is almost twenty, is now living with us. Taylor came out to his parents after spending a semester in Paris, and they didn't take it well, to put it mildly. They threw him out and cut him off, and he came to live with us. He's going back to school this fall at Tulane. Since Frank and Colin are both gone a lot, I'm around Taylor a lot more than they are, which sort of makes me surrogate dad, I guess. He's a great kid—smart, and funny, and adjusting to being gay, young, and living in New Orleans pretty well, all things considered.

Being the same age as his mother hit me a little harder than maybe it should have. I mean, I didn't feel like I was getting old, you know what I mean? But everyone was making such a big deal about me turning forty, I was starting to think maybe it was a big deal.

Or they just liked to give me shit. This was also highly likely.

Oh, yeah, I also used to be a bit psychic. It was a weird thing, really. I didn't have any control over it—it always came and went, and I used to have to read tarot cards for it to really work for me. The Goddess also used to come to me in visions and give me cryptic warnings that never really made any sense to me until later. I even communicated with a dead man once—he channeled through me to help solve his murder. But after Katrina, that all changed. I was angry with the Goddess for not warning me, and I turned my back on her for a while. Then when I tried to commune with her again, she ignored me. Sometimes now when I look at the cards, they're just cards and they don't tell me anything. She did come to me once, when I was in danger, but after that…never again.

I never really thought much about the gift until it was gone. I miss it every now and then, but I've learned to live without it. Frank and Colin and my family knew about it, of course, but I never let anyone else know. I mean, it wasn't something you could just explain without getting laughed at. "Ha ha, what are this week's Powerball numbers?"

No, thanks.

So, forty was looming on the horizon, and it was the hottest summer we'd had in years. Frank was off wrestling, and Colin was due home any day from his last gig.

Little did I know that turning forty was going to be the least of my problems that hot, lazy August…

CHAPTER ONE
TEN OF CUPS
Happy family life, true friendships

You know you live in New Orleans when you leave your house for drinks on a hot Saturday morning in August wearing a red dress.

It was well over ninety degrees, and the humidity had tipped the heat index up to about 110, maybe 105 in the shade. The hordes of men and women in red dresses were furiously waving handheld fans as sweat ran down their bodies. Everywhere you looked, there were crowds of people in red, sweating but somehow, despite the ridiculous heat, having a good time. I could feel the heat from the pavement through my red-and-white saddle shoes and was glad I'd decided wearing hose would be a bad idea. The thick red socks I was wearing were hot enough, thank you, and were soaked through. They were new, so were probably dying my ankles, calves, and feet pink. But it was for charity, I kept reminding myself as I greeted friends and people whose names I couldn't remember but whose faces looked familiar as we worked our way up and down and around the Quarter.

Finally, I had enough around noon and decided to call it a day.

"I don't think I've ever been so hot in my life, and I grew up in Alabama," my sort of nephew, Taylor Wheeler, said in his soft accent, wiping sweat from his forehead as we trudged down Governor Nicholls Street on our way home.

"It hasn't been this hot in a while," I replied, trying really hard not to laugh. I'd been forcing down giggles pretty much all day since he came galloping down the back steps the way he always does and I got my first look at his outfit. "But the last few summers have been mild—this is normal for August, usually." It was true—everyone in town was complaining about the heat like it was something unusual, but we hadn't had our usual hellish summer weather in a couple of years.

Last summer had been not only mild but dry, with little humidity and practically no rain—which was unheard of. Usually it rains every day around three in the summer, when the humidity has gotten so thick it turns to rain.

"I don't even want to think about how much sweat is in my butt crack," he complained, furiously waving the fan he'd picked up somewhere, trying to create a breeze.

I gave up trying to fight it and just gave in to the laughter.

Taylor is even taller than his biological uncle, my longtime partner Frank. Frank is six-two, but while Taylor claims he's only six-four, I think he's taller. He's definitely more than two inches taller than Frank. He's very self-conscious about being so tall, always slouching so he seems shorter. The slouching drives me crazy. I'm constantly telling him to stand up straight and to work on his posture, to embrace being tall since there's no changing it.

It's not working so far.

He's also maybe one hundred and seventy pounds tops—despite eating everything in sight, he never seems to gains any weight. Also like his uncle Frank, he has a high metabolism. Long and lean, with enormous hands and feet, he looked absolutely ridiculous in the University of Alabama cheerleading uniform he'd bought online for the Red Dress Run. The top was intended to be a midriff shirt, but he was so tall it looked like a red and white sports bra with *Bama* written in script across his chest. The pleated red-and-white skirt barely covered his ass. He hadn't shaved his legs or arms or stomach, either, so almost all the exposed, golden-tanned skin was covered with white-gold hair that glistened in the sun with sweat.

Taylor hadn't originally wanted to do the Red Dress Run, an annual event that raises money for local New Orleans charities.

Everyone who participates pays a registration fee, and of course, you have to wear a red dress. There's alcohol, food, and great music and everyone has a really good time.

When I originally asked him if he wanted to do the run, he looked at me like I'd lost my mind or had heatstroke or something. "I have to wear a red dress?" He gave me that oh-so-typical teenage eye roll I was getting to know far too well. "Why would anyone want to do that? In public? And it's not Halloween?"

"New Orleans has a fine tradition of men wearing drag at all times of the year. Not just Fat Tuesday or Halloween," my mom replied before I could splutter out something that would have only made him more resistant. "It's for fun, Taylor, you know what that is, don't you? You don't live in Alabama anymore. Loosen up."

I smothered a laugh as his face turned beet red.

Leave it to Mom. She knew how to handle him far better than I ever would.

It didn't hurt that he worshiped her.

And that was all it took. Once he decided he was going to do it, he dove in head first. "My dress is a secret," he said when I asked him if he wanted to go dress shopping with me. "You won't see it till that day. I want it to be a surprise."

I couldn't have been prouder. New Orleans was good for him, as I knew it would be. He was adapting very quickly. Soon he'd out-local the natives.

So I went shopping for my dress all by myself in the unbearable heat of a July afternoon. Colin was out of the country on another job for who knew how long, and Frank would be wrestling in Jacksonville the Friday night before the Red Dress Run, and there was no way he could get back in time on Saturday unless he drove all night. My best friend David was making his dress—he and some friends were doing a group costume, spoofing those reality shows about rich, Botoxed, shrieking women by going as the Grande Dames of Chalmette. I liked the idea but I can't sew, so that was out. I didn't find anything I liked in the shops on Decatur Street, so I moved on to Magazine Street in Uptown. At a consignment store I found a gorgeous red Diane von Furstenberg wrap dress that required just the tiniest little bit of alteration, and the store had a seamstress there on site. All in all, it was a steal at $60, which included the tailoring. It draped around my body beautifully, hiding unsightly bulges that seemed to have sprouted up out of nowhere and emphasizing my chest and shoulders and slim hips. I used to pretty much be able to wear anything without worrying about how it looked on me, but that wasn't the case anymore. Much as I hated to admit it, it wasn't quite as easy as it once was to keep my body in the kind of shape I was used to. I couldn't just eat everything I wanted to whenever I wanted to anymore.

The fact that I lived with two people who could was just insult added to injury.

The third part of mine and Frank's three-way relationship, Colin, didn't have any weight issues, either. He was built like a muscle tank, a few inches shorter than me, ripped and thick and defined with a tiny little waist and a flat stomach that rippled with muscle.

On the other hand, it was entirely possible I was getting obsessive about it because I was about to turn forty.

"I wish Frank had been able to be here for this," Taylor went on. "I'd love to see him in a red dress." He weaved a bit, and I put a hand on his wet arm to steady him.

He was a bit tipsy. I'd been monitoring his alcohol intake, but with the oppressive heat and the gallons of sweat we'd both lost, the few beers I'd allowed him to have had gone right to his head. I'd mostly stuck to bottled water, with the occasional vodka tonic, but my slight buzz had already worn off before we started home.

Taylor had no head for alcohol.

"I can show you pictures from the last couple of years," I replied, taking another swig from the warm bottle of water I'd bought at the Pub on our way home from the run. It had been ice cold when I'd gotten it, but the heat was so intense the water had warmed up as we'd walked. I was a little surprised there weren't a lot more heat casualties on the run itself. "He'll be home in plenty of time before we go to the party tonight."

Frank had texted me when he'd left Jacksonville to head home, and was probably now somewhere between Mobile and New Orleans. Colin was also due back from his latest assignment sometime tomorrow—he said he'd text me once he'd cleared customs at JFK. I couldn't wait to see him—he'd been gone for several months.

I also hoped the party—which had originally been planned to be outside—was going to be moved inside the house.

I wasn't big on going to parties in the Garden District as a rule. Having grown up in New Orleans, I was very well educated on the ins and outs of the city's caste system. My maternal grandparents lived in a house that was built after the War of 1812 and had always been the Diderot family home. I always thought the Garden District, one of the more expensive and exclusive neighborhoods in the city, was a bit stuffy and full of itself. I generally tried to avoid parties there. They tended to have really good liquor but incredibly stilted and dull conversation, which meant I tended to drink too much.

That never ended well.

But this party was being thrown by Serena Castlemaine, who was becoming kind of a local celebrity—albeit one most locals held at arm's length.

Serena had come to New Orleans from Dallas a little over a year earlier. She had a cousin-in-law who also lived in the Garden District in the old Palmer house; I wasn't really sure of the relationship. The way I understood it, Barbara was old New Orleans money and had married Serena's oil money–rich cousin, or something like that. Serena decided to move to New Orleans for a change and for something new after divorcing either her third or fourth husband, and had gotten a condo at 1 Canal Place. She'd blown into town like a bulldozer, throwing money around at various charities and just being fabulous in general, from everything I'd heard. Of course, being oil money from Dallas was horrifying to the old New Orleans society guard, who were more than happy to take her money for their pet charities but weren't about to allow her into their social circle. Fortunately she didn't care—and when the *Grande Dames* shows decided to have a New Orleans franchise, Serena was more than happy to join the cast. The New Orleans version hadn't started filming yet.

I, for one, couldn't wait for it to start airing.

Frank and Colin mocked me regularly for watching the *Grande Dames* shows, but when I pointed out they watched along with me and knew who all the women were and could quote chapter and verse on their feuds and fights, they both claimed to watch "ironically."

Whatever.

But my sister Rain had gotten to know Serena Castlemaine through working with her on a fund-raiser for Children's Hospital, and when she asked me if we wanted to go to Serena's housewarming party in the Garden District, there was no way in hell I was going to say no to *that* invitation.

Actually, I may have said *you bet your sweet ass we want to go!*

Rain had laughed. "She sees this as a chance to really introduce herself to people, so she's asked me and some others to help her put together a guest list…she collects interesting people, like other people collect dolls or stamps. She doesn't care about backgrounds or anything like that—she just doesn't want to be around boring people. And get this"—she paused for effect—"she bought the Metoyer place."

The Metoyer place!

Cue the dramatic music.

There was no way I was going to miss that party, even if I had to go by myself.

The notorious Metoyer house on Coliseum Street in the Garden District was one of the better-known houses in New Orleans. It was where one of the city's more famous unsolved murders occurred when I was about fourteen.

I actually had a connection to the house. I'd gone to school with Jesse and Dylan Metoyer; identical twins, they were in my class at Jesuit High School. We hadn't been friends—far from it. Jesse had been one of the bullies who'd picked on me in junior high school. Jesse had been the typical Garden District asshole: arrogant, entitled, and horribly spoiled. He'd been on the football team, too—which put him into that crowd of arrogant jocks. *Fag*, they'd hiss at me in the locker room or in the hallways between class, and then burst out laughing. They'd knock my books out of my hands so I had to scramble to pick up everything in the crowded hall as everyone else watched and smirked while they laughed. They'd pants me in gym class, shoot spitballs at me in other classrooms, write things like *Scott Bradley sucks cock* on my locker in Magic Marker. That was why I went out for wrestling—to learn how to defend myself. Finally, one day in the eighth grade Jesse shoved me in the hall, and I used my wrestling training to take him down, control him, and make him cry.

After that, they left me alone.

Despite this bad history with him, I couldn't help but feel sorry for Jesse when his little sister Delilah was murdered. It was one of the first big crime stories to blow up all over the country, winding up on the front page of all the tabloids for well over a year and discussed ad nauseam on any number of cable tabloid shows. The Delilah Metoyer murder was also known—and resented—for launching the career of tabloid television host Veronica Vance, a former prosecutor with a thick North Carolina accent and a habit of shrieking at her guests. Jerry Channing, who had been basically a personal trainer for Garden District socialites at the time of the murder, collected all of the gossip he heard from his clients and wrote a book. He'd even worked for Jesse's mother, Arlene, so he had had access to the Metoyer family itself. The book, *Garden District Gothic*, was a perennial bestseller and had even been made into a really bad movie. You could find the trade paperback in practically every tourist shop in the Quarter, and fans of the book had triggered a cottage industry of its own for a while—for several years, there had been "Garden District Gothic tours."

Every so often, the case would be revived when some player in the case made the news again—usually by dying—and the tabloid shows and papers would be all Delilah, all the time again for a while.

And since this coming October would be the twenty-fifth anniversary of the murder, retrospectives and coverage were as inevitable as the return of the swarms of Formosan termites every May.

No one had ever been charged with the crime—but everyone in town had an opinion as to who the killer was.

"We're almost home," I said to Taylor as we reached the corner at Decatur Street and he stumbled again. "I told you not to drink beer on such a hot day."

As soon as I said the words, I wondered when I'd turned into an old scold.

I hadn't *felt* old before Taylor came to live with us. And deep down, I still didn't really think I *was* old. In my head, I still thought of myself as twenty-nine, give or take—it was always startling to remember that twenty-nine was almost eleven years ago.

I was twenty-nine when I met Colin and Frank.

And so what if I was on the verge of turning forty, and some extra weight was gathering around my waist, and some of my chest hair was starting to turn gray? It wasn't a big deal. *Forty isn't old.*

But I also found myself worrying every once in a while if I was a good role model for a gay kid in college. Frank and Colin were gone a lot, and so I was slowly slipping into the role of authority figure for him. I wasn't sure how I felt about that, to be honest. My own parents had pretty much been free spirits who left us to our own devices, trusting us to make our own decisions. Mom and Dad were all about making mistakes and learning from them. "As long as you learn and grow, mistakes aren't the end of the world," Mom always said. "The problem is when you keep making the same mistakes and don't learn. And no one's perfect—Goddess knows we aren't. Just always try to do the right thing, and when you make a mistake, treat it as a learning experience and become a better person."

I was sixteen when I started slipping into gay bars in the Quarter. I don't remember how old I was when I first started smoking pot, but I do remember Dad rolling the joint from their seemingly bottomless stash. My parents had always been more concerned with our development into fully rounded human beings capable of making our own decisions, rather than seeing how well we could follow rules.

But now that I actually *had* a kid around, I doubted myself.

Stop that! He's not a kid! He's nineteen! And he's a great kid already—you're not going to damage him...and besides, you can't be responsible for his behavior anyway.

I unlocked the gate to the courtyard, and we stepped into the cool shade. The passageway leading back to the courtyard and the staircase to our apartment felt dark and dank. The air felt more stifled, heavier, and there was also a slight musty smell. Had I not already been drenched in sweat, I certainly would have been by the time I stepped out into the sunlight and fresh air of the courtyard. I made a mental note to suggest to my landladies, Millie and Velma, to do something about the ventilation. They'd put a roof up over it after years of my complaining about it being like a waterfall in there whenever it rained—the water cascaded down off the building roofs on either side into the passageway. I've been in showers and gotten less drenched. Maybe putting up some ceiling fans would help—at least they'd help get that mildew smell out of there.

There was a slight breeze rippling through the courtyard, and it felt delicious. I walked over to where the hose was hooked up and turned on the spigot.

Taylor picked up the hose and held it over his head, letting the cold water flow over his body. Goose bumps came up on his skin and he sighed happily, opening his mouth and drinking directly from the hose. He grinned and cupped his fingers over nozzle, spraying me with water.

"Hey!" I started to complain, but the cold water felt amazing. I closed my eyes and let him spray me with the water until I was soaked through and dripping. I wrung out my skirt before heading up the stairs.

Millie and Velma lived on the second-floor apartment. We had the upper two floors. We each had our own bedroom, and technically Taylor and Colin shared the top floor, but when Colin was home he usually slept downstairs in either my bed or Frank's, or we all three piled into mine. And with Colin gone a lot, Taylor had a lovely two-bedroom apartment in the French Quarter pretty much to himself.

No, he wasn't spoiled at all.

On the second floor landing was the enormous energy-efficient washer and dryer everyone in the building shared. I opened the dryer and pulled out two huge bath sheets, handing one to Taylor and using the other to wipe myself down. Millie and Velma were at their condo in Fort Walton Beach for the month of August; otherwise I would have never dared to leave laundry sitting in the dryer like that.

They weren't above dumping it over the railing into the courtyard.

I wrapped the big towel around my waist and unloaded the dryer into the wicker basket I'd left on top of it. Precariously balancing it against my hip, I climbed up to the third floor and unlocked my apartment. A blast of cold air greeted me as I opened the door.

"Oh, that feels good," Taylor said behind me.

"Go upstairs and take a shower, then come downstairs and I'll make lunch," I replied.

I closed the door behind me as he clomped up the stairs, thinking how amazing it was that someone as thin as he was could sound like a herd of elephants—

Stop that. Next you'll be yelling at him to stay off your lawn.

"There you are."

I almost jumped out of my wet skin as two arms snaked around me from behind in the darkened hallway. Frank nuzzled the back of my neck, and despite how disgusting I felt, I couldn't help but lean back into his strong body. I also said a quick prayer of gratitude to the Goddess that I'd sent Taylor upstairs, since his uncle was also naked and clearly feeling a bit frisky. "When did you get home?" I asked, leaning my wet head back against his shoulder. His arms always felt perfect when wrapped around me. We fit together perfectly, and I hated sleeping alone when he was gone.

"About twenty minutes ago," he mumbled as he pressed his lips against my shoulder and let his hands drift downward. "I'm lucky I didn't get a speeding ticket, I think I was doing ninety after I passed Biloxi." He found the buckle for the skirt and undid it. It unwrapped itself and slid down to the floor.

I turned around and put my arms around his neck, hopping up and wrapping my legs around his waist. Frank is very strong and had no trouble walking back into the bedroom while carrying me. He set me down gently on the bed. "I missed you," I said hoarsely as he climbed onto the bed with a wicked grin on his face.

Later, Frank dozed off while I took a shower. I felt so much better with the sweat from the day washed off, and I padded into the kitchen with the towel wrapped around me to get a bottle of water from the refrigerator. I was starving, and with a start remembered that I'd promised to make lunch for Taylor.

Having Taylor around meant we had to be more careful about sex and walking around naked. The first few days Taylor had lived with us I'd walked in on him twice while he was watching porn, and so we'd set some rules and boundaries after that. I didn't want to walk in on him watching porn and I sure didn't want him walking in on us having sex. All three of us had gotten into the habit of walking around in our underwear or naked. I used to be a stripper and had even modeled nude before I finally settled down with Frank and Colin, so nakedness wasn't a big deal for me…but now it *had* to be. With the possibility of Taylor popping in at any moment, we had to be more careful. It was taking some getting used to, but the one rule that seemed to be working was the locked door; if Taylor knew we were home and the door was locked, it meant we were busy. The same rule applied if Taylor's door was locked: he was busy and we were not to intrude.

It was actually easier to just text him before I went upstairs.

My iPhone was sitting on the kitchen counter, so I quickly texted him, *sorry about lunch are you still hungry?*

No worries I figured Frank was home, and yes. Be right down.

I smiled and walked back to my room. I put on my sweats and unlocked the front door before heading back to the kitchen. There were some chicken breasts in the refrigerator I'd broiled a few days earlier, so I got those out and a box of Zatarain's jambalaya mix. Taylor loved jambalaya—although he preferred Andouille to chicken, but I was out of that; I'd have to get some the next time I went to the store. I made a note on the grocery list on the counter and filled a pot with water. I diced up the chicken, added the mix, and waited for it to come to a boil. The front door opened and I heard his heavy footsteps coming down the hall. I opened my mouth to say something about it but then heard my own voice in my head: *Get off my lawn.*

I closed my mouth and smiled at him as he climbed up onto one of the bar stools on the other side of the kitchen counter. He was carrying my battered copy of *Garden District Gothic.* I pointed at it with my wooden spoon. "Are you enjoying that?"

He nodded, absently picking at a pimple forming on his chin. I smacked his hand with the spoon and he sheepishly dropped it. "Yeah, it's interesting." He put the book down on the counter. "But how did he get away with repeating all the gossip people told him in a book?" His eyebrows came together over his nose. "I mean, I'd think people would be *pissed.*"

"I guess maybe because so much of it was true," I replied, turning the jambalaya down to simmer and setting the timer for twenty-five minutes. I shrugged. "You never know what's going to piss people off in New Orleans. He really wasn't *one of them,* so I guess they didn't feel betrayed—it would have been different if someone from their social circle had written it. They thought of him more as a hanger-on, I suppose. I also think people were kind of thrilled to be in it, especially when the book wound up being such a huge best seller. I'm just glad he didn't write about anyone in my family." The Bradley and Diderot skeletons, I reflected, were still safely in their closets.

"You really went to school with Jesse and Dylan Metoyer?"

I nodded, leaning against the counter and taking another swig from my water bottle. "Yeah, they were both in my class, from kindergarten on. We weren't friends." *To put it mildly.* "Jesse was more of a dick—but I didn't really know Dylan very well. I had some classes with him over the years, but he was quiet, didn't talk much. Jesse was what you'd call an attention whore—always had to be the center of attention, was loud, thought he was funny—but he was just a real asshole, bottom line. Although I wouldn't wish what happened to his family on anyone."

"I just can't believe they never arrested anyone." Taylor opened the book back up as I pulled out my stash and started rolling a joint.

"The Metoyers closed ranks, like any Garden District family would." I finished rolling the joint and handed it to him. "It really wasn't a stretch to realize the cops would focus on them more than an outsider."

"But most of the time it is the parents, right?" Taylor was thinking about switching his major from French—he was fluent—to criminal psychology. Frank was a little thrilled by it. Taylor did kind of hero-worship his retired FBI agent uncle, and it wouldn't surprise me in the least if he was trying to be more like Frank.

Frank's pretty awesome. How many people retired after twenty years with the FBI and then pursued their dream of being a professional wrestler in their late forties? And became a star?

I mean, there are worse role models a college-age gay kid could have.

"People thought—*think*—that calling their lawyer before they called the cops meant they were guilty. Of course, those people have never been through a police investigation, either."

My parents had trained us since childhood to only say "I want to talk to a lawyer" when being questioned by the cops. Nothing I'd experienced through my bad habit of stumbling over dead bodies and crimes scenes had proven that to be bad advice. "And yes, when a child is killed, the first people they look at are the parents. It's almost always the parents."

I took the joint back from him and inhaled, picking up the ashtray and my water and walking into the living room. I plopped down on the sofa and stretched out my legs, resting my feet on the coffee table. Taylor sat down in the reclining chair with his book and reached for the joint again. I leaned back on the couch and tried to remember what the Metoyer twins looked like, but couldn't—it had been almost twenty-five years.

And my yearbooks were at my parents' place.

After the murder, with all the attention the family was getting, the Metoyers pulled both Jesse and Dylan out of Jesuit High and hired tutors to homeschool them. Neither had ever returned to Jesuit. I wasn't kidding when I said the Metoyers closed ranks...they shut themselves up in that house on Coliseum Street and rarely came out. I couldn't blame them for wanting to keep a low profile. Reporters and curiosity seekers had camped out in front of the house for months. I'd heard at some point they'd left town and closed up the house. I hadn't known it was up for sale until Rain told me Serena had bought it. I'd never been inside the place, either. My desire to meet Serena, who was actually going to be a *Grande Dame*, was only slightly exceeded by my morbid curiosity to see the inside of the Metoyer place.

"We need to make sure we eat before we go to the party, too," I said as I heard Frank coming down the hallway.

"Won't she have food?" Frank asked, kissing the top of my head and ruffling Taylor's hair. He was just wearing a pair of black Saints sweatpants.

"You didn't sleep for long," I replied, smiling back up at him. "And yes, I'm sure she'll have food—I just don't know if it'll be edible."

There was a new and alarming trend I'd noticed at parties

lately—bad catering. Back in the old days, before Katrina, you really couldn't get away with bad food at any kind of social gathering—people would talk and you'd find people declining your invitations. But the last few parties we'd been to, the food had been terrible. The liquor was good—no one would ever dare skimp on the liquor budget—but this trend toward bad, inedible food was beginning to disturb me. Shrimp creole that was basically just shrimp added to tomato soup, tasteless brisket, overdone meats, and bland chicken wings—I'd had all of it, and there was nothing worse than drinking heavily at a party on an empty stomach.

And since Serena was still pretty new to town, I couldn't imagine she'd had time to find a good caterer yet—especially on short notice.

"I've got jambalaya on the stove," I added, "but I'm sure we'll all be hungry again before it's time to leave for the party tonight."

Frank plopped down on the sofa next to me and draped his right leg over my left. "Do we have to go? I'd rather stay home and just hang out." He took the joint from Taylor and took a deep inhale.

"I want to go, and Rain went out on a limb to get us invited," I pointed out, taking the joint from him and taking another, mind-numbing hit. "Besides, it'll be kind of fun, I think. You don't have to go if you don't want to, of course."

"You're promising me no drama, right?" Frank teased me. "Just a nice time?"

"I can't promise there won't be drama—it's a Garden District party," I replied. "But hopefully there won't be any dead bodies."

Frank laughed. "I can't ask for more than that."

CHAPTER TWO
QUEEN OF PENTACLES
An intelligent and thoughtful woman...rich and charitable

It's only about a three-mile drive from the French Quarter to the Garden District, but the neighborhoods are so different it can feel like going to another country.

This is especially true after dark.

The Quarter comes to life when the sun sets, as the slow sluggishness of the lazy afternoon gives way to the pulsing vibrancy of the night. Bourbon Street clogs with revelers staggering around with go-cups clutched tightly, music blares from every club, and the clouds in the night sky take on a pinkish glow from all the bright neon lights below. Barkers outside strip joints try to lure spenders in, a guy in the hand grenade costume dances on his corner, and everywhere is the smell of Lucky Dogs and grease. Crowds follow guides on ghost and vampire tours, lines form outside restaurants, pedi-cabs speed past, and sometimes, the clopping of mule hooves pulling carriages packed full of tourists being lied to by their drivers about New Orleans history make it seem like time travel is not only possible, but has happened. The Quarter's pulse picks up after the fortune tellers, living statues, and street artists pack up their wares and call it a day, giving way to those who ply their trades in the velvety night.

The Garden District, on the other hand, is much more subdued and sedate. If the Quarter is a painted whore, the Garden District is her much snootier and pretentious sister, narrowing her eyes disapprovingly at the immorality down the river. The people who live in those old mansions on their gorgeous lawns behind their fences will always smirk in the general direction of the Quarter, genteelly sipping tea from heirloom bone china cups held in white-gloved hands…although sometimes the "tea" is actually bourbon. They only venture to the Quarter to drink and dine at the fine old restaurants and pretend that Galatoire's doesn't now have a strip club on either side.

The Garden District has always been quiet and peaceful at night. There are no nightclubs there, no places hawking Big Ass Beers, no one vomiting in the streets—and there never will be.

The Garden District would never change.

But the rest of the city was changing a lot. The Quarter wasn't quite as Bohemian and decadent as it used to be, a hangout for musicians and artists and writers who eschewed the 9 to 5 to create. The classic characters everyone knew like Ruthie the Duck Girl were long gone, and new ones hadn't popped up to take their place. Old businesses were slowly but surely being forced out, and it seemed like condos were being put in everywhere. Yet despite the changes, despite the so-called gentrification, the pulsing heartbeat the Quarter had always had was still there.

When I was growing up in the Quarter, the neighborhood was still kind of sketchy despite its appeal to tourists and college students—and woe to the drunken out-of-towner who mistakenly staggered across one of the Quarter's boundary streets into the Treme, the Marigny, or even the CBD once the sun had set in the west. Change had come to those neighborhoods as well—with old places being renovated and being bought by newcomers, and property values going up as well. Frenchmen Street in the Marigny was beginning to rival Bourbon Street with its bars, restaurants, and live music clubs. The CBD, once a ghost town after five, was thriving at night. The Sewell Cadillac dealership on Baronne Street, notorious nationwide for being looted by some of New Orleans's not-so-finest after Katrina, was now a Rouses grocery store with a CVS right across the street. Parking lots were now eight-story condo megacomplexes.

As New Orleans became more of a mecca for film and television production, stars and celebrities started overpaying for condos or making insane offers for houses in the lower Quarter. A multiple-award-winning actress had offered Millie and Velma such a ridiculous amount of money for our place that I was kind of surprised they didn't take it and retire to their place in Fort Walton Beach—I would have had to think long and hard about it myself.

The makeup of the city was changing, and changing quickly. I wasn't one of those locals who decried every single change—some of the changes *were* for the better, no matter what anyone thought. There were some I wasn't quite so happy about, but I could adapt. Yuppies and hipsters were everywhere, and I couldn't help but feel some of the old charm, the stuff that made New Orleans *New Orleans*, was starting to disappear. A fire had destroyed the bakery that made Hubig's Pies, and the racks that used to hold them next to cash registers in Mom-and-Pop corner groceries had disappeared. The *Times-Picayune* wasn't a daily paper anymore. Seedy dive bars were purchased, closed, and reopened with newly renovated interiors. New restaurants were popping up all over the place. Magazine Street had always been a commercial street, but almost all of the used clothing shops, junk stores, and consignment shops had been replaced with boutiques, gourmet hot dog stands, and specialty food places. There were no new local characters to take the place of the ones who were now gone. The young professionals in their scrubs and the hipsters in their skinny jeans and bowler hats had discovered the blue-collar clubs and chased the old clientele away. Change was inevitable after the destruction wrought by the flood waters after the great levee failure, I suppose.

But I wasn't one of those New Orleanians who looked back to pre-flood days through rose-colored glasses, either. The city has always had problems, and nostalgia for the good old days didn't make that any less true. New Orleans wasn't paradise before the levees failed.

They may not be the same problems we had before, but we still had problems.

Hey, kids, get off my lawn!

"I hope this is going to be a great party," I said as we crossed Jackson Avenue into the Garden District proper, keeping pace with a green streetcar on the St. Charles neutral ground. "Rain says Serena really wants to make a splash."

"She needs to do it now, before *Grande Dames of New Orleans* starts airing," Frank replied. "You know once it does, none of those Garden District ladies are going to want anything to do with her—no matter how much money she throws at their favorite charities."

"I don't think Serena cares about old-line society," I observed. "They weren't going to accept her anyway. She's not from here."

"Who else is going to be on the show? Do you know?" Taylor asked from the backseat, practically sitting on the console between the two front seats.

I resisted the urge to tell him to put his seat belt on while Frank waited for the streetcar to pass before making a left turn onto First Street. "Let me think." I rubbed my eyes. "Besides Serena, there's the local liquor heiress, Margery Lautenschlaeger." I started ticking them off on my fingers. "A writer who used to work for the *Times-Picayune*, what's her name—the woman who inherited the Barron restaurant empire—"

"She doesn't even live in New Orleans," Frank sniffed. "She lives on the North Shore."

There's no bigger New Orleans snob than someone who's gone native.

I named the other three women as Frank drove into the Garden District. I knew it was silly to be excited about a reality show filming in New Orleans—the city was still living down those two horrible seasons on MTV's *The Real World*, but *Top Chef: New Orleans* had been nice.

And that season of *American Horror Story* set and filmed here had been kind of fun.

The narrow streets of the Garden District were lined with parked cars as we got closer to the Metoyer place. Frank grumbled a bit as we drove around in circles looking for a place to park. "So, it looks like everyone in town has been invited to this party."

"Which means it will be even more fun," I replied.

"You'll think it's fun when we end up parking in the Irish Channel."

He finally found a place to park a couple of blocks away, close to the walls around Lafayette Cemetery. I got out of the car into the oppressive heat of the night just as a Garden District security car drove past. The Garden District Association pays for its own patrolling security—one of the perks of living in one of the city's most glamorous neighborhoods. I wasn't sure if the private security served as a deterrent or not, but it made the residents feel safer. I hooked my arm through Frank's as we strolled the several blocks to Serena's. The night was not nearly as hot and humid as the day had been, but it still wasn't remotely close to being pleasant. There were a few clouds in the velvety dark bluish black sky, drifting lazily in front of the stars and the quarter moon. It was quiet and still, other than the rustling of the wind in the massive live oaks.

Serena's house was a historic landmark, designed by none other than Henry Howard himself. It had been built in 1850, and until Serena bought it, was one of the rare New Orleans mansions that had always stayed in the same family. The Metoyers had been extremely wealthy, owning plantations in Vermilion, Iberville, and St. Mary parishes—I think sugar, cotton, and indigo were their main cash crops. They managed to hold on to most of the country land after the Civil War—and then oil was discovered on the St. Mary plantation around the turn of the twentieth century, pouring even more money into the family coffers. The house was gorgeous, three stories high, with galleries encircling the first and second floors, on a huge lot facing Coliseum Street. There was a six-foot-high brick fence on three sides, with a tall black wrought iron fence on the Coliseum Street side. There were black wrought iron fountains in the front yard, and enormous live oaks shaded the lush green lawn. The Metoyers had been relatively scandal-free from the moment the house was built, also a rarity in New Orleans society.

But when scandal finally came to the Metoyers' front door, it came with a vengeance.

One October night twenty-five years ago, the Metoyers' live-in nanny, Robin Strickland, came home from a party around two in the morning. Slightly tipsy, she went upstairs to check on her charge, eight-year-old Delilah, but she wasn't in her bed. Panicked, Robin roused the household, and a search of the enormous house ensued. At some point—no one was really clear about the sequence of events—a bizarre ransom note was found taped to the refrigerator, claiming the little girl had been taken by a political action group whose motivations would be revealed when they called with their ransom demands. A few hours later, Robin found the little girl's dead body on the first floor of the carriage house at the rear of the property.

The story was a wet dream come to life for the tabloids. Delilah's mother, Arlene, was not only Riley Metoyer's second wife, but a former first runner-up in the Miss Louisiana pageant. Her pageant pictures were splashed everywhere, and then the reporters found out that Arlene was also a bit of a stage mother with big ambitions for her pretty daughter. Delilah's head shots were sold to the press, along with audition tapes for television series and movies—and there were a lot of them.

But those were nothing compared to the furor when pictures and video of Delilah participating in the Little Miss Orleans Parish pageant leaked out. From there on, every headline or television news story about the case prominently featured one of the Little Miss beauty queen pictures: highly sexualized, overly made up, and enormous hair shellacked into a helmet.

And of course, the killer had never been caught.

Rain told me that the house's dark history had made it more appealing to Serena, which made me like her all the more.

I thought it was probably too much house for one person, but then again, she'd been born to great wealth and was probably used to living in enormous homes.

We walked along the sidewalk beside the brick fence, which was tilting toward the sidewalk at an alarming angle. I could hear voices and soft jazz music playing on the other side. We came around the corner to Coliseum, and I looked at the house through the tall wrought iron fence.

If I were ever asked to pick the house in the Garden District most likely to be haunted, my choice would be the Metoyer place. Even before Delilah's murder, the place just seemed like it would be haunted, like it should always have black clouds overhead with lightning bolts shooting out. The three-story Victorian, painted a deep fuchsia with black trim, had side porches and balconies and cupolas. A widow's walk on the very top was fenced with black wrought iron. When I was a kid visiting my grandparents, who lived just a few blocks away, Storm and Rain always wanted to come by here, telling me horrifying ghost stories about the house's horrible past. They'd made it all up, of course, but I'd had many nightmares about the house. It always seemed alive to me, and when the shutters were open it was easy to imagine the windows were eyes, watching and waiting. It always seemed to be brooding, and it had always made me uncomfortable. When I was a kid I couldn't get away from it fast enough.

But tonight, it was ablaze with light, and the enormous live oaks in the front yard had festive Japanese lanterns hanging from the lower branches. The fountains were going, and small lights had been sunk alongside the sidewalk to the front gallery of the house. An enormous, thickly muscled security guard wearing a tight black V-neck T-shirt and black slacks stood in front of the gate. There were dark sweat crescents under his arms. An equally sweaty young woman in a white blouse over a black skirt and sensible flat patent leather shoes stood next to him, holding a clipboard.

"Scotty Bradley, Frank Sobieski, and Taylor Wheeler," I said to her, and while she looked for us on her list, I reminded Taylor he was our designated driver. "That means nothing but water or soda, remember—not even a sip of wine."

Hey kids, get off my lawn!

"Shut up," I told the voice in my head, "there's nothing wrong with being responsible."

"Thanks, guys," the young woman said, pushing her glasses up her sweaty nose. "Have a good time. The party is in the back of the house—you can either take the path around the house to the back, or just go up the front stairs and cut through the house, if you want to get out of the heat." She gave us a rueful smile and fanned herself with her clipboard.

The security guard opened the gate and gestured for us to enter. His face looked like it had been carved from stone, and the enormous muscles looked ready to pop through his skin. He didn't say a word as we walked past. He looked familiar to me, but I couldn't remember where I'd seen him before. That's one of the problems with living in New Orleans—it's not that big a town, and everyone looks familiar, but you can't recognize anyone when you see them out of their usual context. The gate clanged shut behind us. The yard looked spectacular. The last time I'd seen the Metoyer place the front yard looked a little... well, *untended*. But now the grass was lush and cut—the smell of freshly mown grass hung in the air a bit—and the flower beds were exploding with blossoms and color. The black metal fountains gleamed in the light of the Japanese lanterns hanging from the lower branches of the live oaks.

Serena had certainly spent a pretty penny on sprucing the place up.

We climbed the front steps, and when we reached the top the front door was opened by a young woman in a black dress with a white apron. "Welcome," she said with a light bow of her head. "If you follow the hallway straight to the back, the door is open to the backyard, and that's where the food and the bars and everything are set up. Many of Ms. Castlemaine's guests have already arrived."

"So the party *is* outside?" Frank asked, giving me a side glance.

"Yes, sir," she replied with a nod. "Ms. Castlemaine has air conditioners set up outside, for everyone's comfort."

"How decadent," I said, grabbing Frank's arm. "Come on, I need a drink."

The house itself was enormous. The ceilings were at least sixteen feet high, and the floors were polished hardwood. The hallway walls were covered with paintings that I didn't recognize but that had incredibly expensive frames. Sets of pocket doors to the rooms off the hallway were closed. A gorgeous hanging staircase led upstairs, but no lights were on up there. The sparkling chandeliers overhead in the hallway were also spotless, the teardrop crystals flashing fire when they caught the light. It was also incredibly cold inside the house. As we walked past the staircase, two gorgeous blue Burmese cats stared at me through spindles just above my head. My heart melted immediately, and I resisted the urge to befriend them, instead continuing to walk with Frank and Taylor down the hall to the backyard. Once we passed through the back door and onto the gallery, I gasped.

Serena had clearly spared no expense.

The live oaks in the backyard, like the ones in the front, had Japanese lanterns hanging from the lower branches, but blinking white Christmas lights were woven around the trunk and branches all the way to the top. Tiki torches burned at strategic intervals. The kidney-shaped swimming pool sparkled in the flickering lights, and lit tea candles floated across the surface. The carriage house—where Delilah's body had been found all those years ago—was also lit up from inside. Through one of the large windows I could see the jazz combo playing. On opposite sides of the yard, two bars had been set up, with huge candelabras at each end, staffed by two bartenders. A massive table in front of the carriage house groaned under the weight of a ridiculous amount of food. A carver was slicing pieces of white meat from a gigantic turkey at one end of the table, and at the other end another carver was slicing a prime rib. Between the carving stations, sterno flames kept chafing dishes warm, and another table set slightly back and to one side held every conceivable type of roll and bread.

And it was, indeed, cool back there. Enormous air

conditioners were humming at strategic intervals around the backyard.

Pretty impressive, I thought as we descended the back stairs.

"Scotty! Frank! Taylor!" My sister Rain materialized out of the crowd and met us at the foot of the steps, kissing us each on the cheek in turn. She looked terrific—she was wearing a simple short black dress with a single gold chain around her neck, and massive high-heeled shoes. "So glad you came!"

"I wouldn't have missed this for anything," I whispered, and she gave me a mischievous smile in return.

"Oh, Serena!" she called. "Come meet my brother and his family."

"Darlings!" Serena came rushing up to us, holding out both hands so she could hug and kiss us each in turn when we reached the bottom of the stairs. She had an electronic cigarette in one hand, the tip glowing blue. I'd only seen pictures of her online (yes, I followed the *Grande Dames* shows online, sue me) but she'd cut her hair since the last pictures I'd seen posted. She used to have a bad case of Big Texas Hair, bleached almost platinum blond. Now it was cut in an asymmetrical bob that actually flattered her rather than the teased and shellacked bird's nest that had added at least another foot to her height. She wore a midnight blue empire-waist dress that pushed her generous breasts almost up to her chin, and the matching shoes had heels of death. In the deep valley between her breasts a gigantic diamond rested on a thick gold link chain, and diamond teardrops hung from each ear. "I'm so delighted you could make it—you must be Scotty," she said, bending down to hug me. She smelled expensive. "Rhonda has told me so much about you I feel like we're already friends."

"Serena, this is my partner, Frank Sobieski," I said, a little overwhelmed. Rain said she had an enormous personality, but that was an understatement. She took a step back and eyed him critically for a moment before turning on her most dazzling smile for him.

"Yes, of course," she enthused, ignoring the hand he was

offering her to shake and throwing both arms around him, crushing him against her breasts. He looked at me for help, and I just smiled back at him. "I'm crushed that Colin couldn't make it. And this must be Taylor." She turned her attentions to him, and he blushed as she crushed him in turn. "Now, darlings, you must help yourselves to food and drink." She waved theatrically and lowered her voice. "I wish I could just stay here and talk to you—some of these people are so fucking boring." She rolled her eyes. "I've never met so many self-absorbed people in my life." She winked at me. "I hardly get a word in edgewise about *me*." She puffed away at the electronic cigarette. "I suppose I should go play hostess." She clearly didn't want to.

"Your cats are gorgeous," I said.

"Baloo and Felice?" She clasped both hands to her cleavage. "Aren't they beauties? Burmese. They're very sweet and smart cats." She leaned in close to me, and whispered, "I actually bought them from Arlene Metoyer herself. She raises Burmese cats now—she has a cattery over on the North Shore, you know—out in the middle of absolutely nowhere." She shook her head. "Not that I blame her, if I were her I'd be living in the middle of the woods somewhere, too."

"I didn't know that." I stared at her as I tried to wrap my mind around it. "Really?"

"I *insisted* on meeting her," Serena went on. "I simply *had* to meet her. She didn't want to, of course, the poor thing, but when my realtor told me she had a cattery, well, there was simply no stopping me. A house just isn't a home without a cat, is it?"

"I guess not," I replied. I've always liked cats, but we never had any growing up because Dad was allergic.

"And you just can't go wrong with a Burmese. Baloo and Felice had several brothers and sisters, and Arlene's price is quite reasonable for a purebred. She agreed to see me the moment I said I needed cats for the house—and I simply fell madly in love with Baloo and Felice the moment I saw them. The poor thing." She linked arms with me and pulled me away from Frank and Taylor, who made a beeline for the food table as she led me in the direction of the bar. "Can you imagine how ghastly it would be to have everyone think you murdered your own child? The poor thing's been living in purgatory for almost twenty years."

"I can't imagine," I replied. "Have you started filming yet? Are you excited?"

"Filming starts next week," she replied. "Next weekend, to be exact. I'd hoped they'd want to film my party"—she gestured with her other hand expansively—"but there were some delays with permits or something nonsensical to do with the city, I don't know, I wasn't really listening once they said they wouldn't be filming at the party." Her eyes flashed. "And yes, I'm very excited. I've been a huge fan of the *Grande Dames* shows ever since they started airing."

"Me, too." I don't think I'd ever admitted that to anyone outside the family before. "I was so excited to hear about the New Orleans franchise!"

"It's truly going to be grand." She laughed. "I was made for these shows, you know. I'm funny and sarcastic and I love to drink. I just hope I get the bitch edit!"

"That would be so awesome!"

"You and I, I think, are destined to be very good friends." She winked at me.

"I hope so!" I was a little starstruck, to be honest. There was just something about her—charisma, charm, whatever you want to call it—and I was enthralled.

She moaned. "Darling, go and get yourself a drink." She brushed her lips against my cheek. "I see another bore I'll have to entertain. But we must have lunch or a drink or something sometime! Come with me, Rhonda, and be my wingman."

She flounced off into the crowd of people without another word, with my sister at her side. I stood there for a moment, trying to catch my breath a bit.

She was pretty overwhelming. She was, I was sure, going to be the breakout star of the show.

I looked around, but couldn't see Taylor or Frank anywhere. It was a shame they weren't filming this party.

Some of my favorite episodes took place at parties.

But I did see any number of local celebrities, and other familiar faces, talking and laughing and drinking and eating. The executive director of the Tennessee Williams Festival was drinking a glass of red wine and talking to one of our local mystery writing superstars. I recognized a number of people who worked on-camera for the local PBS affiliate. One of our local Pulitzer Prize winners was shoveling food in his mouth like he hadn't eaten in days and was washing it down with what looked like Scotch straight up. Venus Casanova, a police detective I'd gotten to know all too well over the course of several murder investigations, was popping a shrimp in her mouth while smiling at a running back for the Saints.

And then I saw a pig.

Well, it was Jerry Channing, author of *Garden District Gothic* himself, walking toward me with an eyebrow raised, what looked like a dirty martini in one hand, and a twisted smile on his handsome face. He was very good-looking, I had to give him that. He shaved his head, and he'd managed to keep the thickly muscled body he'd gotten working as a personal trainer. He always wore loose-fitting jeans and tight black short-sleeved shirts—tonight was no exception.

And one vodka-soaked night in my mid-twenties, I'd let him pick me up at the Pub and spent the night at his place in the lower Garden District.

"Scotty," he said in his deep baritone, nodding in my direction. He toasted me with his martini glass before raising it to his lips.

"Rather ironic to run into you here at the Metoyer place," I said, smiling at him. "I was just going to get a drink."

"Nice to see you, too," he said, walking with me to the bar.

"I'll have a vodka and cranberry, please." I usually drank white wine at parties, but there were bottles of Grey Goose lined up on the bar. Serena was sparing no expense on the booze, for sure, and I wasn't crazy enough to pass up the good stuff. "So, you know Serena?" I was trying to be polite, but it wasn't easy.

Jerry smiled. "Yeah, Arlene banned me from the place after my book came out, and I never thought I'd set foot on the property again." He looked around. "Serena's done a great job bringing the place back to life. I always thought it was a shame the way Arlene just shut herself up here before she left town for good."

And that certainly couldn't have been because of your book, could it? I had enough good manners to not say it out loud. "The twenty-fifth anniversary is coming up," I said, sipping my drink. It was excellent. "I imagine you're going to be doing a lot of interviews…will you be going on Veronica Vance's show again?" He'd been on so many times my mother once joked he should get a costarring credit.

He made a face. "Not a chance in hell." Jerry excused himself and made a beeline for a local mystery author who was a *New York Times* best seller.

Interesting, wonder what happened with him and Veronica? It was probably just a matter of time, I guess. Scorpions always turn on each other, I thought, taking another sip of my drink. I started looking around for Taylor and Frank.

That was when I noticed an *actual* pig and did a double take.

No, I wasn't seeing things. It really *was* a pig.

"Right?" a woman standing next to me said. She was short, a little over five feet tall, maybe, and had reddish blond hair with a green scarf tied into it. She was wearing a full green skirt that matched the scarf and a multicolored silk blouse that hung in folds around her. Her eyes were mismatched—one blue, one green. "I thought I'd had too many martinis myself at first, but it's really a pig." She gave me a crooked smile and stuck out her hand. "Paige Tourneur."

"Scotty Bradley," I replied, shaking her hand but not taking my eyes off the pig, now sniffing around in the grass near the swimming pool.

The pig was quite large, and a gorgeous brown. He was wearing a rhinestone collar—I assumed they were rhinestones, but then again, this was the Garden District—and there was a pink bow on the curly tail.

"His name is Gaspard," Paige went on, taking another drink from her martini glass. "I assumed it was a girl because of the bow—quite a natural assumption, really—and almost got my head bitten off because of my gender stereotyping." She made air quotes as she said the last two words. "And people wonder why I hate coming to parties in the Garden District," she said darkly, finishing the martini in a gulp. She held the empty glass out to me with a pleading, pitiful look on her face. "Would you mind?"

I grinned. "Of course not. I don't mind playing into gender stereotypes."

She blinked at me twice and then roared with laughter. She tucked her hand into the crook of my arm. "Escort me to the bar then, kind sir," she said with a mock Southern drawl, "and I shall get my own dirty martini." As we walked through the crowd, she said, "Gaspard belongs to Alison Strauss, do you know her?"

"The last name is familiar," I replied, scanning the crowd for my guys and not seeing them. Where could they be?

"Her husband is Reggie Strauss." She laughed again. She had a rather infectious laugh, and I grinned back at her. "Reggie Strauss is the developer who's trying to put up those dreadful high-rises in Holy Cross…and Alison, of course—her mother was a Metoyer."

Of course! Reggie Strauss had been all over the news for months. The Holy Cross Historic Association was trying to stop him from getting a height variance from the city council so he could put high-rise condos along the riverfront in the Holy Cross neighborhood—on the other side of the Industrial Canal in the benighted lower Ninth Ward destroyed by the flood after Katrina. "I didn't know his wife was a Metoyer."

"Poor Delilah's first cousin," Paige said as we arrived at the bar. She held her glass out to the bartender. "Another dirty vodka martini, please, with three olives. Make it positively *filthy*." She winked at me. "Buy you a drink, sailor?"

CHAPTER THREE
TEN OF WANDS
One who is carrying an oppressive load

I was taking my second drink from the bartender with a smile and nodded thanks when Paige muttered, "Damn."

"Problem?" I asked. Her face was twisted in disgust.

She sighed. "No—well, yes, kind of." She took a big gulp of her drink. "The problem with being a magazine editor in this town is you have to be nice to people you cannot stand." She forced a horribly fake smile onto her face as she waved at someone. "I have to go make nice with that douchebag now." She fumbled in her purse and handed me a business card. "I'll look for you later, but in case I don't see you, give me a call sometime. Lunch, coffee, a drink—something."

"Thanks." I put the card in my wallet.

She patted my cheek. "Pray for me." She wandered off into the crowd as I took a drink. I scanned the crowd once again for my guys or Rain. I didn't see Frank or Rain anywhere, but over at the food table I saw someone who looked familiar from behind.

I'd know that slouch anywhere.

"How many times do I have to tell you not to hunch over?" I said as I walked up beside where Taylor was standing. He was shoveling food in his mouth like he hadn't eaten for weeks. I sighed. "It's bad for your posture and if you don't stop now, you won't be able to reverse it later and you're going to have all kinds of back problems…" I stopped talking as he straightened up without missing a beat in his feeding.

Goddess, you sound like such a nag. I glanced around to see if anyone had heard me, but fortunately no one was paying any attention to either of us. I took a deep breath and looked over the incredible catering spread. There was so much food on the table, it was practically groaning under its weight. My mouth started watering as I looked over the options. There was a gorgeous prime rib, with a smiling young man standing directly behind it, carving knife and fork in hand. He gave me an inquisitive look and I nodded, hoping I wasn't drooling as he cut off two slices and placed them on a paper plate before drizzling some brown gravy on them. "Thank you," I somehow managed to say as I took the plate from him and started examining the rest of the food. *I can do some extra cardio at the gym tomorrow*, I rationalized as I added a couple of rolls and some butter pats to the plate. I picked up a small bowl and put some rice in it, then smothered it with steaming hot shrimp creole. I added some steamed vegetables to the plate and glanced at Taylor, who was still chewing while adding more food to his plate with his free hand.

I had to admire the skill involved.

And he looked so much better standing up straight.

"Come on," I said, motioning for him to follow me. I walked over to where some tables and chairs were set up underneath the massive branches of an ancient live oak. I sat down at a vacant table, nodding and smiling at people at the other tables who looked vaguely familiar. I started eating just as Taylor folded his long frame into a chair across the table from me, still chewing. His plate was piled high and overflowing—some gravy dripped onto the tablecloth. I put a piece of prime rib in my mouth so I couldn't nag him for making a mess, and moaned in pleasure. The prime rib was perfection—it was so tender it practically dissolved in my mouth. I mopped up some of the gravy with a roll and smeared butter on it. Now I knew why Taylor had turned into an eating machine—or rather, unleashed his inner eating machine. He was contentedly working his way through the plate of food, happy as I've ever seen him.

All of the food was quite excellent, which was a pleasant

change from most of the parties I'd been to recently. The shrimp creole was perfectly seasoned and flavored. It was the best I'd ever had. The shrimp melted in my mouth—I made a note to myself to remember to use parsley and thyme the next time I made it. My opinion of Serena went up another notch. I found myself having to stop myself from shoveling all the food into my mouth at a rather rapid pace. I was still only about half-finished with my plate when Taylor got up to get more. I thought about saying something, but remembered we'd forbidden him from drinking—making him dial it back on eating would be cruel and unusual punishment, especially given how good this food actually was.

I thought about going back for seconds, but standing up reminded me how tight my dress pants were, so I put my plate down with enormous regret on a side table set up for that purpose. "Where's your uncle?" I asked, stretching and reaching for my drink. I was feeling full—a little overstuffed, if I was going to be completely honest.

"I don't know." Taylor finished the last of the shrimp creole and rice on his plate and smiled at me. "He was talking to Rain the last time I saw him, but I was hungry and…" His voice trailed off.

Food was always his top priority.

I was just about to go looking for Frank—the exercise, I figured, would help work off some of the way too many calories I'd just shoveled in—when Gaspard the pig came snuffling up to me, sniffing around at my feet and then looking up at me expectantly. I reached down and scratched his forehead. He grunted contentedly and closed his eyes about halfway.

"Gaspard, it looks like you made a new friend," a woman said, walking up to us both with a broad smile on her face. She held out her small hand. "Alison Strauss."

"Scotty Bradley," I replied, shaking her hand while continuing to scratch Gaspard's head with my other hand.

Alison was pretty, maybe my age or possibly slightly older or younger, it was hard to tell. Her forehead was remarkably smooth, and her eyebrows didn't move much when she smiled. She had dark auburn hair, parted perfectly in the center of her head, that reached down past her shoulders with a slight curl at the ends. She couldn't have been more than five feet tall, if that, with a very slender build and an impossibly small waist. Her short black pleated tennis skirt revealed strongly muscled, tanned legs, and her white short-sleeved blouse was cut low in the front to show off cleavage that had to have been helped by either underwire support or implants. Her oval face was tanned and her greenish eyes danced as she looked back and forth from her pig to me.

"You're Rain's brother, aren't you?" She reached into a pocket and pulled out a small piece of carrot, which she fed to Gaspard. "You kind of look like her. I'm surprised we've never met before. I went to McGehee with your sister, you know. We've known each other forever."

"Did you ever come by our house?" I asked, trying to remember if I had met her. Now that I thought about it, she did look kind of familiar to me.

She laughed. "No, Rain and I ran with different crowds, I'm afraid. We were friends but we never really hung out." She tilted her head sideways and peered at me a little more closely. "You went to Jesuit, though, didn't you? You must have known my cousins? Jesse and Dylan Metoyer?"

"Yes," I said carefully. "They were in my class."

She laughed again. "I can tell by the look on your face you knew Jesse. He was a little shithead, is what he was. He drove me insane. He was such a spoiled, entitled little monster. Dylan wasn't much better. My mother was a Metoyer—Riley was her twin brother, actually. Twins run in the family." She wrapped her arms around herself and looked back at the house. "She died... she died before the trouble."

Trouble was an interesting way to put it.

"I'm sorry."

"I was really young when it happened," she replied. She shrugged her shoulders slightly. "My dad remarried, but I was a Metoyer, so he thought it was important for me to know the rest of my mother's people." She shivered. "I spent some time here when I was a kid. Never really liked it much, you know? I couldn't wait to get back home—especially after Uncle Riley married Aunt Arlene. She was a very strange woman, obviously."

"That must have been rough." I wasn't sure what to say. She had to be sick to death of being asked about Delilah's murder.

"At least most people don't know I'm a Metoyer." She shivered again. "After Delilah died, of course, I never came over anymore. Uncle Riley and Aunt Arlene never really wanted to see people. I can't say as I blame them."

"It must be strange for you, being here now, with someone else owning the house," I replied, "given it was always in your family."

"It's not like I ever lived here," she replied. "Uncle Riley and my mother would have been the last of the family. Now that Uncle Riley's dead"—she again gave that little shrug—"I guess Dylan, Jesse, and I are the only ones left."

"I didn't realize he'd died." It *was* strange. Usually when something happened to someone involved with the case, there was another flurry of interest in the media.

"He took the boys and moved away, once they could. He and Aunt Arlene never divorced though, she kept on living here…I never heard from them once they moved away. I think they changed their names? I was notified—he left me some money in his will—but the lawyer never told me what name they were living under. I haven't seen or heard from Jesse or Dylan since they left New Orleans." She didn't sound like she was particularly sad about it.

Then again, I wasn't particularly close to any of my cousins, either. I made what I hoped was an appropriate noise.

"If you're Rain's brother, that means you're a Diderot—so you're Garden District, too."

"Yes, but I've never lived here. I grew up in the Quarter and still live there."

"We live over on Eighth Street." She laughed. "Still live in the same house I grew up in...no, I never really had any connection to this old place other than tradition, I guess. I was glad Aunt Arlene sold it to Serena, honestly. Exorcize some of the old ghosts. It's past time for that, way past time." She looked over at the building lit up in the back of the yard. "That's where they found her, you know. Like I said, after Delilah died, we never really came around much anymore. Mom and Dad didn't want to have much to do with that side of the family, and they didn't want us around anyway." She made a face. "I tried, a couple of years ago, to try to patch things up with Aunt Arlene...try to, you know, help her out. Things got really bad here for her after Uncle Riley took the boys and moved away." She ran a hand through her hair.

"What do you mean, bad?"

She gave me an enigmatic smile. "Oh, I've been talking your ear off for long enough now, and you aren't interested in our old family skeletons. I should go find my husband. It was lovely meeting you. Come on, Gaspard."

She walked away on the edge of the crowd, her pig walking beside her.

I watched her go, wondering what she meant by *things got really bad here for her.*

How could they have gotten *worse*?

I thought about going to look for Frank again. Taylor wasn't by the food table anymore. I sighed. I wasn't really in the mood to walk into the crowd or look for them. But I needed to do something, move around a bit and work off some of the food, so I walked away from the party toward the pool. Once I was away from the party and the cool air blowing from the humming air-conditioning units, the heat of the night smothered me again. I wiped sweat from my forehead as I got closer to the pool. It was lit from below so the water was glowing bluish green from the paint on the pool bottom. No one was over at this end of the expansive yard.

And just beyond the pool was the carriage house.

I'd seen it any number of times, in newspaper reports and on the news.

The Murder House! the headlines always screamed, with a photo of Delilah with the helmet of massive blond hair, teased and sprayed into an enormous bouffant, her face covered and caked with makeup to sexualize her, superimposed over it.

It was a long wooden building, with a gallery running along the upper floor with doors at either end. There were also doors at opposite ends of the ground floor, and the one on the left was open—the door where they found her body twenty-five years ago. Yet it was lit; every window blazed with light behind closed blinds. I shivered involuntarily despite the hot, heavy, damp air. Curiosity—a kind of nosiness that I wasn't proud to feel, the kind that makes people slow down as they pass car accidents—made me start walking toward the carriage house.

The low murmur of voices startled me, and I looked back at the lit pool. On the far side a man and a woman were talking quietly, close to the edge. The light from the water wasn't bright enough for me to see them clearly, but I could tell it was a man and a woman. He was wearing a dark blue blazer, khaki slacks, and a white racing cap. She was wearing a very short dress that clung to her tightly. I couldn't understand anything they were saying—their words didn't carry across the pool over the sound of the jazz band, and the buzz of the party crowd talking was a dull roar in the background. As I watched, she pulled away from him suddenly and slapped him across the face, so hard I could hear the smack. Her heels clicked against the stones as she ran away from him. She passed directly underneath one of Japanese lanterns, and I saw her face in profile clearly. It took me a second to place her: Kaye Hughes, a successful and very well-known realtor. I'd never met her, but I'd seen her face in any number of ads in the local paper or on signs on buildings for sale or rent. She continued across the lawn until she disappeared back into the crowd.

The man straightened his hat, looked over at me, tipped it slightly to me, and walked after her.

He looked vaguely familiar as well, in that vague way everyone in New Orleans looks familiar.

Ah, Garden District parties, I thought with a slight smile as I walked toward the carriage house. *It's pretty sad when the best-behaved guest is the pig.*

As I got closer to the door, I checked to see if anyone was watching. I knew it was silly, but it felt weird, almost disrespectful, to nose around the place her body was found, even after all these years. Yet I couldn't stop myself. It was some weird compulsion I just couldn't fight off. Even though I knew it was morbid, wrong, and maybe just a little sick, I wanted—no, make that *had*—to go inside and have a look around.

It wasn't really trespassing, was it? No part of the grounds had been named off-limits. Serena hadn't said no one could go back there, or couldn't explore the main house, for that matter. I glanced back at where the rest of the party was going on, under the Japanese lanterns. No one was looking over toward the carriage house, no one was paying me the least bit of attention. Everyone was involved in their eating and drinking and their conversations. The pool area was completely deserted now.

Somehow, knowing no one would notice me slip inside made me feel better.

And I wasn't very proud of that, either.

There was a flagstone walk from the left side door to the pool, and it also continued across the front to the door on the right side. There was a flower bed inside the walk, rose bushes wilted from the heat, the flowers over-opened and dead petals lying in the black dirt. I wiped my forehead and looked back once again. If one person was looking, I wouldn't go inside.

No one was looking.

The door was slightly ajar, and I could hear soft music playing inside, a woman's smooth alto voice crooning a song that was vaguely familiar, but I couldn't place it.

"Hello?" I called softly, pushing the door gently with my fingertips. It swung slowly open. I looked over my shoulder yet another time to see if anyone was watching, but the coast was still clear. I stepped over the threshold and moved the door back to the almost closed position it had been in before I trespassed.

It's not trespassing, she's having a party in the yard and no one said the carriage house was off-limits, and the door wasn't shut or locked.

"Technicalities," I scoffed at myself as I looked around the big room.

There was no one in the room.

In spite of myself I felt a chill. Right over there was where— where they found her. I closed my eyes and said a quick prayer for her soul.

Why is this affecting you so much? I asked myself. *You've stumbled over dead bodies before—this is just a twenty-five-year-old crime scene.*

If I hadn't known that, I probably would have thought the place was charming.

The ceiling was much lower than the high ceilings I was used to, and the floor was slate. The room was the entire length of the building, and black metal spiral staircase led upstairs at the far end. There wasn't much furniture inside. As I recalled from reading *Garden District Gothic*, the Metoyers had primarily used the carriage house as a guest house, but most of the time they used it for storage. Against the far wall was a kitchen counter, a refrigerator, a double sink, and a dishwasher. Cheap-looking plywood cabinets were underneath the counter, and there were matching ones mounted on the wall above the counter. There were also several rows of drawers. There was an iHome player on the counter with an original white iPad. It came to me in that moment what the music was—"Rainy Days and Mondays" by the Carpenters.

My mother loved the Carpenters and used to listen to them a lot when I was growing up.

Now that I was inside, it felt weird being inside the Murder House. In spite of myself, I felt a chill go up my spine. There had been plenty of pictures of the inside—one of the tabloids had managed to get their hands on some of the crime scene photos. Not the ones with Delilah herself, but rather ones with the taped outline of her body on the floor. I closed my eyes and tried to remember the pictures. There had been furniture in the place back then—a small table and chairs, a sofa and reclining chairs, a coffee table—but I remembered that boxes and sporting equipment her older brothers had outgrown that Arlene intended to donate to charity had been stacked and piled up along the front of the kitchen counter.

Oh, yes. There was ski equipment, of course. Jesse and Dylan were both big into skiing. I could hear them again, bragging about the ski trips they took around the world every winter to "get the best snow." They were gone a lot back then in the winter, missing a week here and there, coming back to school with their faces burned from the wind and the sun off the snow, their faces white around the eyes where they'd worn their ski goggles. To hear them tell it, they'd been competitive-level skiers—practically ready for the racing circuit.

I'd never believed a word of it, of course.

God, they'd been insufferable assholes! The kind of guys who bragged about all the sex they were having—which probably meant they were virgins. They exaggerated everything and had a gang of jock buddies who believed everything they said. They were all cut from the same cloth, really. And they'd never bothered me after that time in eighth grade when I took Jesse down in front of a crowd and made him cry.

That memory always made me smile.

I stood there, thinking, goose bumps rising on my arms.

It felt—it felt like I wasn't alone.

I spun around, but there was no one behind me.

The place was empty.

If I was remembering everything correctly—and I probably was, the story had been told and repeated so many times—the night of the murder the nanny, Robin Strickland, came home from a date around two in the morning and went upstairs to check on her charge. She'd had the night off, and both Riley and Arlene had taken Delilah upstairs early after dinner to put her to bed. In two days, Arlene was taking her out to Los Angeles to audition for a role on a television series, and it looked like it could be the big break they'd been waiting for; the producers were very excited about Delilah. So, of course, Delilah had been very excited about it, and it had taken them a while to get her to drift off to sleep. They'd gone back downstairs and watched television until about eleven, and then they, too, went to bed. Robin and her boyfriend had been to a party and had been drinking, so she was a little tipsy when she got home and discovered Arlene was in her bed.

Robin had also been the one to notice, around four in the morning, that the lights were on in the carriage house. The family lawyer was already there, of course—they'd called him immediately upon finding the ransom note—and the police hadn't yet been called because, as the story went, they were trying to decide what to do about the ransom. A lot of people— Veronica Vance, for one—believed it was suspicious they'd called the lawyer instead of the police, seeing that as a sign of guilt. (I could hear that nasal whine of Veronica's even now, twenty-five years later, shrieking into the camera, "What kind of parents call their lawyer first?")

But even as a fifteen-year-old, I could see the fallacy in Veronica Vance's logic. It made sense to me they'd not call the police when she went missing and a ransom note warning them not to call the police had turned up. They were also not thinking clearly. Who would be in that situation?

And there was never any evidence or signs that the Metoyers hadn't worshiped Delilah; even her asshole brothers were part of the weird Delilah Metoyer fan club. I mean, Taylor had only been my nephew—part of my family—for a few months, and if he was kidnapped I would do everything the kidnappers told me to do.

And if they harmed a hair on his head I wouldn't rest until I'd hunted every last one of them down.

The body had been found behind the sofa, which had been on the opposite end of the room from the staircase.

I felt a weird chill again, the hair on the back of my neck standing up.

It had been a long time since I'd had anything slightly resembling a psychic occurrence. My mother's friend Madame Xena, who was the first one who discovered that I had some abilities, believed that as I got older the gift was fading from me. I could still read the cards, every once in a while getting a hint from the Goddess about what was going on, but the days when she came to me in visions and spoke to me through the cards every day were long gone. I'd communicated with a dead man once—but that had been a one-time occurrence, thank you very much. It had been kind of creepy, and I was glad it never happened again. When I stopped to think about it, it made me just a little sad. It was all part and parcel of getting older, I guess, but there was also a sense that it was also tied to me no longer being quite as free a spirit as I used to be. The days when I never knew how I was going to pay the rent, when I'd go down to the Pub and dance on the bar for tips in a thong to make rent, when I'd go home with some hot guy I'd just met and never bothered to learn his last name or remember his first name, the days of dancing for hours on Ecstasy in a crowd of hot shirtless men, the flirting and getting high all the time, personal training and teaching aerobics and drinking too much and having hellish hangovers that could only be cured by a bacon mushroom cheeseburger from the Nelly Deli—I sometimes missed that Scotty. But I was pretty happy with my life, really. It was nice having the money from my trust funds—both grandfathers finally released them to me when I turned thirty—and the quarterly interest payments was more money than I could possibly spend in three months. It was great being in a committed relationship with two great guys who loved me…

But missing my past sometimes didn't mean I didn't appreciate my present and my future.

Whoa there, Scotty. I shook my head and laughed a bit. *That was quite a riff from wondering if you were sensing a dead spirit here, or if the Goddess was going to speak to you again.*

But on the other hand, that was the kind of stream-of-conscious thinking I used to experience when I was about to have an experience based in the gift—

"There you are," Frank said from behind me, making me jump and my heart thud.

"Sheesh, don't *do* that," I said, taking some deep breaths as my heart pounded in my ears. "I could have a heart attack or something."

"What are you doing in here?" Frank frowned, looking around. "Isn't this—isn't this where they found her?"

I nodded. "I can't explain it. I—I just wanted to see it."

"That's creepy, Scotty." Frank shook his head. "I think it's time for us to get going. Rain just left."

"She did?"

Frank shrugged. "She wasn't feeling well, she said. It's so weird—the air-conditioned area and then the rest of the yard—the extremes. I wasn't feeling so hot myself a while ago. And I want to get out of here before the intervention."

"Intervention?"

"Serena tipped me off." He shook his head. "There's some woman here and she is so wasted—her family is going to stage an intervention—"

"At a party?"

"Never a dull moment," Serena said, standing in the doorway. "You can stop hiding, Frank, she's already been carted off to rehab." Her electric cigarette glowed blue as she inhaled. "Honestly. Did you know her daughter had some friends over for a sleepover? I called their parents, and get this—they asked me if they could have a few more hours without the kids!" She threw her head back and laughed wickedly. "I love this city so much! In Dallas they'd be so worried about their precious little snowflakes they would have sent out the *National Guard!*" She coughed. "Besides, the party is already winding down."

"Winding down?" I gaped at her.

"Darling, it's after midnight."

I looked back and forth from her to Frank a few times.

I'd been in the carriage house that long?

What the hell?

It had only seemed like a few minutes.

I followed them back outside, and sure enough, the party was thinned out. Several people were talking louder the way people do when they've had too much to drink, and others were sort of weaving in place. There was a thick cloud of marijuana smoke over by the pool as several people passed a joint back and forth. The catering table was gone, and the bar was being broken down by the bartenders.

Serena held out an elegant hand to be shaken. "Darlings, thank you for coming to my nasty little soirée. Please call me—I do hope we'll be friends."

Frank shook her hand and I kissed her cheek. "I would like that very much," I said as Taylor materialized.

"Are we going?" he asked with a big grin. "I mean, it's hard to top having a guest carted off to rehab. No offense, ma'am, but it's got to be all downhill from here."

"Yes, that will be hard to top the next time I have a party," Serena agreed with a raucous laugh. "Au revoir, my dears."

We made our way to the house, nodding good-byes and smiling at various people we knew slightly. Alison was standing by the foot of the stairs to the house, Gaspard at her side. I said good-bye to Gaspard, who snorted appreciatively as I scratched his head. As we strolled down the front walk to the gate, Frank draped his arm around my shoulders and I leaned into him slightly. I said good night to the security guard. I still couldn't place him, but I knew him from *somewhere*.

We started walking back to the car. We had gotten about halfway to the car when a man about my age stepped in front of us on the next block.

"I'm sorry to bother you," he nodded in the direction of Serena's house, "but is there a party going on at the Metoyer house?"

In the faint moonlight I couldn't get a really good look at him, but there was something about him that looked vaguely familiar. "Yes, there's a party there," I replied as Frank's arm tightened around my shoulders. "but it's not the Metoyer place anymore. The house was sold recently."

He whistled. "Okay, thank you." Without another word, he walked over to a small Honda parked across the street and got in. He started the car and drove off into the night.

I stared after him, unable to shake the feeling that I knew him from somewhere.

"You okay?" Frank asked. "Come on, let's get home." He wiggled his eyebrows at me. "You're looking mighty fine in that dress, ma'am."

I laughed and shook off the feeling. It was probably nothing.

It hit me when we got to our car.

No, you're making things up because you lost time in the carriage house, I thought as I strapped myself into the car as Taylor started the engine.

That man couldn't have been Jesse Metoyer, could he?

CHAPTER FOUR
SEVEN OF WANDS, REVERSED
Don't let others take advantage of you

I was just finishing putting the groceries away when my phone started buzzing.

As I closed the cupboard and picked up my phone, I sighed and considered letting it go to voice mail. I was tired. Every time I'd dropped off to sleep I'd had a horrible recurring nightmare. I was back at Serena's walking to the carriage house—the *murder* house—on a chilly night. It seemed like it was October, and there was no moon. It was very dark, but there were lights on in the carriage house, and even though each step taking me closer filled me with a greater, stronger sense of dread—every fiber in my body was screaming *don't go in there, turn and run, there's still time*—in that horrible way nightmares had, I couldn't stop walking forward. I had to go there, I had to go inside, I was being compelled, the answer was in there, no matter how badly I didn't want to know the truth, no matter how awful it was going to be, I couldn't stop. I would reach the door, smell lilies of the valley, and hear the Carpenters playing, sometimes "Rainy Days and Mondays," the next time "Only Yesterday" or "Close to You" or "Hurting Each Other," Karen's mournful heartbroken voice reaching down into the pain in my soul and grabbing on with both hands and twisting, and I would start to step over the threshold inside and—

I'd wake up, gasping with my heart racing.

At around seven in the morning I got tired of the cycle of sleep/nightmare/wake up and got out of bed. Frank was snoring lightly, his back turned to me, and I knew Taylor was dead to the world upstairs.

This knowledge didn't improve my mood in the least.

I cleaned the kitchen, picked up the living room, and started doing laundry while drinking coffee and trying to shake off the lingering sense of impending doom left over from the nightmare. I thought about getting out my cards—obviously, being at the murder house had triggered something in me; maybe the gift was going to find its way back to me after all this time—but having been disappointed so many times in trying to read the cards, I wasn't in a good enough place emotionally to go through that again.

I was tired and cranky.

I went upstairs and got Taylor's clothes to put in the washing machine. The upstairs apartment was a disaster area. I stopped myself from waking him up and making him clean it. Colin was coming home soon enough, and he'd not stand for that mess.

Honestly, teenagers.

Get off my lawn!

I also decided to go buy groceries. I'd always thought Frank ate a lot, but it was amazing the way food vanished ever since Taylor came to live with us. We were out of a lot of things, and with Colin coming home—usually this was something Frank took care of, since I hated driving, but I needed something to do before everyone got up to entertain myself.

Frank was still asleep when I got back from Rouses, but Taylor had already left for his shift at the Devil's Weed.

I sighed and glanced at my phone. It was Mom, and if she was calling at this hour on a Sunday, she wanted something.

That's incredibly cynical. Just because you're in a bad mood, don't take it out on Mom, I chided myself. *Suck it up and take the damned call. You don't KNOW she wants you to do something you don't want to.*

That made me laugh, but I still didn't want to take her call. With Taylor at work and Colin maybe coming home today, I'd wanted to just spend the day relaxing with Frank. He had to drive back over to Pensacola on Monday to plan out next weekend's wrestling shows and get in some rehearsal time. He always planned to drive back home, but inevitably the day would run late and he'd end up being too tired to drive back. Sometimes he was gone for the whole week, though, so I should count my blessings.

But at least he doesn't have any shows until Friday night, I reminded myself.

It's not easy being in a three-way relationship with two people who are never home.

I also wanted to get to the gym before church let out. Despite being a decadent city known for debauchery and sin, the best time to do anything on a weekend in New Orleans was on Sundays during church. During football season, that window opened up even more. The city turned into a ghost town during Saints games.

I sighed and looked at the clock. It wasn't quite noon yet. Mom was rarely up before noon. I picked up the phone and clicked Accept. "Hey, Mom. What are you doing up so early? I was just getting ready to go to the gym—"

She cut me off. "You can go to the gym anytime. You need to come over. Right now. It's important."

"Mom—"

"See you in fifteen minutes. And bring Frank." She hung up.

I sighed and put the phone down.

I knew I shouldn't have answered.

Don't get me wrong, I love my mom. She's amazing. But her definition of *important* could mean anything from "we have to go bail your brother out of jail" to "we HAVE to do something to stop big oil destroying the wetlands!"

Not that both aren't equally important. But I *really* wanted to go to the gym.

Mom was a force of nature. Sure, her passionate determination could be annoying at times, but her heart was always firmly in the right place. Once I moved into my own place, she dealt with whatever empty nest pangs she had by collecting what we call in the family her strays. Emily Hunter had started out as one of Mom's strays. A cute lesbian who'd come down from Chicago for Mardi Gras, she decided to stay and met Mom on Fat Tuesday at some party in the Quarter. By the time they'd finished talking, Mom had hired her to work at the shop and found her an inexpensive studio apartment in the Quarter. Emily sang with a band—her voice was amazing—that played gigs around town most nights of the week, and of course she still worked days running Mom and Dad's tobacco shop, the Devil's Weed. I'd come to think of her as another sister—and she was just *one* of Mom's strays. She took to both Colin and Frank immediately, and she'd welcomed Taylor into the family the moment she met him, hiring him to work part-time at the Devil's Weed, which was on the first floor of the building she and Dad owned on the corner of Dumaine and Royal streets. "You have to have a job," she said patiently when she let him know he was going to be a part-time employee, right after he came to live with us. "Otherwise you'll be spoiled. And if you're going to work, you might as well work for family. You're never too young to learn the value of hard work and a dollar."

Of course, now she was spoiling Taylor much worse than I ever dared to even try. She was always buying him little gifts and clothes, and forcing food on him.

Well, trying to, at any rate. Mom and Dad were strict vegetarians. Taylor's feelings about tofu were very similar to mine—I'd rather eat one of my shoes.

Taylor worshipped both her and Dad.

The joints of the best pot available in Louisiana that she was always slipping into his shirt pockets didn't hurt, either. Mom and Dad were unrepentant stoners and always had a supply of the best money could buy on hand. They often stayed up until dawn, smoking and drinking wine and having long discussions about politics and art and the state of the world with whatever friend or family member had stopped by the night before. As far back as I could remember, our apartment on top of the store had always reeked of marijuana smoke. I'd lost count of how many times she and Dad had been arrested at protests.

She was always making sandwiches and taking them out to the street kids spare-changing on Decatur Street. She taught all of us to donate shoes and clothes that were still wearable to homeless shelters rather than throwing them away.

She was amazing. A gay kid couldn't have asked for better parents than mine. She was a great mother—she'd always been supportive of all of us kids. She'd been thrilled when I came out to them when I was fifteen, joining PFLAG and marching in Pride parades, daring any homophobe to challenge her. She was passionate about things she believed in—protesting nuclear power plants, women's rights, civil rights for all, health care. She'd marched and protested I don't know how many things, and had been arrested any number of times. The joke in the family is my brother Storm became a lawyer because legal fees were sending us to the poorhouse. She'd recently been arrested for slugging the homophobic lieutenant governor, which started an investigation that resulted in his eventual arrest and conviction for corruption. She and Dad were both what people would probably call hippies, and from the moment they were married they'd lived over the Devil's Weed, which is where we all grew up. My mother had inherited the building from a great-aunt who was very similar to her, a Quarter bohemian who wanted nothing to do with the stuffy Garden District society she'd been born into. Mom could be a bit much to handle sometimes, but like I said, the good far outweighed the bad. It had really warmed my heart to see how Mom and Dad both had taken to Taylor, treating him like the grandson they'd always wished to have. I suspect he was probably not the best employee at the Devil's Weed—every time I walked by there when he was working he was reading a book with his feet up on the counter.

And after the horrible experience he'd had with his own ultraconservative religious family, it was kind of nice to see him in the bosom of my family.

Although I did worry he'd taken to the pot smoking a little too much.

Get off my lawn!

Seriously, I reminded myself. *Get over yourself. Mom and Dad had you smoking pot by the time you were thirteen and look at how—*

I stopped *that* thought dead in its tracks.

Frank walked into the kitchen with a joint in his hand.

"I thought we were going to go to the gym," I said, taking the joint out of his fingers.

"Just waiting for you to finish putting everything away." Frank leaned over and kissed my neck as I pinched the joint out with my thumb and forefinger. "Besides, I focus on my workout better if I have a bit of a buzz."

"How far you've come from the FBI agent who was horrified by my family's drug abuse," I replied with a smile. "That was Mom on the phone. She wants us to come over—in fifteen minutes, to be exact."

"And didn't say why, of course." He made a face. "I suppose there's nothing to do but go, right? We can hit the gym later."

"Yeah. I just hate putting it off." I sighed. "But you have to make me go later if I don't want to, okay?" I was getting into the very bad habit of finding excuses not to work out—which explained those pesky extra pounds and my unintentionally tight clothes. Back when I was a trainer, I used to caution my clients about this very behavior.

Former trainer, heal thyself.

"Of course I will." He pushed away from the kitchen counter. "Come on, we'd better get moving before she calls back."

Mom and Dad only live about six blocks or so away from our place, and most of the year it's a gorgeous walk. I usually walk up Chartres Street, past the Ursulines Convent and the Beauregard-Keyes House on nice days. But in the brutal heat of an August early afternoon, it felt more like several miles than just six blocks. Just getting the groceries in from the car had drained my energy, yet another exercise in learning to live in clothes soaked in sweat. My clothes had dried a bit, but my socks were still wet. I changed into fresh clothes and tucked a spare pair of socks in my shorts pocket to change into once we got to Mom and Dad's.

There's *nothing* worse than wet socks.

Another thing that was different now was we no longer had an off-season from the tourists. Before the flood, the Quarter was a ghost town in the summertime before the hordes of gay boys descended on us for Southern Decadence over Labor Day. That always signaled the end of the off-season, and until the heat really kicked into gear again the next June, the city was always filled with tourists. In recent years we weren't getting that breathing space anymore. The last few summers had been much more pleasant than usual and I wondered if that was why the tourists didn't take the summers off anymore. But this summer—this horrible, blast furnace of a summer—hadn't affected the tourist trade as much as I would have thought.

The tourists were few and far between as we escaped out the front gate onto Decatur Street. I was already sweating, and Frank even took off the baseball cap he usually wore to protect his shaved head from the sun and shook sweat out of it as we stood there in the shade. The tourists were staying out of the heat, like anyone with a brain.

I hated seeing the windows of the business on the first floor boarded up. It had been a Mom-and-Pop grocery store for as long as I could remember, owned and operated by the Duchesnay family for years. The building had been Molotov cocktailed the Southern Decadence before Katrina (long story) and burned down. Mama Duchesnay chose that opportunity to retire. It had then become a costume shop for a brief while before Hurricane Katrina, and was empty for about a year before a coffee shop went in. The coffee shop had shut down at the start of the summer—the business owners skipped town owing God and everyone money. Millie wouldn't say how far behind they were on the rent, and the subject always made her face get thunderous, so I never pursued the subject. Because of the big glass windows in the front were a break-in hazard with the place unoccupied, Millie and Velma had the windows boarded up while they looked for a new tenant. It was a prime location, and the rent they were asking wasn't, given how insane rental prices had shot up, too bad. I figured someone would snap it right up, but nothing had worked out yet. I suspect this had more to do with Millie and Velma being much stricter about whom they rented to than anything else. Millie and Velma decided to give up for the month of August while they were at the beach, and let a real estate agent keep looking. As far as I knew, no one had even looked at the place since they'd gone to Destin.

But who would want to start a business in August in New Orleans?

I could feel the heat from the sidewalk through the soles of my shoes, and I took a gulp from my bottle of water. The heat index was somewhere around 115. The power bill for our apartments was going to be outrageous, but it was worth every penny. It was worse on the fourth floor in Taylor's apartment because the small attic above his roof wasn't insulated and all the building's heat rose, of course. I'd noticed a few times going up there he had the thermostat set to arctic...but I couldn't blame him. When the summers got bad, Colin usually stayed down with us on the third floor.

"This better be important," Frank complained, pulling his shirt up and wiping his reddening head as we turned the corner onto Royal Street. The blond hairs on his abs were dark with sweat.

"It could be anything," I replied, pressing my now lukewarm water bottle on the back of my neck as we kept trudging along. "I may not leave there until the sun goes down."

"God, I can't believe how hot it is." He wiped at his face again. His face was completely red as we crossed St. Philip Street.

"Hey, Colin's been in the Middle East all summer," I protested in response. "It could be worse. Just one more block."

It seemed to take an eternity in the heat, but finally we got there. I unlocked the gate to the back stairs. The doorknob on the back door was so hot I jumped back with a cry when I touched it. Frank wrapped his shirt around his hand and pushed it open. The cold air blowing out through the open door felt heavenly. I pulled the door shut behind us as we stepped into the darkened kitchen.

I could hear Pink Floyd music playing softly in the living room—"Comfortably Numb"—and I could also smell pot smoke. "Don't smoke any more or we'll never make it to the gym," Frank whispered as we crossed the kitchen to the big double doors leading into their living room.

I gave him a dirty look as we walked through the big doors into the living room, which was only lit by scented candles. Jasmine, if I had to hazard a guess.

Mom and Dad sat side by side on the couch. There was someone else sitting in one of their easy chairs. My eyes were still getting accustomed to the lower light after the brightness of the sun outside, but I could see Mom was taking an enormous hit from a dragon-shaped glass bong. She was wearing one of her Moroccan muumuus, her graying hair tied in its customary ropelike braid down her back.

"Boys!" Dad said, getting up and crossing the room to hug us both. He was wearing a pair of cargo shorts and a baggy Grateful Dead tour shirt. Dad's tall and lanky, and his graying hair is always pulled back into a ponytail. His glasses had slid halfway down his nose, and he hadn't shaved in a couple of days. One of the biggest disappointments in his life was his inability to grow a beard. But still he tried, every once in a while. "Scotty, an old friend of yours dropped by to see us." He turned slightly and gestured to the person in the easy chair.

My eyes had adjusted enough to realize the stranger, getting up now with a tentative smile on his face, was the same guy I'd talked to outside Serena's house the night before…and I realized, with my heart sinking, that I hadn't been wrong. It was Jesse Metoyer.

My old bully.

Delilah Metoyer's older brother.

"Hey," he said, sticking out his hand. "I thought that might have been you outside the house last night but I wasn't sure. It's really nice to see you again. It's been a long time."

"Yes, yes it has," I replied stiffly, shaking his hand and letting go as quickly as I could. "This is my partner, Frank Sobieski. Frank, this is Jesse Metoyer. We went to school together here when we were kids."

Frank raised his eyebrows questioningly, but was too polite to do or say anything other than shake Jesse's hand and murmur "nice to meet you."

"Sit down, sit down!" Dad said, gently nudging Frank and me over to the love seat. We sat down, and Jesse took his seat back in his chair.

"Do you boys want any wine?" Mom asked, but we both declined. She held the bong in our direction with an inquiring look on her face. I was tempted, but when Frank said no I reluctantly shook my head. "Suit yourselves," Mom replied, taking another hit.

I couldn't stop staring at Jesse Metoyer in the dim candlelight. We'd been sophomores at Jesuit High when Delilah was murdered. I was a star on the Jesuit wrestling team then, and he played on the football and baseball teams. Our social circles certainly didn't overlap, so by then I only really saw him in the hallways or if we had a class together.

Much as I hated to admit it, I'd been kind of attracted to both twins when we were in high school—but Jesse more so than Dylan. Dylan was also on the football and baseball teams, but he seemed a pale imitation of his brother rather than his equal. Dylan kept more to himself, always looked a little disheveled and confused—his shirts never tucked in right, his tie slightly askew, his hair a mess. Jesse was always impeccably put together. He wore his clothes tighter to show off his muscles and his body. We had PE together that year, and I found myself watching Jesse when no one was looking—stealing glances, watching the way the light made the sweat on his body glisten, looking across the locker room to catch a glimpse of him in his tight white briefs. He was always loud, always talking about his sexual conquests of girls from Sacred Heart or Newman or any other school, giving the impression that all he had to do was flash his crooked grin at some girl and she'd drop her panties for him.

Sometimes at night, alone in my bed, I would remember those images from the locker room, from gym class, or just seeing him strutting down the hallway with his entourage in tow, and would get aroused.

I hated myself because of this attraction to him. I hadn't come out to my parents yet, and so my sexuality was a deep dark secret I was keeping from everyone, and I'd wondered if I'd deserved to be bullied, deserved to be treated the way I was. How did he know? I wondered to myself in the quiet of my room with the lights off and the door locked. How did they all know about me?

They'd left me alone since Storm had convinced me to go out for wrestling.

We were in the eighth grade when Jesse bumped up against me hard in the hall with his idiot buddies around him. "Watch where you're going, fag," he sneered at me. "How many dicks have you sucked today?"

I took him down and within thirty seconds had complete control of him, his arm twisted back to the breaking point, and he was crying, begging me to stop hurting him. After that they all left me alone, but I knew they still said shit about me behind my back like the cowards they were.

Because I'd hear the snickering when I walked past them in the halls at school—but I also knew none of them would ever have the nerve to say it to my face ever again.

And somehow I was attracted to this guy, this louse of a person, and fantasized about him.

Then Delilah was murdered, and neither Metoyer twin was ever seen again at Jesuit High.

Is there anything worse than being attracted to your bully?

But he'd been a good-looking kid, with his thick dark brown hair parted in the center and his big brown heavy-lidded eyes. He hadn't had the pimple problem so many of us did, and he hit the genetic jackpot with his body, too. Maybe it was all the skiing he bragged about, or playing sports, but he had a great body in high school. Broad shoulders, narrow waist, perfect bubble butt, big arms…but now?

He hadn't aged well, to be honest. His once luxuriant dark brown hair was thinning badly in the front, but he wore it long on the sides and the back in a really bad and obvious attempt at hiding it. He hadn't quite reached the comb-over stage yet, but it looked like he would have no problem once he went bald on the top. His hairline had made a steady retreat at the temples, but there was still a solitary lock in the direct center that he grew long to try to hide the exposed forehead on one side. Over the years he had let his body go a little to seed. He was thicker in the waist, there was a bulge to his stomach underneath the red polo shirt, and his skin was pale. White hairs stuck out of the collar of his shirt, and I suspected the strange brown color of his hair wasn't natural. His big brown eyes were just as pretty as they'd been when we were teens, but now they seemed sunken, with enormous dark circles underneath them. The eyes were bloodshot and he was blinking oddly, which meant he was probably wearing contact lenses that weren't entirely comfortable. There was a cheap sports watch on his wrist and a big gold class ring from the University of Florida with a gaudy, cheap-looking stone on the ring finger of his right hand.

My skin was still damp with sweat, and I shivered a little in the air-conditioning. Mom and Dad always kept their apartment at a temperature in which meat wouldn't spoil, in direct contradiction to their green save-the-planet lifestyle. "How have you been, Jesse?" I said carefully. "It's been a while."

He shifted a bit uncomfortably in his chair. "Yeah. I haven't been back to New Orleans in a long time. After…" He hesitated. "After Delilah was murdered and the press started to die down a little bit, Dad took me and Dylan to live in Florida. We always had a place in Pensacola Beach the press never seemed to know anything about, so when Dad left Arlene we went to live there."

He cleared his throat. "They never divorced, actually, but the pressure—the strain, was too much for them."

"You both went with your father?" This was from Frank, in a very even, professional FBI voice. "That's unusual."

"Arlene wasn't my mother—she was my father's second wife." Jesse shifted uncomfortably in his seat. Frank has that effect on people when he goes into interrogation mode; even though I know he loves me, it works on me, too. He has these amazing, piercing blue eyes, and the way he can just tilt his head and infuse a particular word with meaning makes you want to confess to just about anything he wants you to. "It's a long story," Jesse said slowly. "Do I need to really explain about my sister? You all know the story, right? Everyone does." He sighed, rubbing his eyes tiredly. "Or at least they think they do." He sank down even farther into the seat. "Your mom said you're a private eye now, Scotty—you and your partner, right?"

"Yes, we're licensed," I said carefully. It wasn't a lie—we'd gotten licensed in Louisiana the year before Katrina, and we've always kept our licenses current, more from habit than anything else. We've never had any official clients—which was weird, considering how many murder investigations we've been involved in over the years. But we've never actually been *hired* by anyone. My brother Storm used to pay me to do some background work for him, but I never really counted that as actual detective work.

"I want to hire you both." He looked over at my parents.

Taking a cue, they both rose and excused themselves, leaving the three of us alone in the living room.

"To do what, precisely?" Frank asked.

He swallowed. "I'm not going to lie to you both, okay?"

"Well, that would be counterintuitive," I replied. "If you want us to help you, you have to be honest with us."

"Delilah's murder destroyed my family," he said, turning beet red. "It broke up my father's marriage and ruined both my life and my brother's." He sighed. "My brother died a couple of years ago—suicide. Suicide. He hanged himself. I managed to keep it quiet and out of the papers—he was teaching at a junior college in Tampa, and we changed our names anyway when we moved. Dad didn't want anyone to know who we were, just wanted to us to have as normal lives as we could, so no one knew Dylan was Delilah Metoyer's brother...he used to tell me that the Metoyer name was cursed now. Maybe Dylan was right, maybe there is a curse on our family, I don't know." He held up his hands like he was surrendering to something. "It was hard, you know, being a Metoyer, still is. I took the name back when I got out of college. Dylan told me I was crazy. I get asked every once in a while if I'm *that* Jesse Metoyer, and I always deny it." He laughed bitterly. "Anyway, what I'm here for, what I'm wanting you to do..."

"You aren't asking us to find your sister's killer?" I asked. "Because I don't see how we could, if the police couldn't. The case is almost twenty-five years old, and it's been gone over so many times..." In spite of what I was saying, I was starting to get interested.

But still—he'd been such a *dick* to me in junior high.

"Well, no. I don't think we'll ever know the truth about Delilah." He took a deep breath. "But if you want to poke around, see what you can find out, that would be great. But what I really want—what I really want you to do—is find my mother." He swallowed. "I barely remember her. She left us when I was maybe eight or nine. And then Dad married Arlene."

"You never saw her again after she left?" Frank glanced at me.

He shook his head. "I've always wondered...I mean, especially after...after Dylan's suicide, how different things would have been if she hadn't just disappeared from our lives the way she did."

In spite of myself, I felt sorry for him. "Did your father ever say anything?"

He bit his lower lip. "When we asked he'd just shake his head and say he never heard from her, he was sorry but he couldn't make her get in touch if she just didn't want to." His voice broke, and he wiped at his eyes. "Sorry, even now...but with Dylan dead now, and Dad gone…I just thought it would be nice to see if she was still alive, ask her why, you know?"

Maybe that was why he was such a dick in junior high. Aloud, I said, "And have you asked Arlene? What does she have to say about your mom?"

"I haven't seen or spoken to her since we left New Orleans," he replied. "I don't even know where she is now. I didn't even know she'd sold the house." He added harshly, "Which would have been nice to know, I mean, maybe *I* wanted it."

Sounds like you have a lot of unresolved issues with your stepmother, if you ask me. "So what you really want us to do is look for your mother," I heard myself saying. "And if we stumble over something that might have to do with your sister's murder, you want us to pursue it? Do you really want to rehash all of that again?"

"It's always bothered me that her killer got away with it." He sighed. "I mean, I know what people said about us…about my family. It would be nice to get it all resolved once and for all… but I also know it's not likely. Not after twenty-five years." His face twisted. "I hate that Dad and Dylan both died not knowing the truth. But the priority is my mother. I want to find her. She doesn't even know that Dylan's dead." He hesitated. "She may not care, but he was her son. She has a right to know."

"Why now?" I asked without stopping to think. "Why after all these years are you interested in finding her?"

He bit his lower lip. "Something there isn't right." He shook his head. "I accepted my mother left us a long time ago. It wasn't easy—you wonder what you did to make your mother leave, you know? Why didn't she love us enough to stick around? It wasn't until I was older and put it all together—Dad was having an affair with Arlene while he was married to Mom. After Mom left, Arlene started coming around. She was really nice to me and Dylan, you know. Every once in a while I would wonder about Mom, but I finally got to the point where I was like, well *fuck her*, if she doesn't want to be around us, fine. Who needs her? But when Dad died a few months ago…well, I was a little surprised to find out a few things. Dad…well, Dad went through almost all of his money. There was hardly anything left. But Mom's money…it's just been sitting there in the bank ever since she left."

"Your mother has never touched her money?" Frank asked. "Not once?"

Jesse nodded, biting his lower lip. "Mom's money was separate from Dad's. She had her own trusts and everything her parents set up for her. When my grandparents died they left everything to her and my aunt, in separate trusts they had access to. My mother—she never touched or accessed hers after she left us."

Frank and I exchanged a glance. "Why do you think we might have success after all this time?" Frank asked. "It's been over thirty years, right?"

"I don't. I don't know that you'll find her. But it's very strange, don't you think?"

We both nodded.

"And as for Delilah, you have me to help you with that." He gave us both a hesitant grin. "I never talked to reporters, I never talked to the police without a lawyer there who never let me answer anything. That Jerry Channing didn't know shit about our family, you know? That whole *Garden District Gothic* book is bullshit." He rubbed at his eyes. "So, yeah, sure, poke around and see what you can find out about my sister, too. Find my mother, shake some trees about Delilah, see what falls out." He paused. "I also want you to find Arlene for me."

"Your stepmother?" Frank replied. We looked at each other and then back to Jesse.

He took a deep breath. "Look, you got to understand how it was in our family. My dad—he always thought Arlene killed Delilah. He went to his grave believing that. She always denied it, but he never believed her. And she—she always thought I did it." A tear slipped out of one of his eyes, and he angrily wiped at it with his right hand. "Arlene thought I killed my sister, isn't that great? So no, I never had any desire to see or talk to her again either, after we left. I don't think anyone can blame me for that. And Dad did give her the house when they separated. There was a legal agreement…but I want to know why she didn't let me know she was selling it." He swallowed. "And…she might know something about my mother. She was around back then, she might have known her, maybe Dad told her something, I don't know. But it's worth a shot to ask her, right?"

"What about the rest of your family? You mentioned an aunt." This was from me, remembering Alison and her pig at Serena's party the night before. "There must be cousins, on both sides of the family."

"My aunt—my mother's sister—her name is Lorita Godwin. She still lives in the Garden District, in the house that used to belong to my grandparents." He gave me a bitter look and just shook his head. "I tried reaching out to her when Dylan—when Dylan killed himself. She never responded, never called me back. I shouldn't have been surprised…what few relatives there were always treated us like we had the plague after what happened to Delilah. They didn't want anything to do with any of us. So much for blood." He held out his hands to us. "What do you say, guys? Please?"

"Why us?" I heard myself asking. "Why not some other firm?"

He looked surprised. "I know you, Scotty, or at least I used to. We went to school together. We may not have been close but we were friends, right?"

I was so stunned I couldn't speak.

Frank said, "We'll be glad to take the case, Jesse. We can't promise anything, of course."

He sighed in relief. "Terrific. Look, I've rented a place over in the Marigny, on Touro Street. I'm going to be in town for about a week." He held up his hands again. "How much do you charge?"

I bit my lip and glanced over at Frank, who very smoothly said, "Two hundred a day, plus expenses. You can give us a deposit for the first few days, and we'll give you a report on, say,

Wednesday. If you want us to continue, then we can take another deposit."

He pulled out a checkbook. "Okay, great. I really appreciate it, guys. Hopefully, you can get a line on Arlene sooner rather than later."

I smiled back at him. "I don't think that will be a problem."

All it would take, really, was a phone call to Serena.

Chapter Five
Queen of Wands, Reversed
She is strict to a fault and domineering…

Of course, it started raining as I drove onto the causeway bridge heading for the North Shore.

Great, I thought with a sigh as a gust of wind rocked the car, *like crossing the bridge isn't bad enough on a nice day.*

The Causeway Bridge is twenty-four miles long, stretching from Metairie just outside New Orleans across Lake Pontchartrain to Mandeville and what we call the North Shore. You don't have to drive very far onto the bridge before Metairie disappears from your rearview mirror, and all you can see is the bridge stretching out in front of you and the grayish brown water of the brackish lake on your left and right. Now, with the wind howling and fat drops of rain splatting on the windshield, there were whitecaps out on the water. I had to reach down and turn on the headlights so I could see. This was going to be one of those horrific summer storms, the kind that are a nightmare to drive in—when you have to slow down to a crawl, the pavement covered in an inch or so of water, and the day turns as dark as night.

"I can drive," Taylor said from where he was slouched down in the passenger seat, playing a video game on his phone. "I mean, you're white-knuckling the steering wheel already, and I know how much you hate to drive."

"I'm fine," I said, slowing down and cursing the bad luck that had me driving to the North Shore in a thunderstorm in the first place.

I wasn't convinced that helping out my former bully was such a great idea anyway.

The way my luck usually ran, dead bodies would probably start dropping out of the sky at any moment.

Frank had left for Pensacola at the break of dawn this morning, promising to get back as soon as possible. Still no word from Colin, either—which also had me a bit on edge. He'd originally said he'd be back on Saturday, and now it was Monday, without any word.

"Just trying to help," he replied in that sulky teenage voice I was getting to know all too well.

"Sorry, I didn't mean to snap." I glanced over at him. "I'm just worried about Colin." *Like always*, I added to myself. I hated when he was overdue. I have a very active imagination, which can be a curse.

"He'll be home soon," Taylor said with the confidence of youth, putting his phone back in his pocket. "How are we going to handle Mrs. Metoyer when we get there?"

"She just thinks we're looking for a kitten," I replied. I'd called Serena to get her number last night. Serena bought the pretext that I'd fallen in love with her kittens so much that I wanted one of my own. I knew she would—all pet owners love their pets so much they think everyone should have a similar one. I'd then called, hoping there were still kittens available. There were, and so I'd made an appointment for the next afternoon. "I'm not entirely sure all this is necessary." I flinched as one of those enormous pickup trucks shot past us at a ridiculous speed, splashing water up onto my windshield so I couldn't see for a moment or two. "Asshole," I muttered.

"He really hasn't seen her in twenty years?" Taylor asked.

"That's why Frank thought we should get the lay of the land first before letting him know where she is." I could see headlights coming up behind us very fast in the left lane in my rearview mirror. The big fat drops were hitting the car so fast and hard it almost sounded like machine gun fire. "I guess it makes sense.

It would be a big shock for both of them if he just turned up on her door."

We'd walked Jesse back to his place on Touro Street after we agreed to take his case. As we walked in the horrific heat, Frank talked to Jesse about things that didn't matter—where he went to college, what he did for a living, was he married, and what his life had been like since he'd left New Orleans. He and his brother had gone to a Catholic boys' school, St. Thomas Becket, over in Pensacola, but they had pretty much kept to themselves, not being involved in afterschool activities or sports. They didn't make friends, never invited anyone over; it was just the two of them against the world. As Jesse put it, "we tried to be as inconspicuous as possible. We were worried the more public we were—activities, sports, and so on—the more danger there was that someone might recognize us and we'd be fucked, we'd have to move and start all over again. It was hard, but it was really hard on Dad."

Once we got to the nice little Creole cottage he was renting and were inside in the cool, he told us more.

Riley Metoyer had never really held a job, despite an MBA from Emory. He just managed his inheritance investments, and he continued to do that in Pensacola while keeping a low profile.

But he'd also started drinking.

"We never heard from Arlene again once we left, and Dad— he just kind of lost interest in women," Jesse said. "They never got a divorce or anything. But as far as I know, there wasn't any communication between them. I was really surprised to find out he'd signed the house over to her...I just wish she would have come to me before she sold it...but it doesn't matter. None of it matters. There's been too much death...she may not want to make peace after all these years, but when he was dying, my father told me to try." He rubbed his face with both hands. "That's when he told me she thought I'd killed Delilah. Dad thought she was just...just trying to deflect attention away from herself, but Arlene worshipped Delilah. There's no way she would have killed her. Delilah was her whole world, and I can see why she would have thought I did it...or Dylan."

"And why was that?"

He sighed. "We were never really close to her. I guess on some level we blamed her for getting rid of our mother. I mean, she was around almost as soon as our mother was gone, and we never heard from Mom again..." His voice trailed off. "I mean, it hurt when we were kids, maybe Dylan...but she was just gone. And Arlene tried, but we—we weren't very nice to her. She always thought we were jealous of Delilah, but that wasn't true. Both Dylan and me—we loved Delilah. The stories about her being a spoiled brat, the bad behavior, all that stuff the gossip rags said? Delilah wasn't like that at all. She was a sweet little girl, and she worshipped both of us. But the night she was killed..." He took a deep breath. "We had a terrible fight at dinner, Arlene and I. Delilah had just gotten this callback audition for a sitcom, and if she got it, they'd have to move to LA because the show would shoot there, obviously. And if they were in LA filming...well, we had a big ski trip planned that winter. Switzerland. Dylan asked what would happen to the trip if she got the show, and Dad said we'd go out to LA to visit them instead of taking the trip. I kind of lost it. We were all screaming at each other." He took a deep breath and exhaled. "Before I stormed out I said I wished Delilah had never been born. It was a horrible, horrible thing to say. Delilah was crying the whole time...and I never said I was sorry to her. I was so mad I just went up to my room and slammed the door. And the next morning she was—she was dead."

I sat there watching him as he told us things no one outside the Metoyer family had ever known about the night his sister was murdered. I couldn't believe he'd made me so miserable, bullied me so harshly, and didn't remember a damned thing about it. I couldn't believe he remembered we'd been *friends.*

But given what was going on in his house at the time...

"You said your father thought Arlene had killed Delilah," Frank said, "Why would he think that?"

He sighed. "I don't know," he said. "Arlene—I don't know

what you know about my stepmother, or what you think of her, but she wasn't anything like they made her out to be. She worshipped Delilah—we all did. Dylan and I were awful to her, yes, but she stopped trying once she had Delilah. It was like me and Dylan didn't exist anymore...she finally had her own child, a girl to spoil and dress up and everything. Arlene was very talented, no one ever remembers that or talked about it back then. She was amazing. She could listen to a song on the radio and then sit down at the piano and play it. She could have been a star."

"Why didn't she pursue a career, then?" I asked, remembering. Jerry Channing had painted Arlene Metoyer as someone who'd dreamed of stardom but didn't have the ability to pull it off, the star quality and talent necessary to make it big—so she tried to make her own dreams come true by pushing them onto her eager-to-please daughter. He made her look like the stage mother from hell.

"She wanted to be a mother," he replied simply. "She didn't have any ambition for herself, no matter what Jerry Channing may think. Whenever anyone heard her play or sing, they would ask her why she wasn't a professional and she would say being a mother was more rewarding than applause. She'd been in the Miss Louisiana pageant, and I think that convinced her she really didn't want to be in the limelight. People always said Arlene forced Delilah into pageants and all that." He shrugged his shoulders. "Delilah loved it. She loved being the center of attention. If she didn't want to rehearse, or go to practice, or anything, Arlene never made her. It was all up to Delilah...no one ever believed that, of course."

"What happened that night? Besides the argument at dinner?"

"I don't know—I was in my room. Dad came by my room later to talk to me, but I wouldn't let him in...Robin—Delilah's nanny—she had a date, so I guess Arlene spent the evening with her after dinner. She usually did anyway, Robin had the world's easiest job—she was more of a glorified babysitter/chauffeur for

Delilah if Arlene wasn't available or had to be somewhere else and couldn't take care of her. Arlene usually put Delilah to bed around nine. I just stayed in my room and did my homework—we had to write a paper for US History, remember, Scotty?"

I nodded. I'd forgotten, but he was right. I'd written a paper about the Yankee occupation of New Orleans during the Civil War. I'd gotten an unfair C.

"And then I went to bed. I was tired because we'd had football practice, and I think it was about ten o'clock. I went right to sleep." He brooded for a moment, and then went on. "About one in the morning Dad woke me up because Delilah wasn't in her room and he wanted me to help look for her. I barely remember the rest of the night, or the order of things, but sometime after that they found the ransom note in the kitchen and Arlene had hysterics, I remember that, and Dad called our lawyer—Jack Fenelon—and he came over, and it was just around dawn when Robin found her." His eyes stared off into space. "It had been a terrible night, but the real trouble was just getting started."

"And Arlene blamed you?"

"She never said that to me…I had no idea she felt that way until Dad told me. She never acted any different to me or Dylan. In those months…the years after…we were all really close. I thought we'd gotten closer as a family. And then Dad told us we were moving to Pensacola, and we left."

We'd promised Jesse to get started on his case first thing Monday and walked back to our place.

An eighteen-wheeler passed us on the left, throwing up yet another huge stream of water just as lightning flashed in the east and thunder rumbled. It was really pouring now, my windshield wipers barely able to keep up with the rain. I cursed at the asshole truck driver—when visibility was low on the bridge it wouldn't take much for a car to go through the low guardrail and pitch into the choppy waters of the lake.

I'm not a particularly good swimmer, either. I imagine desperation would keep me going for a while, or at least until I could get to one of the bridge supports to hold on for dear life while hoping someone saw me go over the side and called for help.

This is one of the reasons I hate driving on the causeway—well, that and the fact I'm not a good driver.

I should have rescheduled this once I saw the weather forecast, I thought bitterly, also worried I was having to drive so slow we wouldn't get there on time. I gritted my teeth and sped up.

"It's kind of weird that Jesse's mother just disappeared, isn't it?" Taylor asked. "I mean, what kind of mother doesn't stay in touch with her kids?"

"I don't know." I sighed. "It seems weird to me, but we also don't know what went on back then. Maybe she had a really good reason for leaving, who knows?"

We rode the rest of the way over the bridge in silence. The rain finally let up just as I got off the bridge on the North Shore. I could make the appointment easily enough—her cattery was just outside of Rouen, which was about another thirty minutes or so away.

Half an hour later I was checking the GPS as I approached an unpaved driveway.

There wasn't a name on the black metal mailbox at the foot of the driveway, but there was a hand-lettered sign just to the right reading CAMPBELL BURMESE KITTENS with a phone number listed underneath.

When I was looking for her website, I wasn't sure I'd found the right one. The name she had listed on it as proprietor was simply "A. Campbell," and it took a little more research for me to find out Campbell was her maiden name; she'd dropped Metoyer in what I assumed was an attempt to fly under the radar. The picture of the woman on the website bore very little resemblance to the pictures of the former beauty queen/bereaved mother I remembered, either. When she'd been a Garden District wife and mother, she'd been ridiculously thin, impeccably dressed, and perfectly made up. The picture of A. Campbell on the cattery website showed a blowsy woman carrying about fifty or sixty pounds of extra weight with thick gray hair pulled into pigtails on either side of her face.

I also doubted that Arlene Metoyer would have been caught dead in the Garden District wearing greasy, paint-spattered overalls, either.

I'd spent most of Sunday night looking for information about the case online. Despite not ever paying much attention to it, I'd remembered most of it right—although there were some details I'd either never known or had simply forgotten.

Delilah Metoyer was eight years old when she was murdered. Her body had been found, like I remembered, in the carriage house. I hadn't remembered that the carriage house had been converted into a studio for her mother's hobbies—it wasn't just a storage place, like I'd remembered from reading *Garden District Gothic*. Arlene had a variety of interests, including photography, sewing, and painting. She'd actually made a lot of Delilah's costumes herself and had taken all of her headshots and portfolio pictures.

I didn't know Delilah won her first beauty pageant when she was eight months old. She'd been in and out of the pageant world quite a bit in her short life. Apparently, she was either a natural or took to it with righteous abandon, placing first or second in every single pageant she'd entered. I found an old interview Arlene had given to a news station in Monroe where she talked about "how much Delilah loves competing and performing for audiences" and "if she ever says she doesn't want to do it anymore, then she's done." That confirmed what Jesse had said—but was that the party line he'd been trained to repeat? That interview was a few years before Delilah was murdered, when she was five years old.

It was kind of amazing how much interest still remained in the case. The level of dedication and devotion to Delilah Metoyer out there on the Internet was almost cultlike, and more than a little unsettling. There were websites and blogs devoted to Delilah's memory, and tracking down her killer. There were sites with old videos of her competing in pageants or auditioning for film/television producers—some of the websites actually charged fees, which seemed a bit distasteful to me. There were websites insisting that Arlene had killed her daughter, and just as many that defended her. Some thought it was one of her brothers, the nanny, the cook, or her father. Speculation still raged out of control almost twenty years later. Every blog entry had hundreds of responses. The level of hatred and vitriol the different camps threw at each other in comments on blog posts about the case turned my stomach.

There were sites in French, German, Spanish, Chinese, Polish—every conceivable language. I'd known it was a phenomenon, but I'd never had the slightest clue just to what extent.

There were countless books on the case, and almost as many books on the murder's impact on society and culture itself. I counted twenty doctoral theses before giving up with a shake of my head. One article I found claimed the murder had created an industry with about a hundred-million-dollar impact on the US economy alone. I found that a bit hard to believe, or did until I looked at the statistics quoted. Tabloids with Delilah's picture on the cover almost doubled in sales, and ratings jumped every time a news program covered the story. Jerry Channing's book was a number one best seller for over a year and still sold extremely well in both hardcover and paperback editions. Almost every book about the case had made a profit for its publisher, no matter how sleazy or badly researched it was. Another pageant mother, Violet Parlange, whose daughter had competed against Delilah, wrote her own two-hundred-page paperback original book about her and her daughter's memories of Delilah and the Metoyer family. It had sold over a hundred thousand copies and gotten Violet on every talk show that would have her. Violet was from Ascension Parish, and somehow I doubted that Arlene Metoyer of the Garden District would have picked a small-town beautician from rural Louisiana as a confidante.

As I scrolled through blogs and websites, I noticed that Jerry Channing didn't emerge unscathed. He and his book were dissected, trashed, and his character assassinated. The kindest criticisms called him a manipulative exploiter. The worst called him homophobic slurs I hadn't heard since college. He also had defenders, but if pressed I'd have to say the Internet seemed to be divided equally between his supporters and his enemies.

Some even went so far as to say Jerry himself either was the killer or had at the very least assisted the murderer with the cover-up.

One thing everyone could agree on was that the NOPD had botched the investigation, and the district attorney's office wasn't much better. The lead detective, Rocky Champagne, had been beaten up pretty badly in Jerry's book as well as in the press. The district attorney at the time, Michael Gargaro, had also taken a beating. Gargaro hadn't run for reelection, and there really wasn't much about him online after he left office. Champagne seemed to have left the NOPD within a few years.

But if the case had wrecked some careers, it had made others.

Veronica Vance had been a mere legal correspondent for one of the twenty-four-hour news cable channels back then, and had become a "star" thanks to her coverage of the case. She'd parlayed that popularity into her own show and several best-selling books, and to this day, every night at eight p.m. central time she could be found slandering people and hurling vicious accusations with absolutely no evidence to back her claims. The sound of her voice always turned my stomach, and I couldn't bear to watch her show under any circumstance. She was one of the most loathed broadcasters in the country, yet her ratings remained solid enough to keep her on the air.

I made myself sit through some of the Veronica Vance news coverage, which was posted either on YouTube or on veronicavance.com. She was just as sickening then as she is now. The only difference was she was younger. She'd had the same hairstyle and makeup for almost twenty years. Her "reporting" style hadn't changed one bit over the years, either. She'd always been a vitriolic shrew who cut off and shamed anyone who disagreed with her. The notion of her as a prosecutor for any district attorney's office frightened me, but better she be a bitch on a cable show than actually perverting justice in a courtroom somewhere.

I had also been right about their live-in nanny being the first to notice she was missing. "I always checked on Delilah before I went to bed," Robin Strickland had told the *Times-Picayune* tearfully, "and when I saw she wasn't in her bed I immediately woke up Mr. and Mrs. Metoyer." The house's alarm had been on when Robin had come home. She'd had to punch in her code and rearmed it after locking the front door again.

The ransom note simply read *Do not call the police and this capitalist princess won't be harmed. We will be in touch.*

It was the use of "capitalist princess" that had some convinced it was some radical socialist group, like the Symbionese Liberation Army that had kidnapped Patty Hearst back in the 1970s. There were still theories everywhere online that it had been a botched kidnapping, and when the kidnappers had accidentally killed her, they dumped the body and ran.

They didn't find Delilah's dead body in the carriage house until after the sun had come up. Just like she'd been the first to notice she wasn't in her bed, Robin Strickland was the one who found the body. At that point, the Metoyers still hadn't notified the police, had sat around waiting for the kidnappers to call with their ransom demand. But things changed once Robin's screams woke up pretty much the entire neighborhood.

Their detractors always liked to point out that the Metoyers had called their lawyers before they called the police once they knew their daughter was dead. Their lawyer was at the house with them when the police arrived, and controlled the questioning. That didn't sit well with anyone. *Why did they need their lawyer if they had nothing to hide?*

It made sense to me. It's always a good idea to have your lawyer with you anytime you are talking to the police. But on the other hand, who was calm enough at that time to think "hey, we should have a lawyer with us when the cops get here"? Who is that calm when your child has just been murdered?

It *did* look suspicious.

And of course when all of her little girl beauty pageant pictures and audition tapes somehow got into the media, Riley and Arlene Metoyer became two of the most hated people in the country.

I'd made a lot of notes and bookmarked a lot of sites on my laptop, but wasn't sure why.

One thing was for sure, though. A whole lot of crazy had built up online over the last twenty years. I also needed to reread Jerry's book. I'd read it while I was a student at Vanderbilt and had always meant to reread it but had never gotten around to it.

I turned into the driveway and drove through the towering pine trees. The narrow paved driveway cut through a forest, and I'd gone maybe about a half mile before I came around a curve and into a clearing. A small clapboard house in need of paint with a screened-in porch sat in the center of the clearing, and a weathered small barn was set about a hundred yards farther back. There was a filthy white Dodge Ram truck parked facing the driveway between the house and the barn. The screen door to the porch opened and a short woman stepped out onto the stone steps. She was barefoot and had a baseball cap pulled down low on her forehead. She wore a ratty old LSU sweatshirt and black leggings.

She was also carrying a shotgun, and the look on her face indicated she had no qualms about using it.

"Stay in the car," I muttered to Taylor as I pulled to a stop and turned off the engine. I opened the door and plastered a smile on my face. "Hi, are you Arlene?" I called, waving and making my voice as friendly as I could. "We made an appointment to see some kittens?"

"You have to make an appointment," she shouted back at me. The screen door slammed shut behind her and she scowled. "You can't just show up. You just turn that car around and get out of here, you understand me? You need to fill out an application on my website. I don't give my kittens to just anyone. You have to pass a background check, and I don't just let people show up here and look at my cats. That's an invasion of privacy!" She pointed back at the driveway. "Now go! I'll forget you invaded my privacy if you go now. Or you won't be getting one of my cats. *Go!*"

She screamed the last word at me, but she didn't raise the gun to aim.

"I *do* have an appointment." I held up both hands. "I'm Scotty Bradley? I emailed you?"

"Oh." She frowned at me. "You're early. I wasn't expecting you for another hour."

I looked at my watch. It was five minutes past one. "I'm sorry, I thought I'd made the appointment for one."

She came across the parking area, still carrying the gun, stopping finally a few feet from me. "Why do you want one of my kittens?" she asked in a soft voice.

I gestured to Taylor in the car. "My nephew—he's a college student—his cat—well, we had to have his cat put to sleep a few weeks ago," I lied glibly. "And we were at Serena Castlemaine's housewarming party this past weekend, and he was so taken with her kittens, I thought we'd get him one."

She smiled. "Tell him to come along, then," she said, gesturing for me to follow her, turning away from the car and stumbling a little. I realized she was a little drunk. I waved at Taylor, who got out of the car with a curious look on his face.

"They're in the barn," she said, walking across the gravel. "Come on, I don't have all day."

She stopped in front of the barn door, and scowled at us. "I only have one left," she said with a scowl, "and he's not cheap."

"Okay," I replied. "What do you mean by not cheap?"

She unlocked the padlock and opened the door. "Three hundred. But he's been chipped and had all his shots. I had him neutered as soon as he reached three pounds." She shared a smile with me. "I have them all fixed once they reach the right weight. The ones I'm planning on selling, anyway." She stepped inside and flipped a switch.

The barn wasn't very big, but it felt cool inside and I couldn't smell anything other than straw and litter. What had probably once been stalls for horses had been converted to enormous cages. There were four of them, and each housed a pair of cats. She led me to the end cage and opened the door, gesturing for me to step inside. Sleeping in a white plush cat bed was an orange kitten, which opened its eyes. It blinked at us and yawned, completely unconcerned as Arlene stepped around me and reached down to pick him up. He curled up in her hands, and she held him out to me.

I stepped forward and reached for him. He was warm, and as soon as my hands closed around him his eyes half shut and he started purring so loudly the cats in the next cage came bounding over to see what was going on. I held him close to my face, and he reached out with one of his paws and touched my nose, still purring. "We'll take him," I said without even stopping to think.

"Let me have him!" Taylor's eyes were wide as he reached for the kitten. "Oh, who's a pretty kitty?"

She laughed. "Let me get a carrier for him. You didn't bring one by any chance?"

I shook my head. "Not with me."

She nodded and walked out of the cage, gesturing for us to follow her. She picked up a small carrier and opened the gate in its front. "Put him in here, and we'll go back into the house."

Taylor didn't want to let go of him, and he let out a pitiful little meow as he put him inside the carrier. She closed it before he could leap back out, and Taylor took the carrier from her. We followed her back to the house, Taylor murmuring to him the whole way. "Go ahead and get in the car," I said. "This won't take long."

He made a face at me that I ignored, but I heard him get into the car. I went up the stairs behind her and into the house. It was cute, and cozy, if extremely cluttered. She cleared a stack of magazines and books off a reclining chair, and I sat down. She walked over to a white file cabinet and pulled the top drawer open. The pile of papers on top wobbled a bit when she closed it after retrieving some forms. "I don't take checks," she said, handing me the forms, a clipboard, and a pen. "Cash or credit cards only."

I took a credit card from my wallet and handed it to her.

"The carrier is thirty dollars," she said. "If you want to bring it back sometime, I'll refund the thirty bucks."

"I may just keep it," I replied, "I don't get over here that often. It doesn't make sense to drive all this way just for thirty dollars. And we'll need one, anyway."

She nodded and took my credit card with her. She sat down at a desk and booted up a computer. "Burmese cats are pretty smart," she said over her shoulder as she ran my credit card through some website. "Burmese can be a handful. Do you work at home?"

"Yes."

"Well, if you have to leave him by himself, my advice to you is to close him up in a room with food and water and a litter box—he's also box trained. He won't like being left alone at first—he'll howl as long as he thinks you can hear him. You said you live in an apartment?"

"Uh-huh." It was hard following what she was saying while filling out her paperwork. It was more in-depth than the paperwork for my last car loan. The woman took her cat adoptions very seriously.

"Then if your walls are thin, you're going to need to apologize to your neighbors about his yowling until he gets used to being left alone." Her printer began spitting out a receipt, and she spun around in her chair. "Of course, he might just continue to yowl to make you feel guilty. But once he's used to your apartment—give it a week or so—it'll be okay to leave him to wander around during the day."

I signed the last form, swearing under penalty of forfeiting my money and giving the cat back that I wouldn't have him declawed (as if I would maim a cat), and handed everything back to her. I signed the receipt and took a look around. The walls were covered with framed pictures of cats—all Burmese, every age and color and size—but there were no pictures of family; neither the two sons nor Delilah were depicted on her living room walls. "Do you have any family?" I asked, trying to keep my voice as casual as possible as I folded my copy of the receipt and slipped it into my wallet.

"No," she replied. She stood up. "Okay, if you have any questions about him, my number and email address are on your receipt." She handed me a manila envelope. "Here's his medical records, his family lineage, and his chip information—you're going to want to get that on file with your own veterinarian as soon as possible. Your vet can of course contact me directly with any questions about medical history—my vet's card is in your packet, so your vet knows who to reach as well if I'm not available for any reason." Her eyes got wet. "I'm going to miss Scooter."

"Scooter?"

"I get attached to all of them, unfortunately." She didn't look up at me, and her voice was shaking as she answered, "I name all the kittens. Of course you can name him whatever you want."

"I like Scooter." I stuck out my free hand. "Thank you very much."

She nodded and picked up a glass with amber liquid in it. "Just take care of him."

I put my hand on the doorknob and hesitated. I wasn't sure if I should say anything or not. "Can I ask you a question?"

"You know who I am." It was a statement, not a question.

My mouth got very dry. "Yes, yes, I do."

"You didn't just come here to get a kitten. Are you a reporter? Because I'm not going to talk to you." She took a drink from the glass, and gave me a half sneer, half smile.

"I'm not a reporter. I'm—I'm a private eye, hired by your stepson, Jesse. He wants to see you." I shrugged. "I do want the kitten, though."

"And you've found me." She waved her hand, gesturing at the room. "What are you going to tell him?"

"He just wants to talk to you. Just to see you?" I didn't mean for it to come out as a question, it just did.

"Why does he want to see me?" She tilted her head to one side as she reached for the bottle to refill her glass. "I haven't seen him in years. Why does he care all of a sudden?"

"He wants to find his mother."

The glass froze on its way to her lips. "I don't know where she is," Arlene finally said, after a few moments of silence. "Tell him I don't want to see him. Now go."

I walked out of the house and got back into the car. Taylor was still talking baby talk to Scooter, who was mewling back at him. "His name's Scooter," I said as I started the car.

"Did you ask about—"

I nodded as I turned the car around, the tires crunching on the gravel and clamshell mixture. "Yes. She's Arlene Metoyer, all right. As soon as we get home I'll call Jesse and let him know we've found her. Then it's up to him."

"What did she say? Was she upset?"

"She wasn't thrilled. She said she doesn't want to see him." I drove down the driveway. "I guess I can't blame her for that, if she thinks Jesse killed Delilah." I paused at the foot of the driveway, waiting for an eighteen-wheeler with a load of lumber to go past. "And she said she didn't know where his mother was."

"Did you believe her?"

I pulled out onto the road and accelerated. "I don't know. She reacted very strangely when I brought her up." I shook my head. "But hey, at least this part of the investigation is over. We've found his stepmother. I'll call him and let him know—and then we can start looking for Melanie Metoyer. Who knows? Maybe finding her will be just as easy as finding Arlene was."

At least I hoped so.

The sooner we were done with the Metoyers, the better.

CHAPTER SIX
EIGHT OF SWORDS
Restricted action through indecision

After leaving Arlene's cattery, my stomach started growling as we headed down the road that led to I-12. Both sides of the highway were littered with every conceivable fast food place. Taylor can always eat, so I asked him if he had a preference.

"Arby's!" he said excitedly, almost bouncing up and down in his seat with excitement.

Honestly, you'd think we starved him.

I turned into that parking lot and parked in a space near the front door.

I handed him a twenty. "Get it to go. I'll just have a sandwich and a bottle of water. I'll stay here with Scooter. I'm going to go ahead and call Jesse."

He snatched the twenty out of my hands and was out the door before I could say anything else. I sighed and looked at the cat carrier in the backseat. Scooter tilted his head to one side and meowed. "We'll be home soon enough, Scooter," I said with a sigh, hoping neither Colin nor Frank were allergic to cat dander. Or that Millie and Velma didn't care about me getting a cat. Maybe I shouldn't have been so impulsive.

But being impulsive used to be part of my charm.

Get off my lawn!

I got my phone out and scrolled till I found Jesse's number. I hit Dial and waited as it connected and started ringing. Almost immediately it went to voice mail. "Hey, Jesse, this is Scotty. I've found Arlene, and I've confirmed it is your stepmother. She's using her maiden name, Campbell, and she's running a cattery on the North Shore, just outside of Rouen. In fairness, though, I have to say she didn't seem particularly enthusiastic about seeing you. She also said she didn't know anything about your mother's disappearance." I flipped my little notebook open and read off her phone number, as well as the email address. I hung up and slid my phone back into my pocket.

I scribbled an idea into my notebook: *find out when exactly Melanie left Riley, when they were divorced officially, and when Riley married Arlene.*

Scooter was still meowing. I leaned over the seat and put my hand against the carrier gate. He started purring and rubbing his head against my fingers. "Well, that's done, Scooter," I said, rolling my eyes when I realized I was crooning in a babyish voice. "I don't know how we're going to find his mother, or solve Delilah's murder when the police couldn't...but at least we got this done."

As Scooter continued to rub against my fingers, I couldn't remember ever reading anything about Delilah's murder, including Jerry's book, that pointed out that Arlene was Riley Metoyer's second wife and not the boys' mother. I guess it wasn't relevant to Delilah's murder, but it was a weird detail for everyone to overlook.

I hated feeling sorry for Jesse.

Real mature, Scotty, I scolded myself. *His sister was murdered, his brother committed suicide, and his father's dead. He hasn't seen his real mother since he was a kid and he hasn't even seen his stepmother for over twenty years. Be a better person and let it all go, already. You're not in junior high school anymore.*

And really, what harm had his bullying done? Sure, he'd made me miserable and self-conscious at the time, but I survived, hadn't I? And maybe, just maybe, being treated so badly by him and his asshole friends had made me a better, more empathetic person.

And holding the grudge now is hardly empathetic.

I closed my eyes and said aloud, "All right. I forgive you,

Jesse. I don't know what your home life was like back then, I don't know what kind of suffering was going on behind that smirking face. But I survived. You didn't harm me. And I forgive you now for the unhappiness you caused me."

I exhaled and opened my eyes.

I felt better.

Letting go of bitterness was always a freeing feeling.

I went to the web browser on my phone while I waited for Taylor to come back out and did a web search for *Riley Metoyer first wife*. The little wheel spun around for a moment or two—I always hated how slow my phone was out in the country—and finally a list of links popped up. The first few I knew from experience were websites that required payment to use, but the next one on the list was from the *Times-Picayune's* website. I touched the link with my finger, muttering, "Might as well settle in for the winter now," but the link opened almost immediately. It was a wedding announcement:

METOYER-GALLAUDET

All of their friends believe that Riley Augustine Metoyer and Melanie Anne Gallaudet were just meant to be. "They were born two days apart in the same hospital, started going steady in junior high school, dated all through high school, got engaged in college, and now they're married," maid of honor Alexandra (Alex) Mackesy said, wiping a tear from her eye as they drove off from the reception to their honeymoon. "I've never known any two people who loved each other as much as they do."

In another display of serendipity, their parents were also best friends. Riley's parents, Gerard and Virgilia, were best man and maid of honor at Melanie's parents' wedding; Beau and Leslie Gallaudet returned the favor a month later at Gerard and Virgilia's wedding. The Metoyers and the Gallaudets live only a block away from each other in the Garden District; growing up, Riley and Melanie were in and out of each other's houses all the time as the families remained close.

"Virgie and I used to joke about it when they were kids," Leslie Gallaudet remembers with a fond smile. *"Wouldn't it be wonderful if our kids fell and love and got married? And then we had mutual grandchildren? It was almost too much to hope for, you know?"*

Virgilia *"Virgie"* Metoyer agrees with a laugh. *"I wanted to hope, but was afraid to,"* she confesses with a wink, *"I figured they knew each other so well they'd grow up thinking of each other as brother and sister. And when they started getting involved romantically, I was almost too afraid to hope. But they were always so adorable. They always finished each other's sentences, always knew what the other was thinking, and now they're married and going to spend the rest of their lives together."*

Taylor opened the door and slid into his seat. He handed me an icy bottle of water wet with condensation and popped a large Coke into the cup holder on the armrest between the seats. Scooter started meowing again as Taylor handed me a hot sandwich wrapped in foil paper. "Calm down, Scoot!" he said, unwrapping his own sandwich. He gave me what I'd started calling his puppy eyes, which he always did when he wanted something.

"Whatever it is, no," I replied, biting into my sandwich. I don't eat fast food very often—there are no fast food places inside the Quarter, and no fast food burger is good enough to get me to walk all the way down to Canal Street to get one when there are any number of better burgers to be had on the way— but this was actually kind of good. It was maybe a little too salty for my taste, but still—not bad.

"Yeah, it's probably not a good idea to take him out of the crate in the car," he said with a bit of a pout. It amazed me how big his lips could get when he wanted to.

"Yeah, that's so not going to happen." I finished my sandwich and tossed the wrapper into the bag. I put the car in reverse and headed back out on the highway.

The rest of the way to the causeway I listened to him chew the other two sandwiches he'd gotten, and the French fries, and slurp down his Coke, all over the nonstop chorus of meowing from the backseat. And the minute he finished his food, he unbuckled his seat belt and climbed over into the back. I glanced in the rearview mirror. He turned the carrier sideways and was playing with Scooter through the gate. I could hear Scooter's purring now over the sound of the tires against the pavement. I smiled.

Maybe Colin and Frank were right. Maybe I did spoil Taylor a bit.

But it made me happy, and it didn't hurt him.

The sun was shining on the wet pavement as I drove back onto the causeway bridge heading to the south shore. I kept looking in the rearview mirror at Taylor and Scooter. Scooter was still alternating between meowing and purring as Taylor kept talking to him and stroking him through the gate with his fingers.

I supposed it was no wonder Scooter was meowing. After all, he was just a baby and his whole life experience so far consisted of Arlene's barn. The sound of the car, the vibrations of the tires on the pavement, the confined space of the carrier, and the unusual smells had to have him completely terrified. I was tempted to let Taylor take him out of his carrier, but I am not a good driver under the best of circumstances. A loose orange Burmese kitten in the car was just a major accident waiting to happen.

At least it wasn't raining anymore. The lake was calm, the sky was blue, and the sun was shining. The wet pavement was the only evidence of the downpour we'd experienced before.

"How's he doing?" I looked back in the rearview mirror. "Have you had a cat before? I've never had a pet. Are cats a lot of trouble?" I was sure hoping not. I'd never hear the end of it if Scooter was a pain in the ass.

Taylor laughed. "Cats aren't any trouble. You just have to

clean their litter box regularly and make sure they have food and water." I saw him frown in the rearview mirror. "He's fixed, isn't he?"

"She said he was."

"Well, then he won't spray. At least, I don't think he will."

Spray?

Scooter let out a really loud meow and the car filled with the stench of a really foul bowel movement. My eyes watered and my gag reflex engaged.

"Holy shit," I said, quickly cracking every window from the master control panel on the driver's side door. It was without question the most foul thing I'd ever smelled, and the rain-fresh lake air was a blessed relief to my burning nostrils and my streaming eyes. "Well, Scooter, is that how things are going to be when we get you home?" I glanced back in the rearview mirror and grinned. Taylor looked a little green and had pulled his shirt up to cover his nose and mouth.

He meowed.

I laughed.

I hated leaving Scooter trapped in there with the foul smell, but didn't really have a choice.

We were approaching one of the turnabouts that dot the causeway every mile or so, and I signaled. I pulled into one of the parking spots, grabbed the Clorox wipes out of the armrest, and tossed them back to Taylor. "I think there's a towel in the back," I said, putting the windows back up. "Pass him up here to me, and you can take it outside and clean it...just throw the towel away when you're done with it." Taylor opened the gate and pulled Scooter out. He put him into my outstretched hands, and once I had a good hold on him, Taylor got out with the fouled carrier and slammed the door behind him.

"You're not going to be any trouble, are you?" I asked him, looking into his adorable little triangular-shaped face. He put his right paw on my nose and started purring.

My heart melted.

I hated handing him back to Taylor when he got back in

with the freshly cleaned carrier, but I had no choice. I did so with a reluctant sigh and then had to wait for some speed demons to go past before I could safely get back on the southbound lanes.

The rest of the drive home passed without further incident.

And by the time I was parking the car in our lot, there was no way that kitten was going anywhere. If Frank or Colin were allergic, well, there was medication they could take, wasn't there? Or Taylor could just keep him upstairs, and I could go up to visit him. There was no way I was taking Scooter away from Taylor.

Or me.

I left the car running and got out of the car, opened the back door, and grabbed the carrier. "You need to go get supplies," I said to Taylor, handing him a credit card. "A litter box, litter, toys, whatever you think Scooter might need. I'll take him in and look up a vet online."

"Where should I go?"

I made a face. "Look it up on your phone."

I started carrying Scooter home. He started meowing again, trying to get to me. I talked to him, my cheeks turning red when some pedestrians gave me a funny look. "New kitten," I said and walked faster. A dog across the street at Café Envie started barking as we passed. I walked even faster and went around the corner.

What have I done?

"You've spent a lot of money for a new responsibility," I muttered to myself as I unlocked the gate. "And you didn't check with your partners. Nice going."

I carried him upstairs and into the living room. I set the carrier down on the living room table and slowly opened the gate. He stuck his cute little head out. I reached inside—he didn't weigh anything, and he was so little! I picked him up, cuddling him to my chest. He was purring so loud it was like he had speakers. He started kneading my chest with his front paws, walking up my chest and head-butting me. "Aren't you the sweetest boy?" I said, wondering if that was how you talk to cats.

He seemed to like it. He fell asleep on my chest.

Gently I got up and carried him over to the desk. I sat down, holding him in my lap. He stretched a bit, yawned again, and curled up into a ball as I touched the space bar with my free hand and brought the computer back to life. I opened a Word document and started writing up notes on my meeting with Arlene, my impressions and thoughts:

Arlene Metoyer now lives on the North Shore and operates a cattery, breeding and selling Burmese cats. She has gone back to living under her maiden name, Campbell, and seems to live a quite solitary existence except for the cats. While the cattery itself is well kept, organized, and clean, her small house seems cluttered and dusty. She also seemed to smell slightly of liquor, and I noticed her recycling bin had rather a lot of empty wine, whiskey, and vodka bottles. I doubt she's recently had a party. She wasn't friendly at first, either, threatening me with a rifle until it was determined I had an appointment and had arrived early for it. There's some paranoia there, clearly, but that can certainly be understood given her past. Outside of the dust and the clutter, there was nothing unusual about her house other than the absolute absence of any photographs or anything personal, mementoes, etc. The house could have belonged to anyone.

She's put on weight, and she doesn't seem to care as much about her personal appearance as she used to; I don't know what that means other than every picture or television appearance I'd seen of her before, including candids from paparazzi, she always seemed immaculately groomed—not a hair out of place, perfectly made up, and her clothing perfectly pressed and worn. It is that impression of her that probably made the way she was today so startling to me; I would never have imagined seeing her in dirty, soiled, unkempt sweats, without makeup, her hair not styled and graying, and the extra weight. I am maybe being unfair here; she's obviously been through a lot and her life has changed a lot in the last twenty-five years or so.

I tried several times to engage her in personal conversation in a generic, someone-you-just-met polite manner. She deflected each attempt abruptly—polite, not rude, but made it very clear she wasn't interested in talking to me about anything other than the welfare of the kitten, and whether I could provide him with a good home.

I even mentioned that I became aware of her because I had been given her name by Serena Castlemaine and that I was interested in a Burmese kitten because of Serena's two; she dismissed this attempt and I saw no way of bringing up that I knew who she really was—that she'd sold not only the kittens but the house to Serena—without making her angry and risking being kicked out. As I mentioned before, she greeted me with a shotgun when I first arrived—and I wouldn't have been surprised had she kicked me out with the shotgun aimed at me as well.

My impressions? I felt sorry for her, more than anything else. She doesn't seem particularly happy, other than when talking about the cats. I got the feeling that she has left the past behind, or really wants to, and wouldn't necessarily welcome it being brought up. Again, I can't blame her for this; I can't imagine what it would be like to live with the kind of notoriety she has.

She said she wasn't interested in seeing Jesse or talking to him. This wasn't a surprise, since Jesse himself said she thought he had killed Delilah.

I also feel sorry for Jesse. It occurred to me on my way back that it might not be a bad idea to check out Jesse's mother's family. Her wedding announcement in the Times-Picayune online archive said she had a brother and a sister—so there may be Gallaudets still left in New Orleans, even though Jesse said he had no other family.

But we've found his stepmother for him. I called and

left a message on his voice mail. All we have to do now is find his mother.

And look into his sister's death.

I leaned back in the chair and stared at the computer screen, the blinking cursor.

He wants us to try to solve a twenty-five-year-old murder that the police couldn't solve. That's not only crazy, but also a waste of our time and his money.

Okay, that was probably a little harsh. I mean, if Rain had been murdered when we were kids and the killer never caught, I don't think I'd rest until I knew the killer was in jail.

How awful it would be to never know what really happened.

Why don't you ask the cards?

I bit my lower lip and stared at the blinking cursor, then looked over at the couch.

I hadn't used the cards in a long time.

What would it hurt?

You don't want to try because it hasn't worked in years.

I liked to think if I needed her, the Goddess would talk to me through the cards again. She'd come back a couple of times, helped me in a couple of situations. But it had been years since the cards spoke to me. It had been so long since I'd gone into a trance and She'd come to me.

Admit it, you know what you did. Ask her for forgiveness. You've never done that, you know. She's come to you when you've been in danger, hasn't she? She will forgive you. If you could let go of the bitterness about Jesse…

"Scooter's asleep," I said aloud. "I don't want to disturb him."

That's stupid, because it's not like he won't fall asleep again, I berated myself, yet I still sat there, staring at the document. Finally, I saved it under the file name "first contact with Arlene Metoyer" and put in a folder marked *Metoyer.*

I called Jesse again, but just got his voice mail again. I didn't see any point in leaving another message, so I disconnected.

Garden District Gothic was sitting there on the desktop, spine up and bent open to mark a page. I picked it up and saw Taylor had left it open at the page about the voodoo priestess Arlene had consulted in an attempt to find her daughter's killer.

I'd forgotten about that completely.

How much else have I forgotten?

I leaned back in my chair and started reading.

I always thought that part of the appeal of the book was that it supposedly gave outsiders a view into what it was like to be Garden District society. I'd read an interview with Jerry in the paper on the twentieth anniversary of the book's publication, where Jerry said that very thing. "Outsiders are fascinated with New Orleans," he'd said, "and even people from New Orleans who aren't a part of Garden District society are fascinated by it. They want to know what it's like to come from an old family, to live in one of those old houses, to belong to Rex and Comus. The book feeds that fascination, and then you add in the Delilah Metoyer murder…even if the book was written in words of one syllable, people would have bought it."

And enough people had bought it to make Jerry Channing a mint of money.

Jerry had littered the book with bon mots about real people and what they were like, sometimes disguising their identities with false names (he was particularly fond of using Fontenot) that didn't fool anyone in New Orleans; it was always pretty clear who he was talking about. It amazed me the first time I read it—all the gossip and secrets he'd laid bare for the entire world to see…surely he would have to leave town? My grandmother had once talked about some really talented novelist who wrote a fictionalized account of some Garden District people's story, and she'd been cut dead, wound up having to leave town.

Yet Jerry still was invited to the best parties.

The passage Taylor had left the book open at was a good example.

I don't know if Arlene Metoyer actually consulted a voodoo

priestess, but I was pretty certain that if she had, it hadn't gone down the way Jerry described it in his book:

Madame Laroux (not her real name) was a Creole woman of indeterminate age; she could have been anywhere from thirty to seventy. When asked her age she just smiled, showing some gold teeth, and said "Black don't crack, love." She claimed to be descended from Marie Laveau herself and made a point of laying flowers at the tomb of her ancestress once a month, when the moon was full and the night filled with good ju-ju. It was rumored she had summoned Papa Legba himself on several occasions, and not only did she summon him but took him as her lover. In the New Orleans voodoo community, Madame Laroux is the woman you go to when you need powerful magic, the kind most practitioners won't touch or even talk about except in hoarse whispers before saying they won't do it. Madame Laroux fears no spirit, no god; they say she is the modern-day incarnation of the famous Voodoo Queen.

Madame Laroux told Arlene Metoyer to meet her, at midnight, in Lafayette Cemetery Number One, only a few blocks from the Metoyer house. Arlene went, and that night Madame Laroux wrung the neck of a chicken and cut its throat, using its blood and some other magic powders to call on Papa Legba to find out who killed Delilah and to cast a protection spell over Arlene so the police would never arrest her, that she would never be tried for the murder of her daughter. Papa Legba refused to come that night, or any other night when Madame Laroux tried to call him for Arlene Metoyer.

"That mean Papa Legba think she guilty," Madame Laroux told me, her gold teeth flashing in her mouth as she drank red wine with a shrug. "But Papa Legba enforce the spell because I asked him to—Miz Metoyer will never be tried for her daughter's murder. She will never go to jail for it."

"Doesn't Papa Legba know?" I asked her, refilling her glass of wine. "Doesn't he know if she is guilty or not?"

"Papa Legba not distinguish between what happen and what in the heart," she replied. "I not know if she kill her daughter or not. But she wanted her dead, that I do know. In her heart she wanted her dead, and that is all Papa Legba need to know. That all I need to know."

I closed the book and put it down.

It had come out when interest in the case around town had died down somewhat, that I did remember. The news crews from the twenty-four-hour cable networks had moved on to the next big headline case that drove up ratings; the tabloid reporters were gone, and if anyone talked about Delilah Metoyer's murder, it was always with a fatalistic shrug. No one thought a Metoyer would ever be arrested. No one believed a Metoyer would ever go on trial. That wasn't the way things worked in New Orleans back then, and it probably held true today. But when Jerry's book came out, it was all anyone could talk about. It was of course a national best seller, and tourists came to New Orleans in droves to check out the places he talked about, to see the Metoyer house, to try to track down the real names of the people he'd tried to disguise.

It had actually become a parlor game for New Orleanians that year—trying to guess the identities of the people whose names he'd changed to avoid libel suits. No one knew who Madame Laroux was, and there was a theory that he'd made her up completely. Arlene Metoyer of course never commented on the book—and again I wondered how it had made her feel. Then again, by the time it came out she'd been raked over the coals in ways no one could have even imagined before. But she still had to have felt incredibly betrayed.

I placed a piece of paper inside the book to hold the place and tapped it against my chin.

Much as I hated to admit it, if we were going to have a chance of finding Melanie Metoyer and figuring out who actually had killed Delilah twenty-five years ago, we were not only going to have to interview most of the people in Jerry's book, but the best place to start was with Jerry himself.

Maybe Frank would do it so I wouldn't have to.

Get over yourself, you slept with him well over ten years ago— closer to fifteen.

I hadn't known who he was when I slept with him.

He'd looked familiar that night at the Pub, but that doesn't mean anything in New Orleans—everyone looks familiar here. It's a really small town, and you often see the same people all the time—the cashier at Walgreens, the bartender at Good Friends, the waiter at Irene's—but when you see them out of their usual context, all you know is they look familiar. So when he walked into the Pub that night in a tight black muscle shirt and loose khaki shorts that showed off a strongly muscled ass and legs, he looked familiar to me as I danced around on the bar with dollar bills stuck into my thong and wads full of damp bills shoved into my socks inside my boots. It was around one thirty in the morning, and the crowd had thinned down considerably as guys took their drugs and headed upstairs or across the street to dance until dawn. I got off at two in the morning and my legs were getting tired. I'd been flirting and dancing since ten and I'd made more than enough to pay the rent for the month, maybe even some extra to go out for a nice dinner one night, and was already starting to think about who I was going to go home with when I was done. I was drenched in sweat—even as low as their air-conditioning was turned down, dancing up on the bar in a crowded room made it hot—and I was wondering if I should go home, drop off the money, and take a quick shower before heading back, or if it made more sense just to head down to the bathhouse. I could lock my tips in a strongbox at the check-in window and just shower there, maybe sit in the steam room or sauna or the hot tub to ease the stiffness in my muscles. The other added bonus of going to the bathhouse was none of the usual pickup games applied. The bathhouse was more honest than picking someone up in a bar. No one was in the bathhouse because they were looking for someone to date or to fall in love with or for Mr. Right.

They were in the bathhouse because they wanted to get laid, period, and names weren't necessary.

But he motioned to me when he stood at the bar, and I danced my way over there. He was hot. Had a great body. Oozed sex appeal from every pore. I knelt down and he stroked my quads with each hand, a smirk on his face. "I want to fuck you," he said simply, sliding a twenty into my thong.

I smiled back at him, taking the twenty out and giving it back to him. "I'm not a bottom," I replied, putting my free hand on his shoulders, "and if I take money from you I feel like a whore. I prefer to keep my status amateur."

He laughed at that, and thirty minutes later I was in his Porsche speeding through the CBD to his place in the Lower Garden District. The sex wasn't great—he was one of those "I'm so hot all I have to do is lie here and you'll be aroused" guys, the worst—but I fell asleep there, and when he woke me up the next morning he couldn't hurry me out of there fast enough.

Not something I ever cared to repeat.

I suppose I could have pushed off interviewing him on Frank, but him putting the moves on Frank wasn't something I wanted to deal with.

No, I was going to have to do it.

I heard the front door open. "That was quick," I said, getting up and carrying the still sleeping Scooter in my arms to the hallway—

—where I was grabbed and lifted up into the air.

CHAPTER SEVEN
THE DEVIL
Domination of matter over spirit

Scooter howled and clawed me as he shot out of my arms like a
bolt of lightning. I stumbled backward, losing my balance, and
started going down just as two incredibly strong arms deftly
swung me up like I weighed nothing and spun me around in the
air a couple of times before gently setting me down on my feet
and pulling me in for a big, wet, sloppy kiss.

Colin is lucky he's a good kisser. I got lost in the heat from
his kiss, and all I could think about was not swooning rather than
being pissed at him.

My heart was pounding from both adrenaline and the kiss
when he finally pulled his head back from mine. Our bodies
were still pressed tightly against each other. I could smell his
cologne—he always wore Christian Dior's Fahrenheit—and
beneath that his own musk and sweat.

He apparently was also very glad to see me.

I gasped and took a few deep breaths. "Dude, you scared
the crap out of me." I lightly spanked his right butt cheek with
my hand. "I hate when you do that." Part of his training as an
international espionage agent included being able to move
without making a sound. It's unnerving. It's so ingrained in him
that he does it all the time. I'll think he's in another room and
turn around to see him standing right behind me, smiling like he
was now.

His grin got even bigger, his big white even teeth glowing

in his deeply tanned and slightly peeling face. His dimples appeared, too.

He really is too good-looking for his own good. He's only about five feet five inches tall and weighs around two hundred pounds of solid, thick muscle. His olive skin is always deeply tanned, and his amazing green eyes are so bright they almost glow in the dark. His thick, curly bluish black hair was buzzed down to the scalp. He was wearing a gray Tulane T-shirt that looked like it was a couple of sizes too big and a pair of black khaki shorts. His mirror sunglasses were pushed up onto the top of his head, and there were sweat spots under his arms.

"Sorry I almost knocked you down," he said sheepishly. "What can I say? When I saw you I got a little overexcited. It's your fault for being so sexy." He squeezed my ass with both hands and kissed my neck. I moaned a little and felt myself getting even more aroused. "Was that a cat?" He let go of me and raised an eyebrow.

Still a little wobbly from the now-fading adrenaline rush, I put a hand out to the wall to help steady myself. "Yes, I bought a kitten today, and his name is Scooter. I just brought him home. He's a Burmese, and you undoubtedly scared the piss out of him. I hope we can coax him out from wherever he's hiding." As my legs started feeling like they could support me again, I cautiously let go of the wall. "You're not allergic, are you?"

"No, I love cats. I just—you know, with my line of work, I've never been able to have one because it wouldn't be fair, being gone so much. I never really thought about having one." He scratched his head. "I *am* sorry I scared you. And him." He opened his eyes wide contritely.

I sighed. I can't ever resist him when he gives me puppy-dog eyes, and I wasn't that mad in the first place. "I'm just glad you're home," I said, giving him another hug and a kiss on the cheek.

I meant it. It's not fun having a boyfriend who's basically an undercover agent for hire, the person foreign governments— and sometimes our own—turn to for covert actions when they need plausible deniability. We never know where he is, what he's doing, or how long he's going to be gone. Frank and I push it to the back of our minds as much as possible, try to pretend the worry isn't there, but when he comes home safely, or his boss contacts us to let us know he's on his way home, the feeling of relief is like, I don't know, having a five-hundred-pound weight lifted off your shoulders.

And you can breathe again.

You can learn to live with the worry, but it's not something you can ever get used to. You can pretend when he leaves for an assignment that it's not dangerous, but there's always that little voice in the back of your mind reminding you *he may not come home*.

I wish he would quit, but I can't ask him to do that. He loves what he does, he believes in what he's doing, and he feels like he's making a difference in the world. He may not ever be able to tell us exactly what he was doing when he comes home, but I know he thinks he's doing important work.

And really, how many people ever get a chance to make a difference the way he does?

So yeah, you learn to live with it, even though you hate it.

"How long will you be home this time?" I asked. "Do you know?"

"Well, unless something truly drastic comes up, Angela has promised me a few months off," Colin said, flashing his teeth in another smile. "She was really pleased with my work this last assignment, so unless…"

"Unless some government somewhere is overthrown?" I teased, walking into the living room.

He laughed, following me into the living room. "I don't get involved in that kind of thing."

"Liar."

"No, I do think Angela really meant it. She said I deserved some time at home." He grabbed me from behind and pulled me back into him, kissing the back of my neck again. "I've missed you and Frank. And Taylor, too. It'll be nice to have some sort of normalcy for a while."

Angela was Angela Blackledge, owner and operator of the Blackledge Agency. I've never met her and I have no idea what she looks like. I've spoken to her on the phone a few times—she's always friendly and pleasant, with a deep throaty voice and a great laugh, but I never feel completely comfortable with her. She recruited Colin when he left the Mossad in his late twenties, and he's worked with her ever since. I've tried researching her online a few times when I'm bored, but there is nothing to be found anywhere. It's like she doesn't exist. Whenever Colin's off on a job and something happens somewhere—an assassination, or a terrorist cell being blown up—I sometimes wonder if that's where Colin is.

It's a weird life. What can I say?

"Cool! We've missed you, too." I got down on my hands and knees. "There you are," I said, spotting Scooter under the couch, his eyes open wide and breathing very heavily. He looked absolutely terrified. "Come here, baby. Colin didn't mean to scare you," I said in my most soothing voice, which I hoped he would recognize or whatever it is cats do. I reached for him and he didn't run away. He just head-butted my hand and gave me the wide-eyed look again. "You are the most adorable thing, Scooter," I cooed at him, grabbing hold of him and dragging him out gently. He started purring again almost immediately.

"What a little cutie," Colin observed, scratching the top of Scooter's head. "We had a cat when I was a kid…" His voice trailed off. His family had moved to Israel after his father died. When he was in college, a suicide bomber in a café killed his mother and younger brother.

I bit my lower lip, but he smiled and said, "Cats are very sweet, you know."

I hadn't realized I'd been holding my breath until I exhaled.

"Why a cat? Why now?" He smirked. "Let me guess, Taylor wanted one?"

"I do *not* spoil him! Stop saying that! You and Frank are going to give me a complex!" I sat down on the couch, the purring kitten in my hands. Colin sat down next to me, his leg pressed against mine.

"I'm just teasing you," he replied. Scooter crawled out of my hands and up Colin's chest, head-butting him a few times. "I don't really think you spoil him too much—"

So, of course, that was the moment Taylor chose to come running in with the packages from the pet store, his face aglow with excitement, practically bouncing up and down and off the walls. "I think I got everything we needed—COLIN!" He dropped the plastic bags with a rather loud crash—I thanked the Goddess that Millie and Velma were out of town—and came bounding around the coach to give him a hug.

Colin, the bastard, smirked at me and raised an eyebrow at me over Taylor's shoulder, as if to say *yeah, you're not spoiling him at all, are you, Uncle Scotty?*

I sighed.

I wasn't going to win this argument.

"Taylor, why don't you take Scooter upstairs with you and get the upstairs all set up for him?" I said wearily. "Do you mind?"

He got a puzzled look on his face. "But—" Then he stopped, looked back and forth between us, and got a big grin on his face. "Sure." He winked at me. "Come on, Scooter."

He scooped the kitten up off my chest and disappeared down the hall with the bags. I heard the door open and shut behind him. I leaned against Colin, who slipped an around my shoulders. "Maybe I spoil him a little." I said, listening to his heart beating. He was so damned cuddly. "I can't help it. I just feel so bad for him."

"Yeah, his parents definitely gave him a raw deal, no question about that." Colin ruffled my hair a little bit. "But he has us, and your family, now. I can't imagine how awesome it would be to be a college student living in New Orleans with your family around."

"I think that's why they sent me away to Vanderbilt," I replied with a short laugh. "I was a handful in high school. But

I worry about him. It's weird, I think about all the things I used to do when I was his age, now I think, *my God, I must have driven Mom and Dad crazy with worry.* I mean, I know he's not stupid, and he's smart enough to take care of himself, but...at that age they think they're indestructible. And they aren't. When he's out at night I can't sleep until I hear him on the stairs coming home." I sighed. "When did I turn into such an old man?"

He kissed the top of my head. "You're not an old man, Scotty, far from it. Believe it or not, you've always been a nurturer. You always want to take care of everyone. It's just who you are. You want to protect him because he is so young. That's normal. I want to. I worry about him. Frank really worries about him, you know. We all do. Which is great for him, but we have to let him experience things, too. He's going to have problems, he's going to be hurt, and we can't shelter him from the world. And we can't *spoil* him, either."

"Yeah, well. I'll keep that in mind. But just so you know, I bought the kitten for me, not him. I had no idea he'd take to it."

"How did that come about?" He kissed the top of my head. "You just suddenly decided you wanted a cat? You've never mentioned it before."

"Believe it or not, we have a case!"

"What?" He shook his head.

"Someone actually hired us." I laughed. "Someone I knew from high school. He went to Mom—and she...well, you know how she is. Frank and I tried to get him to hire an actual working private eye—"

"You and Frank may not get many clients," he interrupted me, "but the three of us have solved some pretty tricky cases, haven't we?"

"Agreed."

"So stop with the self-deprecation. Got it?"

"Okay." I sat up and shrugged. "But it's Jesse Metoyer. To make a long story short, he wants us to find his actual mother. He also wanted us to find his stepmother, Arlene—which I did today. And he wanted us to kick around, revisit his sister's murder, see if anything new turned up." I deliberately didn't go any further than that. I wanted to see if he recognized the name.

He didn't, but he frowned. "Aren't the police looking into it? The cops are better with murders than we would be." He laughed. "Well, I guess we've caught a few killers over the years. But they have resources we don't."

"Since she was murdered twenty-five years ago, I doubt it's still considered an active investigation." I folded my arms. "It's a cold case."

"Well, at least you didn't stumble over another body this time," he teased. "So what does this have to do with the cattery?"

"Well, there's a bit of a story." I went on to tell him about Serena's party, her cats, and that she'd bought the Metoyer house. "So, finding Arlene was pretty easy. I made an appointment to look at a kitten, and once I saw Scooter I wanted him, so I bought him."

"And you didn't tell her—what was his name? Jesse?—was looking for her?" He frowned. "Why do those names sound familiar to me? Have I met the Metoyers before?"

I laughed. "I've kind of been dicking you around, Colin. Does the name Delilah Metoyer sound familiar?"

"Delilah? Seriously? Her name was Delilah?" I watched and waited as it slowly started dawning on him. "*Delilah Metoyer?*" I could see the light bulb turning on in his mind. "The child beauty queen? That *was* in New Orleans, wasn't it?" He shook his head. "*You went to school with her brother?*"

"New Orleans is a small town." I decided not to share that Jesse had bullied me in junior high. It wasn't relevant, and besides, I'd forgiven him.

"What does he think we can find out that the police didn't? It's been what, thirty years?"

"Twenty-five," I replied, "and I had the same reaction. I mean, what else is there to find out? That case has been picked over for decades. I kind of have a funny feeling about it." I shook my head. "I don't know. Something doesn't seem right to me about it." I hesitated. "I mean, why is he looking for his stepmother? Okay, she raised him. But his *own* mother left when he was a kid—his dad was cheating on her, and she just walked out of their lives, got a divorce, and was never heard from again."

"That is weird. What did Frank think?" He made a face. "Come to think of it, where is Frank?"

"Pensacola. He'll be home either late tonight or tomorrow morning. We didn't really talk much about the case before he left. We were just 'hired' on Sunday, and Frank had to leave early this morning." I crossed my legs. "And she was local, Colin. Her parents and her husband's parents were close friends, they grew up a block apart…" I sketched out everything Jesse had told us, with Colin listening and nodding when it was appropriate. "Did you ever read *Garden District Gothic*?"

He shook his head. "No. What is it?"

I laughed. "A very famous book someone peripherally connected to the family wrote, you've seen it in shops—it's everywhere."

"Oh, that." He made a face. "I don't really like those nonfiction novel things. I had to read *In Cold Blood* in college, but it really bothered me how he made things up when he couldn't have known what happened, you know? Like conversations the dead family had amongst themselves? It makes the whole thing suspect to me. So, what was Arlene Metoyer like? Besides a crazy cat lady?"

"I don't know that I would say she's a crazy cat lady," I said slowly. "True, she's kind of crazy and she does have a lot of cats, but she's a breeder, it's not like she keeps them. I kind of felt sorry for her. I mean, maybe I should have brought up Jesse while I was there, but…I don't know. There's something about her that seems broken, I guess? I don't know how she'd react to actually seeing him, but I don't think it's my place—our place—to initiate that contact between the two of them. All he wanted was for us to hunt her down, and we did that…I called him and just got his voice mail, but I told him where to find her. I'll call him again later to make sure he got the message."

He whistled. "A twenty-five-year-old murder…and an even

older disappearance." His voice trailed off and he stared off into space, thinking. "Talk about the trail going cold…it's going to be almost impossible to find Melanie Metoyer all these years later. Witnesses, anyone who might have known her…hell, even the killer might not be alive anymore."

"Trust me, I've been thinking about this all day," I replied glumly. "And there's so much information out there—news coverage, articles, opinion pieces—to sift through. Who knows what's good information or bad? It's kind of hopeless." I glanced at him out of the corner of my eye. Colin loved a challenge.

"Well, you can just forget about any of that shit." He shook his head. "All that is good for is getting names of potential people to interview. What we need is the evidence file, the police report. That's where we start."

"I know the guy who wrote *Garden District Gothic*," I said cautiously. No need to let Colin know we had a past. "He knew the family, was around. He might know some things—things he couldn't put in the book."

"Did you sleep with him?" he asked, grinning and raising an eyebrow.

"A long time ago." I grinned back at him impudently. "There wasn't a repeat performance, either."

He laughed. "That good, huh?" He winked at me. "So, you're our inside man with the guy?"

"Jerry Channing. And I'd prefer not to be called the inside man." I gave him a sour look. "He was at Serena's party. Let me give her a call and see if she has his number." I pulled my phone out of my pocket.

"Do you think Venus would get us the police file?"

"Yes. I'm sure she'd be more than happy to risk her job to help us out," I said with a big eye roll. Venus Casanova and her partner, Blaine Tujague, were New Orleans police detectives, and our paths had crossed many times over the course of murder investigations. I used to annoy them, but now I think they've grudgingly come to respect me a little. I've helped them catch more than a couple of cold-blooded killers over the years, and

Venus doesn't always have that exasperated look on her face when I talk to her now. That's progress, right?"

"Hmm." Colin gently pushed me aside and got up, walking over to the computer and sitting down in front of it. "I wonder… it's been twenty-five years, though." He started clacking his fingers over the keyboard. I started to get up and walk over there, but decided it was probably smarter to stay on the couch. If he was going to hack into the New Orleans Police Department's computer system—Colin has crazy-mad hacking skills—it was better I not know anything about it. Plausible deniability is very important.

"I wonder if anyone ever filed a missing persons report on Melanie?" I said loudly.

I wasn't *asking* him to hack the information, after all. I was just thinking out loud.

Plausible deniability.

I called Serena, but the call went to her voice mail. I left a message, telling her what I wanted, and then tried Jesse again. I hung up when it went to voice mail.

"So what was the story with his birth mother?" Colin may not have said anything about it when I mentioned it, but he was sharp—he never missed anything.

"She walked out on the family when he was a kid. The dad remarried, had Delilah with Arlene. He's never seen his mother again since the day she left. And he's pretty certain she left because Arlene was having an affair with his dad."

He whistled. "And she's been missing for over thirty years?" He snapped his fingers and rolled his eyes. "Yeah, this is going to be a piece of cake. Doesn't look like anyone ever filed a missing persons report on her. There's nothing in the database with her name on it. Although if it was before they were computerized… they might not have gone back and loaded old cases into the database."

"Can you toss me that book?" I called from the couch, and a few seconds later the battered copy of *Garden District Gothic* came flying at me. I nimbly plucked it out of the air and opened it to the back. As I remembered, there wasn't an index. *How can you write a nonfiction book without an index?*

By writing fiction and passing it off as nonfiction, that's how.

I couldn't remember the name of the detective who'd headed the investigation. But I did remember Jerry mentioning him in the book, and not kindly, either. The detective in charge had gotten a lot of bad press at the time—he was widely assumed, by Veronica Vance and many others, to have botched the case from the very beginning.

For that matter, he'd gotten a lot of bad press ever since as well. Just about every show I'd seen over the years had savaged him.

I paged through the book until I came across the name: Detective Rocky Champagne. Jerry's description of him was brutal:

> *Rocky Champagne looked like he had been sent out from Stock Casting for a role as the stereotypical redneck Southern cop, from the buzzed haircut to the belly bulging over his straining belt holding up polyester pants to the perpetual sweat stains under his armpits to the red sweaty face that always looked like he was on the verge of having a stroke. The only thing missing was the chewed-up cigar dangling from his lips. You knew just by looking at him that he drove a battered old Chevy pickup with a Confederate flag decal in the back window, a gun rack, and a horn that played the LSU fight song when he wasn't driving his official vehicle. He had the look of a high school jock who'd sadly gone to seed; high school had been his glory days—the time when his life had peaked, and it had been all downhill ever since. Probably either the star running back or quarterback on a mediocre football team at some segregated public school outside of Orleans Parish, maybe even the Homecoming King. The big man on campus gone to seed, trapped in a marriage to one of the cheerleaders he'd probably knocked up right after high school (if not their senior year), he'd become a New Orleans*

cop and watched, bewildered, as the old world he'd known,
one of racism and segregation and the superiority of the white
man, was slowly dismantled and "the coloreds" given equal
(or, as all racists believe in their heart of hearts, preferential)
rights.

Harsh, right?

If I were Rocky Champagne, I would have sued the hell out of him.

Sadly, though, I knew exactly the type of man Jerry described. The Rocky Champagnes of the world didn't sue people. They waited to catch the person who'd wronged them in a dark and lonely place.

In their minds, lawyers were for pussies.

I shuddered.

"Google Rocky Champagne, New Orleans police," I called over to Colin as I kept paging through the book, looking for other mentions of the unfortunate police officer. "He was the poor sucker who was in charge of the investigation."

Jerry wasn't any kinder anywhere else he mentioned Rocky in the book; almost every mention of him was mocking at best, insulting at worse. I hadn't read the book in a long time, but I did remember feeling bad for Detective Champagne when I read it the first time. Rereading some of these passages reminded me why.

He hadn't been treated well by any reporters, really— the general consensus of everyone covering the case was that Champagne had blown it almost from the very moment he showed up at the Metoyer house in the wee hours of that morning. I shook my head. He had no idea when he got woken up from sleep that night that his life was about to become a living hell. Most people felt he'd been far too deferential to the Metoyers, not pressing them hard enough, not getting a search warrant for the main house for several days, giving them plenty of time to get rid of evidence.

It was impossible not to feel sorry for him once the vultures started circling over his head. The district attorney for Orleans Parish at the time—whose name I also couldn't remember—and the mayor's office had been all too happy to let Champagne take the rap for the failed investigation and the lack of an arrest.

The local press had been kinder to him, not that it mattered. The local reporters understood what it was like to be a cop in New Orleans, investigating a murder in the Garden District involving an old society family. It had to suck, having the bad luck to be assigned the case. He couldn't have had any idea when he went there that first morning what was going to happen. No one could have known it was going to become a national media sensation, something that people still talked about twenty-five years later, or that a cottage industry was going to spring up around it. Murders in New Orleans were usually drug-related or heat-of-the-moment type things where very little investigation was required. Children of Garden District families just weren't found murdered in the carriage houses on their estates. Garden District families weren't suspects themselves. Arlene Metoyer might not have been New Orleans society, but the family she'd married into had history here and lots of powerful connections. I didn't blame Rocky Champagne for handling them with kid gloves. One false move and he could have lost his job and his pension. And how could he—or anyone—have foreseen just how big a circus the case would turn into?

This case was way above Rocky Champagne's skill level.

And even the Metoyers took their turn ripping him a new one. As the investigation dragged on, not getting anywhere, the Metoyers' lawyers turned on the police, called them bunglers who'd ruined any chance of finding justice for their daughter, ruining their lives.

"He retired about twenty years ago," Colin called over from the computer. "And yes, he was in charge of the original investigation. It looks like he was pretty much assigned to desk duty—ah, here's his death announcement. He died shortly after he retired." I could hear the frown in his voice, and looked over the back of the couch at him. "He was kind of young to retire."

"My guess is they forced him out," I said, reaching under the couch for my deck of tarot cards. I store them in a cigar box wrapped in blue silk, to keep them safe from outside vibrations. Like I said before, the gift I once had has faded with time; I don't really get the answers from the cards the way I used to. But I still kept the worn deck safe under my couch the way I always had, and sometimes the cards speak to me the way they used to. I don't really mind the way the gift has faded, to be honest. It did at first, because I thought I had angered the Goddess after the levees failed. But Frank explained it to me in a way that made a lot of sense to me and made me feel better about it. He said that she couldn't hold my anger after the flood against me, as it only stood to reason I would be angry at what happened to the city. Frank felt that she used to come to me because she felt I needed her help, that I needed her guidance—but now she no longer felt that I did. She now felt I was capable of working things out for myself, and that if I ever truly needed her help she wouldn't fail me. And she hasn't. She's come back a few times when I've needed her—but I haven't needed her all that much. And not knowing whether she would answer me caused me to start solving problems and issues on my own.

I was using her as a crutch, and now I could stand on my own two feet.

I opened the box and looked at the cards, swathed in their blue silk. But I hesitated. Did I really need to ask her anything? Was it something I could figure out for myself?

I closed the box but put it on the coffee table instead of back under the couch. I got up and walked over to where Colin was reading on the computer and rested my forearms on his muscled shoulders. "What are you doing?"

"His wife is also dead." Colin started typing again. "But he had a couple of kids that are still alive. Most of them no longer live here—I don't know if it was Katrina related or they just left New Orleans or what. But his oldest son still lives in the city. He's apparently a plumber and has his own business."

"Plumbers make good money in New Orleans," I replied,

resting my head against Colin's. He smelled remarkably good for someone who'd been traveling all day. "Good for him."

"Do we have anything that a plumber needs to look at?" Colin kissed my right forearm. "Leaky faucets, slow drains?"

I shook my head. "No, afraid not. What's the address?"

"He's on Tchoupitoulas Street—the business address anyway." He pulled up the website for CHAMPAGNE PLUMBING—*the best plumbers in Orleans Parish. "Why have wine when you can have Champagne?"*

"Clever marketing," I said. "That address is pretty far uptown, close to Rain's place, if I'm not mistaken. Near Children's Hospital, maybe? Definitely uptown of Jefferson Avenue."

Colin wrote the address down on a notepad. "It's a good place to start, I think. He might remember some details about what went on back then."

"His dad kind of took a beating over the case," I said. "He may not want to even talk about it. I should try Jesse again." I picked up my cell phone and pulled up the contacts, touching Jesse's number and also touching the call button. It went immediately to voice mail, which meant his phone was either off or he was still on the other line. I frowned. "Hey, Jesse, it's Scotty Bradley again, can you give me a call? Like I said, I've found Arlene." I disconnected the call and put the phone back down.

Colin kissed my forearm again. "Shall we lock the door and make up for some lost time?"

I kissed the top of his head. "I thought you'd never ask."

CHAPTER EIGHT
THE MAGICIAN, REVERSED
Use of power for selfish gains

I pulled up in front of Jerry Channing's house and tried to steel my nerve to get out of the car.

I'd rather have had a root canal than go knock on his door, but it couldn't be helped.

A woman in her eighties, wearing a black T-shirt with WHO DAT written in gold glitter across her rather large breasts, walked two enormous poodles with glittering collars past, undoubtedly on her way to Coliseum Square, the park at the end of the block. A Cox Cable truck rumbled past me, followed by a couple of shirtless, sweating joggers who were clearly insane—the heat index was hovering around 105, even at this early hour. A hipster wearing cut-off brown slacks with long strings hanging down his legs came around the corner riding a bicycle, his long kinky beard almost reaching the handlebars of what appeared to be an 1980s-era Schwinn girl's one-speed, complete with a white basket with plastic daisies affixed and pink and white streamers from the handlebars.

Given the porkpie hat, I assumed he was riding the bike ironically.

I took a deep breath, summoned my courage and nerve, and opened the car door.

The heat hit me in the face like a bitch-slap from an angry drag queen. I could feel my armpits, feet, and forehead getting wet with sweat. It was too damned hot to dress in long pants or anything with sleeves, but Frank and Colin both insisted I dress "business casual" since this was actually a professional interview.

It was just as well. I didn't like the idea of going to Jerry Channing's wearing a tank top and cargo shorts or anything clingy and revealing, no matter how hot it was.

To be honest, I hated the idea of going to Jerry Channing's house, period.

I leaned back against the car, delaying some more. It was actually a nice house, a late nineteenth century Victorian double he'd bought and renovated into a single. Even as a double, the individual units had been gigantic—they had to be at least two thousand square feet each. Why he wanted four thousand square feet of house was beyond me—we had more room with our two twelve-hundred-square-feet places than we knew what to do with, and there were four of us. He'd been able to get it on the cheap, too, before the Lower Garden District's renaissance in the late 1990s sent the price of houses there into the stratosphere. When I was growing up the Lower Garden District was an undesirable, high-crime area with crumbling houses, and Coliseum Square itself was a known drug dealers' hangout. Now, of course, it was gentrified—the St. Thomas Housing Projects and the partially demolished highway on-ramp distant memories.

Jerry had done some of the renovation work himself, hiring contractors to do what he couldn't—plumbing, electrical wiring, things like that—and it took him just over two years to complete. The house was raised about six feet above the ground, and the front porch, painted a dark emerald green, had square columns. The gallery deck above it had a lovely black iron railing, with roses and fleur-de-lis designed into it. In the little yard area between the black wrought iron fence and the porch, roses bloomed and a black wrought iron fountain with several naked cherubs bubbled and splashed. Bees flew lazily around the roses. There had originally been two front doors at either end of the porch when the house had been a double, but he'd taken out the door on the left and replaced it with an enormous window matching the other two—which were at least ten feet high, and started level with the porch. All the shutters, painted dark green, were closed and probably latched. The house itself was painted a traditional Caribbean Creole coral color. There was a cobblestone driveway to the right of the house, behind an electronic gate, also made from matching black wrought iron; behind the gate I could see a red convertible BMW with a white Lexus SUV parked in front of it.

Not only does he have too much house, he owns two cars. Because of course one person should have two cars. He has so much money he doesn't know how to spend it all.

I started to reach for the buzzer, but noticed that the gate was unlatched. *Oh, that's right, he's expecting me, how thoughtful,* I thought with an eye roll, opening it and stepping inside. I wiped sweat off my forehead before it could run into my eyes. Getting out of the heat was a great motivator to get me to go knock on the door. I walked up the steps, ducking a bee as it went past my face, and pushed the doorbell.

I'd tried again this morning over breakfast to get out of coming to interview Jerry. Colin and Frank, who'd gotten home late last night, had overruled me.

"You have a personal connection with him, after all," Frank said, not even having the decency to hide the grin, "and so he'll be more comfortable talking to you. Just try not to sleep with him this time." They'd both laughed, the wretched bastards.

There are times when I miss being single.

I could hear footsteps approaching the front door.

I never thought I'd ever set foot inside this place again.

In fairness, it was a nice house—if you didn't mind living in a museum.

Both sets of my grandparents' homes—the Diderot place in the Garden District and the Bradley place on State Street, farther uptown—were houses like that, and I always wondered how my parents stood growing up there. Both places were filled with antiques and artwork, old oil paintings of dead ancestors hung on the walls, expensive Oriental rugs spread over hardwood floors polished to a mirrorlike sheen. I never felt comfortable enough to relax in houses where everything was in place and there wasn't a speck of dirt anywhere, or any signs that people actually lived in the house.

I'm always afraid I'm going to break something or spill something. Nana Bradley had banned red wine after my perpetually drunk Uncle Skipper had spilled some on a white rug—twenty years ago.

And she loved red wine.

I did not understand people who prioritized rugs over wine.

That deeply regretted night so many years ago that I'd gone home with Jerry, we'd left the Pub after I was finished dancing at two. He waited for me, nursing a bottle of water, out in the bar while I got dressed and counted my money. I'd wanted to just go back to my place—when you're carrying over three hundred dollars in sweat-dampened cash, you don't really want to go anywhere else—but he insisted we go back to his place. I was horny, and when he pulled me into a deep, open-mouthed kiss there in the bar, well, it wasn't too hard to convince me. He drove a silver Porsche 911 Carrera convertible back then, and he was parked on Burgundy Street. He was sexy, and he kept stroking my back and my ass as we walked. I'd seen him around before in the bars and had always thought he was kind of hot. He gave me all the specifics of the car when we got to it—how much it had cost, how fast it could go, how much it cost to insure it in New Orleans. All I could think was *why would you spend that much money on a car in a city riddled with potholes and no one knows how to drive?* I was already beginning to regret my decision as he started the car and zipped out of the parking spot. My legs were aching from dancing, and I was worried about falling asleep on him.

Not because I was tired, but because he was boring me out of my skull.

I didn't need to say anything besides "cool" and "wow" and "okay" in the twenty minutes or so it took to get from the Quarter to the Lower Garden District. I'd met, and danced with, gay porn stars who didn't reach the level of narcissism this guy possessed. All he talked about was himself: his workout routine, the kind of supplements he took and the ones that didn't work, his trip to Italy and how he wouldn't go anywhere he couldn't fly in first class, on and on and on.

A couple of times when we were stopped at a traffic light, I debated the wisdom of getting out of the car and running home.

And the minute we'd walked in the front door of his house and he'd turned on the lights I was convinced staying in the car was the wrong decision.

He was the kind of gay man who had marble columns with statues on them strategically placed for maximum impact, with small lights hung from the ceilings spotlighting them—just like a museum gallery. The perfectly placed furniture didn't look comfortable, or like it had ever been used for anything other than being looked at. The art on the walls looked like the kind of art that gallery owners don't understand anything about other than they can talk someone with money into spending a lot of cash on it by spouting a lot of bullshit babble. He insisted on giving me the grand tour of the house. It was gorgeous, and he should have been proud of it, anyone would be—but I didn't need to know the cost of everything or that the marble columns had come from Ferrara ("that's in Italy, you know"). I just didn't care. I wanted to get laid and I wanted to get out of there—and the longer I was there, the less I was interested in getting laid. And the more he showed off his stuff, the later it was getting, and the less in the mood I was getting.

But he finally did lead me upstairs to the expansive bedroom on the second floor, which also contained his office.

That was when I realized that Jerry was Jerry Channing, the guy who'd written *Garden District Gothic*. There wasn't any escaping it. Only an idiot wouldn't have figured it out. There was no artwork in the bedroom/office. Instead, the walls were covered with pictures of him with celebrities, with the Oscar-winning director who'd made the film of his book, with Meryl Streep, Bridget Fonda, Nicolas Cage, and any number of other A- and B-list celebrities. The *pièce de résistance* was the area around his desk. The wall around the desk contained a framed poster of the book cover, the movie poster, framed reviews of the book, and framed magazine covers with his smiling face on them.

All in all, it was quite a lovely shrine to Jerry Channing.

As if all this wasn't bad enough, the sex was terrible—which made the rumors Jerry had been a sex worker when he first came to New Orleans hard to believe.

Finally, the door front opened and a delicious welcome arctic blast of cold air washed over me.

Jerry smiled and reached over to hug me, giving me a kiss on the cheek. "Scotty. It's so nice to see you again so soon! Come on in and get in out of that horrible heat." His voice was much friendlier than I'd been expecting, given how he'd been when I'd called him earlier.

Then again, maybe it was just as awkward for him as it was for me.

If so, he seemed to be making the best of it. Maybe pretending that night had never happened was the best way to go.

I can be just as phony as anyone, even if I don't like doing it.

"Thanks," I said, kissing his cheek in return. "Thanks for letting me come over on such short notice."

He shrugged and raised an eyebrow, smirking slightly. "I just finished a piece for *Street Talk*, and now I have to figure out what book I want to write next." He stood aside so I could enter. "I thought I had a great story—a murder/suicide twenty years ago in Redemption Parish that might have been more than it seemed…but I couldn't get anywhere with it. So it's back to the drawing board." He shut the door and turned the deadbolt.

"That must be disappointing," I replied. It was at least thirty degrees colder inside the house than it was outside.

It's amazing how cold seventy degrees can seem.

The front room looked completely different from what I remembered. The wooden staircase with the white banister was still there, but instead of being covered with expensive Oriental rugs, the floor was completely bare. The hardwood was polished to a mirrored finish. The four-foot-high columns with the statues were gone. I recognized the artwork he now had on the walls—it was all from local emerging artists and not terribly expensive. The splashes of color and the art itself blended in with the walls tastefully and made the room seem cozier. There were several overstuffed couches and matching chairs placed at strategic intervals throughout the room. He'd torn out the wall separating the two sides of the house, so this front room was enormous. The shutters on the side windows were open, so the room was filled with sunlight. If I remembered correctly, the door to the right of the staircase led to a formal dining room, and there was another door on the other side that led to a sitting room. The kitchen ran the width of the house in the back, with a laundry room and pantry behind it. There was another porch in the back of the house. The two-story carriage house in the back was a combination library/office/guest house where he actually worked; the office in his bedroom was more for mundane things like paying the bills and business matters.

"It's different," I said. "I like it."

"Yes, that's right, you've been here before." He sighed. "I feel like I owe you an apology."

"You do?"

He nodded. "That night—it seems like a million years ago, doesn't it? Anyway, I don't think I made a very good impression on you." He folded his arms. "Back then…well, my success was new to me. I didn't handle it well." He gestured around the room. "I got tired of living in a showplace and decided I wanted a home. The old décor wasn't very comfortable, and I finally realized I didn't need to show off." He was wearing his trademark black muscle shirt over a pair of black Saints sweatpants and sandals. "Come, have a seat in the sitting room." He gestured and I followed.

The sitting room, which had been incredibly austere in black and gold, with cream walls and brass fixtures, now had overstuffed maroon reclining chairs with footstools, a large coffee table with magazines spread across the top, and a full wet bar on the wall opposite the windows. "Have a seat." He waved in the general direction of the chairs and walked over to the mini refrigerator, retrieving a green bottle of Pellegrino and twisting off the cap. "Would you like some Pellegrino? I showered after the gym, of course, but am still feeling a bit dehydrated."

He was being ridiculously polite. "Yes, sure," I said, sitting down in one of the chairs and getting a notepad out of my backpack.

He handed me a cut crystal water glass and I smiled my thanks as he sat down in the other chair and smiled at me. "You know my story, right?"

"I've heard—things," I replied carefully.

He laughed. "Of course you have! It's New Orleans." He spread his hands out expressively. "My parents threw me out when I was sixteen for being gay. I came to New Orleans, worked as a hustler and a stripper, and paid my own way through college because I always wanted to be a writer. I worked as a personal trainer for several years…and then I wrote my big book." He made a face. "I wanted to be a fiction writer, you know, write important novels. But one day I realized my journal could be turned into something…I had no idea what it was going to turn into."

"You were Arlene Metoyer's trainer, weren't you?"

He smiled. "Yes. I was the Garden District trainer. I charged $150 an hour. And all those women talked to me. Their husbands didn't mind me because I was gay and I kept their wives' bodies tight and hard."

"I charged thirty-five dollars when I was a trainer."

"The money was always in going to the client, rather than having the client come to you," he said. "Lorita Godwin was my ticket to the Garden District."

"Ah." I tried not to smile. I hadn't been sure how to bring her into the conversation, and now Jerry had done my work for me. "Wasn't she Riley Metoyer's sister-in-law?"

"You've done your homework." He sounded impressed, and he smiled. "Yes, she was the first Mrs. Metoyer's sister, born Lorita Gallaudet. Lorita and Melanie were twins, in fact. They didn't get along, weren't close…anyway, Lorita has always had a thing for gay men. She collects them, like commemorative plates. She hired me at the gym where I worked, and she was the one who introduced me to her friends, got them to hire me. And those bitches loved to talk." His voice took on a bit of bitterness. "I was the help, of course, so I was never invited to dinner or to parties…but I knew more about them than their own husbands. Their kids. Their friends."

"And they still talk to you, even though you wrote a book about them."

"Are you kidding? They *love* talking to me." He laughed. "I could have dinner somewhere every night of the week if I wanted to—eat every meal out on some matron's husband's credit card. Only now I get invited to the parties, too."

"But Arlene Metoyer wasn't one of them, was she?"

He sipped his water. "No, she wasn't. Lorita knew her—felt sorry for her, in spite of—of everything. I always thought it was interesting…everyone believed the reason Melanie left Riley was because he was fucking Arlene…but like I said, Lorita and Melanie weren't close. Lorita really wanted to help Arlene, but there wasn't anything she could do for her—she couldn't invite her to dinner parties, or those woman would have cut Lorita dead. But she tried, whenever she could. Lorita introduced her to me. Arlene was having trouble losing weight after she had Delilah." He winked. "And she had to keep Riley interested. If Riley lost interest…" He clucked his tongue. "Well, it wasn't like he hadn't cheated on a wife before."

"Did you know Melanie Metoyer?"

"She was long gone before I came along." He shook his head, the scalp gleaming in the sunlight coming through the window behind him. "Like I said, Arlene was his mistress—and she wasn't the first. But Melanie finally had enough and left him, never to be seen or heard from again." He circled his index finger around his temple. "From what I heard, Melanie wasn't exactly stable. Of course, it's not like either Lorita or Arlene were reliable sources when it came to the first Mrs. Metoyer…he divorced her and married Arlene."

"That's just so weird to me—that she just vanished like that. And you say Lorita was nice to Arlene?"

He nodded. "Lorita wanted to be close to her nephews, I guess."

"Did she ever hear from her sister?"

"Not that I know of. Melanie left town and didn't look in the rearview mirror once, I guess."

"Why would she do that to her sons?"

"Crazy, I guess. The Gallaudets...weren't the most stable, you know." He smiled. "The boys blamed Arlene, of course. They hated her. And she tried, you know, she really tried. But the boys were horrible to her." He refilled his glass from the bottle he'd set on the table. "That wreaked some havoc on the investigation, you know. I think Riley thought the boys might have had something to do with it—I know Arlene did. She was convinced one or both of the twins had killed her precious baby." He looked at me. "Do you really think you can catch the killer after all this time? Or find Melanie? She's probably dead now." He laughed. "Lorita's no spring chicken, all the surgery to the contrary."

"Maybe." I smiled back at him. "I don't know. But it doesn't hurt to try."

"Especially when someone's paying." He laughed and held up his hand. "No offense. God knows I've made a fortune off that tragedy."

"Do you get tired of talking about it?"

"You have no idea. When I wrote my book I had no idea it would turn into such a cottage industry. Every single time something happens, or someone involved in the case dies, everyone wants me to go on television and talk about it, write a retrospective, something." He shook his head. "Yeah, it gets old, but I don't really have much choice. My book is the one everyone remembers, the one people still buy. There were other books, of course...quick-and-dirty tabloid-type paperbacks that came and went pretty fast." He set his glass down and put his feet up on a footstool, crossing his legs at the ankles. "I always thought someone—you know, someone like Ann Rule—would eventually do the definitive book about poor Delilah and people would forget about mine. And then I'd have to find a new gravy train." He laughed. "But no one ever did, and here we are."

"Who do *you* think killed Delilah?"

His eyes opened wide. "That's really the question, isn't it?" He laughed a little bit. "You know, Delilah is always made out to be this wonderful little girl—I even did it in my book. 'Everyone loved Delilah.' It wasn't true, of course. Delilah was a spoiled little monster who threw screaming fits when she didn't get what she wanted. Those screams cut right through your soul." He shuddered. "There were times when I was there training Arlene, and Delilah wanted her attention. My God, I could have gladly wrung her little neck myself." He steepled his fingers together. "I always thought that was what happened, you know. She pitched one of her fits and someone snapped…once they realized she was dead, they hid her in the carriage house and wrote the ransom note." He gave a little shrug. "Who that was, I couldn't say."

"If you had to hazard a guess…" I replied.

"I've obviously thought about it a lot," he replied. "You've read my book, of course."

"Of course."

He took another drink from his glass, emptying it. The bottle was also empty. "Do you want some more?" he asked, getting up and walking over to the refrigerator.

"I'm good."

"I knew Arlene the best, of course," he said, his broad back turned to me as he refilled his glass from the green bottle. "She was a first runner-up Miss Louisiana. Everyone always got that wrong, always. But it made better press to call her a former Miss Louisiana. She was definitely a former Miss Plaquemines Parish, though. She was a nice woman…but she was in way over her head in the Garden District. She actually met Lorita volunteering with the New Orleans Symphony—Arlene had always wanted to be an opera singer, you see. She loved classical music. I always felt bad for her…a Campbell from Plaquemines Parish whose father was a shrimper was never going to be a part of the Garden District, no matter how many pageant crowns she won or how pretty she was or who she married." He gave me a sly look as he sat back down. "You know what those bitches in the Garden District are like."

Another dig, but rather than rising to his bait I kept the smile plastered on my face. "Yes, they are terrible snobs, aren't they?"

"Delilah didn't get into McGehee," he went on, like I hadn't said anything. "Arlene was crushed, and Riley was furious. I always thought there was more to it than what I was told...so they took her to Sacred Heart instead." He frowned. "I can't imagine the nuns were any happier about Arlene's ambitions for Delilah's show business career...that's what the pageants were about. Practice for Delilah so she could learn how to perform. She was a talented little girl."

"I've only seen the clips they show of the pageants on television."

"You were what, a teenager when she was killed?" He cocked an eyebrow up at me, like he was trying to figure out how old I was.

"Yes." My cheeks were starting to ache with the effort of smiling. "I actually went to Jesuit High School with her brothers."

"Is that who hired you, Scotty?" He set the glass down on the end table with a clink so hard that sparkling water splashed over the sides. "Jesse or Dylan?"

"Does it matter?"

"Of course it matters, Scotty." He settled back into his chair, gracefully crossing his ankles again on the footstool. "You'll find out the more time you spend on this, everything matters when it comes to Delilah Metoyer's murder." He took a deep breath. "I always thought it was Jesse."

"I beg your pardon?"

"I always thought it was Jesse. That killed her. That family dynamic was very fucked up." He sighed. "They thought Arlene couldn't have any more children after Delilah was born...and since she had no real friends in New Orleans, she kind of made her entire life about her daughter. She gave her way too much attention…and I think if society had accepted her, let her in, who knows, maybe it wouldn't have happened. She wouldn't have pushed Delilah to be a star, and maybe all of this could have been avoided." He sighed. "Arlene wasn't an evil woman, the way she was made out to be, the way the boys thought she was. Yes, she was the other woman, but being married to Riley wasn't easy."

The way you made her out to be in your book.

"All she had was that kid, and her own broken dreams of what she wanted from life. She gave up what she thought could have been a big career in show business to marry Riley and be a high-society lady in New Orleans…only the other society women would have none of it. Delilah was her chance…her chance to get the stardom she always wanted, to pay those women back who thought she was parish trash and not good enough for their clubs and their parties…I never knew who blackballed Delilah from McGehee. If I had, I would have put all of that in the book." He smiled. "There was a lot of stuff I left out."

"You really think Jesse killed his sister?"

"Jesse hated Delilah, it was clear to me every time I set foot in that house. You went to school with him—you know what he was like. An arrogant little asshole who thought the world belonged to him, that he deserved everything." He picked up the glass again, mopped up the little spill with a napkin. "And a homophobic little shit at that. I bet he made your life a living hell at Jesuit, didn't he?"

I started. *How could he know that?*

He laughed a little bit. "I was right, wasn't I? You may think I'm a jerk, Scotty, and you're right—when we first met I was a jerk. But I can read people pretty well."

"You think Jesse was jealous of Delilah?"

"She got a lot of attention from her father, even though Riley was at best a distant parent. So who knows?"

"I don't—"

"There is one thing I couldn't put in the book—I think Riley was cheating on Arlene. I didn't know who—Arlene certainly thought he was cheating." He spread his hands again. "Cheaters generally don't change. I'm always amazed when someone who was the other woman is surprised when her husband cheats on her. I guess they think they're special, it won't happen to them. Riley had cheated on her several times, but this time Arlene thought it was serious."

"You don't think Riley could have—"

"No. Riley wasn't a killer. A cheater, certainly, but not a killer. My money was always on Jesse."

"Really."

"It's the only thing that ever made sense to me." He went on slowly, "Why they called their lawyer immediately when the body was found—who does that?"

It was a question everyone had asked over and over again, and it was also one of the reasons people thought Arlene or Riley had killed the child—the call to a lawyer *first*, when it was possible that the killer might have been caught if they'd called the police instead. They called their lawyer and waited for him to come, consulted with him, and then called the police.

"Most people thought it meant they were guilty," Jerry said. "But Riley and Arlene worshipped that child. They didn't even *spank* her. Robin, the nanny, wasn't allowed to do anything but scold her in a reasonable tone and put her in time-out when she misbehaved…no one was allowed to yell at that little girl…and I'm supposed to believe Arlene or Riley just lost their minds completely one night and killed her?" He shook his head. "No, I think it was either Jesse or Dylan, more likely Jesse. Dylan was afraid of everything. I can't see him having the gumption to do it. That leaves Jesse."

"And outside of Robin, there was no one else in the house but family?"

"The maid and the cook came in every morning and left by five every night, with dinner cooking." Jerry folded his arms. "It had to be Jesse."

"Who was Madame Laroux?"

"You want me to give up all my secrets?" He laughed. "Her name is Madeline Lefort, and she lives in the Treme now." He pulled out a notepad, wrote her name and phone number down, and passed the paper to me. "Tell Miz Madeline I sent you, or she won't talk to you."

I folded the paper and slipped it into my pocket suspiciously. "Thank you."

He glanced at his watch. "Sorry, I have to go. Call me if you have anything you want to ask."

"I will."

The front door shut behind me. *He sure gave me the bum's rush to get me out of there. Ah, well, maybe I'm being overly suspicious.*

I started the SUV and dialed Jesse again.

"Hello?"

"Hey, Jesse, didn't you get my messages?" I said, irritated. "Look, I—"

"Is this Scotty Bradley?"

My heart sank. This couldn't be good. I knew that voice, and it wasn't Jesse.

"Yes, this is Scotty Bradley."

"And this is Detective Blaine Tujague with the New Orleans Police Department," the voice went on, sounding annoyed. "Do you want to explain why you're calling a cell phone I've found at my crime scene?"

CHAPTER NINE

SIX OF CUPS, REVERSED

Living in the past rather than the present

It only took me about ten minutes or so to get to Serena's place.

I couldn't turn onto her block of Coliseum, since it was blocked by a fire truck. Since I couldn't turn, I drove down to the next block and parked there in the shade of a massive old live oak tree. Hopefully, that would keep my car from turning into an oven. I got out of the car and walked back to the corner, sweating. Serena's block was nothing but chaos. Another fire truck blocked off the other end, and people in uniforms were swarming in the street and along the sidewalk in front of her house, talking into walkie-talkies, checking cell phones, or talking amongst themselves.

In addition to the fire trucks blocking off the street, the crime lab truck, an ambulance, and multiple squad cars were parked up and down the street on both sides. I sighed and wiped sweat off my forehead. Other than the low buzz of conversation and the occasional burst of static from a radio, the neighborhood was blanketed in an eerie silence. In any other part of the city, pedestrians and neighbors would be gathered at an almost-but-not-quite discreet distance, talking and gossiping and wondering what was going on. But the Garden District wasn't that kind of neighborhood—coming out to stare and talk would be considered much too vulgar for the delicate sensibilities of the city's elite.

No, the ladies of the Garden District whose windows had a view were sipping brandy, surreptitiously glancing through the curtains, and talking on their cell phones in a hushed, excited whisper to friends without a view.

As I stood there, hesitating, a van from the local Fox affiliate came screeching to a halt up the street, the side door opening and camera and sound men in jeans spilling out, followed by a perfectly coiffed young female reporter wearing an eggplant-colored suit.

Another murder at the Metoyer place was going to be big news. If I was going to get in there without showing up on the evening news, I was going to have to hurry.

Keeping my eye on the news crew, I strolled up the sidewalk as nonchalantly as I could. I felt like I was sweating to death in my polo shirt and jeans, and cursed myself for not bringing a weather-appropriate change of clothing along with me in the car. There was a uniformed cop standing guard at Serena's front gate. A couple of firemen came out through the gate, not speaking, and wandered down to the fire truck at the other end of the street.

I took a deep breath and crossed the street.

The cop on guard weighed well over two hundred pounds. His uniform shirt was tight to the point that I didn't see how his blood was circulating in his arms. His polyester navy blue pants looked painted on. His arms were folded in front of his massive chest, his arm and shoulder muscles bulging. There were some enormous, angry purple pimples on his upper arms. I could see orangish-red whiskers on the sides of his head below his cap, and his face was red and wet with running sweat. He had the look of a steroid user. He held up his big hands in warning and said, as I approached the gate, "You can't get in there. It's a crime scene."

"Would you mind calling Detective Tujague on your radio and letting him know Scott Bradley is here, as he requested?" I gave him what I hoped was my winningest, most nonthreatening smile. I've always found it smart to be polite to cops, no matter what Mom says.

Or does, for that matter.

He scowled in response and pressed the button on the radio

clipped to his collar, but before he could say anything the front door of the house burst open.

"*Scotty!*" Serena shrieked, loud enough to be heard in the Quarter. "Scotty darlin'! Thank God you're here!" She came running down the front steps of the house and down the walk, no mean feat as she was wearing high-heeled feathered mules and a flowing leopard-skin print negligee that left very little to the imagination. The cop turned when he heard her calling my name, and his face turned an even deeper shade of red, almost maroon. When she reached the gate, she swung up it open and dramatically threw her arms around me, almost smothering me in her enormous bosom.

I hadn't realized how tall she was until that moment.

"I'm so glad to see you, darlin'," she said in her thick Texas drawl as she continued clutching me with an iron grip. She was also a lot stronger than I would have thought. "It's all right, Officer," she said over my head, "he's welcome to come inside, he's a dear friend and I need all the support I can get with this horrible tragedy!" Her tone was friendly but also made it very clear she wasn't going to let him stop her. As she spoke, she was pulling me inside the gate. "Thank you, darlin'," she said to the cop, "you're doing a wonderful job! Can I send you out some water or something to drink?"

"No, thank you, ma'am." He actually saluted her and smiled. "Just doing my job, ma'am. And no need for thanks."

It was amazing how different he looked when he smiled.

Once we were safely inside the gate she relaxed her death grip. "Come on inside," she said loudly, as she took me by the hand and dragged me up the walk. She muttered in a low breath out the side of her mouth, "Don't say anything until we're safely inside the house, okay?"

Confused, I followed her up the steps. *Safely inside? What did she mean by that?*

Once we were safely inside the house and she'd shut the door behind her, she let out an enormous sigh of relief. "Sorry." She gave me a 100-watt smile, her white even teeth sparking in the light from the chandelier above. She was wearing pale pink lipstick, and the rest of her makeup was very subtle. "I've got to be careful." She rolled her eyes. "We were supposed to start filming today—just some interviews, you know, the talking head things about our backgrounds and our interests that they'll weave into the show as they edit it together, we don't start shooting actual scenes until this weekend, and this has got me all tied up." She ran a perfectly manicured hand through her blond hair. She shook her head. "This is *not* how I envisioned my story on the show going. Come on." She gestured for me to follow her as she stalked down the hallway like a caged leopard.

I followed her through a doorway into the sitting room. The leopard print was flowing out behind her as she walked over to the bar along the far wall between two sets of French doors leading out to the side gallery. She grabbed a bottle of Jim Beam from the shelf and poured herself several fingers into a crystal glass. Felice and Baloo stared at me from the other end of the bar, blinking. "Serena—"

"Can you believe the fucking luck?" She exploded after throwing the whiskey back in one shot and refilling the glass. "You want anything?" She gestured at me with the bottle.

"No, thanks." I sat down in a beige wingback chair. One of the cats hopped down from the cart and leaped into my lap, curling up into a ball and purring. I started scratching its head. The gold color around its neck read BALOO in rhinestones...then again, they were probably diamonds. Serena didn't strike me as the fake jewel type. "What's happened? Who's been killed? I should probably be finding Blaine—"

"That attractive Detective Tujague?" She smiled as she sat down in a chair facing me, and the other cat hopped up into her lap. "He's gorgeous."

"He's also gay, Serena."

"That figures. Of course he's gay. Are all the good-looking men in this town gay?" She made an extravagant gesture, accompanied with a dramatic eye roll, and let out her breath in a large, melodramatic sigh. "Of course, there's no telling how long the body's been out there—"

"Body? Whose body? All Blaine told me was that someone had been murdered. He didn't say who." I was hoping it wasn't Jesse—but his phone being there wasn't promising. Then again, Blaine had said *Why are you calling a phone at my crime scene*, not *why are you calling a dead man's phone?*

Okay, maybe that was splitting hairs, but he didn't seem to know whose phone it was.

Which meant Jesse wasn't the victim.

"You're a private eye, aren't you?" She raised an eyebrow as Felice started head-butting her and trying to nip her chin. "Rain told me that."

"Yes, but—"

"I don't think I'll need one," she went on, like I hadn't spoken. "I haven't done anything, but it's just my bad luck that someone has to go and get themselves *killed* on my property. I should probably call my lawyer—do you think I need my lawyer? What are my rights in this situation, anyway? Yes, definitely I need to call my lawyer."

I help up my hands. "*Stop.*"

She goggled at me.

"Please, Serena, start at the beginning."

She sipped her whiskey. "Oh, there, that's better now. Off with you, Felice." She pushed the cat out of her lap. Felice howled in protest and galloped out of the room. Baloo leapt from mine and followed. "I was out late last night—I didn't get back here until, oh, I don't know, three in the morning maybe? I love that the bars here don't close…anyway, I was out with some friends having some drinks and took a cab back here, and I just went up to bed. The alarm was on when I get here, and I turned it back on, of course, before going upstairs." She frowned. "I think I may need to have some live-in staff. This place is too big for a woman living alone."

"You're probably right," I replied, "or at least hire security guards to patrol the grounds for you." The Garden District's private security force couldn't be everywhere all the time, after all, and crime was a concern in every neighborhood.

"So obviously, I had no idea what had happened in the carriage house, or when."

"The carriage house?" I felt the hairs on the back of my neck standing up.

In my mind, I could see the inside of the carriage house, and sensed the danger there. The dusty ski equipment, piled in the corner. The Carpenters playing in the background, this time "It's Going to Take Some Time This Time." Something bad was going to happen…

"Right?" Her eyes bulged as she got up to retrieve the whiskey bottle. She refilled the glass and took a healthy gulp. "And the body is *right where* Delilah's was found. The. Exact. Same. Place." She shuddered. "Maybe I should just sell this place. It's obviously cursed."

"Whose body…I mean, who was it?"

"Arlene Metoyer, can you believe it? The poor thing." She gulped down the whiskey and winced. "I should probably stop drinking, in case they do want me to film later…"

"Arlene?" I stared at her. I don't know what I was expecting to hear, but that wasn't it.

"Yes, can you believe it?" She rubbed her temples. "But why was she even here? And in the carriage house, of all places? You'd think that was the last place on earth she'd ever want to see again, wouldn't you? I haven't seen her since I bought the kittens, and she never has been here. I wouldn't have met her had I not insisted…so what on earth was she doing here?"

"Arlene?" I couldn't wrap my mind around it. Serena was right—it didn't make sense.

What on earth had Arlene been doing here, and why? And why was Jesse's phone—

Jesse.

My client.

Who'd hired me to find his stepmother.

Who was now dead.

And his cell phone was at the crime scene.

"And they're certain it was foul play?" I heard myself asking. *Of course it was, you dumb shit. The cops wouldn't be here otherwise, and she wouldn't be drinking her weight in whiskey if it wasn't murder.*

"Yes." She took a deep breath. "Yes, it was murder. Definitely murder. I went out for a swim this morning—swims are the best thing for a hangover, you know—and I noticed the carriage house door was open. It didn't make sense. I don't use it for anything, really, I have to figure out what to do with that space, but the door is always locked."

"Not always." I said. "It was open the night of your party."

"No, it couldn't have been." She shook her head. "Like I said, it's always locked."

"I was in there," I replied. The hair on my arms joined the ones on the back of my neck in standing up now. "The lights were on, a stereo was playing some music. I went in…and—"

"The door should have been locked," she insisted. "There are only two keys, and the master. The master and the spare are locked in my desk drawer, and the other is on my key ring. I didn't unlock the carriage house. I never do. It's not possible, Scotty."

Someone else, then, either had a key or had access to hers. "Go on." *We'll figure that out later.*

"So I walked over there, and I screamed when I saw the body. It didn't seem real, you know, like a mannequin or something." Her face began to redden again and her eyes watered. "And then the minute I realized it was Arlene, I came running back to the house and called the police." She frowned, and tilted her head to one side. "Why are you here? You just happened to turn up on my door the day I find a body in my carriage house?" She laughed. "Rain was right, you *are* a detective!"

"I came here because…" I bit my lower lip. How much could I tell her? Ah, it was all going to come out sooner or later anyway. "I was hired by Jesse Metoyer to do some things…one of the things was to locate Arlene for him. I called him this morning to let him know I'd found her—"

She interrupted me, smiling, "So *that's* why you needed her phone number! You didn't want a cat after all!"

"Well, we did get a cat." I smiled back at her. "But yes, that was why. Anyway, when I called Jesse's cell phone this morning, Detective Tujague answered, and wanted to know what I was doing calling a phone at his crime scene. He also wanted to talk to me." I got up. "I guess I'd better get out there—I've delayed long enough."

She waved and filled her glass again. She was going to be pretty hammered soon. "They're all in the backyard."

I thought about reminding her she might be filming *Grande Dames* later, but hey, it's also not every day you find a dead body.

It's happened to me several times, and I'm still not used to it.

I excused myself, went down the hallway to the back door, and stepped out onto the back gallery.

The carriage house looked busy—crowds of crime lab technicians doing their thing, and I'd apparently gotten there just in time to see the body being removed. It was already in a body bag. Blaine accompanied it out of the carriage house, his partner right behind him. He had a grim look on his face that grew even grimmer when he saw me standing on the gallery. He said something to his partner. She grimaced and started walking across the grass toward me.

Venus Casanova is probably the most senior police detective on the force, but I don't know how old she is. She keeps her hair buzzed pretty close to the scalp, but I'd noticed in recent years the dark black was now shot through with gray. Her face was wrinkle-free, and the high cheekbones and slightly reddish tint to her dark skin probably indicated Native American blood back in her family tree somewhere. She was tall, well over six feet, and always wore stiletto heels that made her look even taller. She had a wiry build—I'd heard she'd put herself through college on a basketball scholarship—and her arms, which were bare, were well-muscled. She was wearing a pair of dove-gray slacks and a sleeveless pink blouse. She'd undoubtedly ditched the jacket because of the heat, but there were no signs of sweat on her anyway. Her strides were long, and the look on her face would have put fear into the heart of a lesser mortal.

I've dealt with Venus many times over the years, so she no longer scares me the way she did in the beginning. As everyone likes to remind me, I have a bad habit of stumbling over bodies, or just having them turn up in my general vicinity. One time one even fell out of the sky and landed on my balcony.

Hey, it's not my fault!

Anyway, Venus can be very intimidating, but over the years I think she's gotten used to me.

At least, I hoped so. She was a lot nicer to me than she used to be, at any rate.

She already had her notepad in one hand as she came up the back steps. "Damn, that ceiling fan feels good," she said, fanning herself with the notebook. "It's too damned hot to be outside today. Come on, let's sit here and talk." She gestured to the table underneath the ceiling fan. "No need to be out in the damned sun if we don't have to be."

Her friendliness was a good sign. Usually, if they were going to play the good cop/bad cop game with me, she was the bad cop. It never worked. I figured the mentality was since Blaine was also gay, that was supposed to make me feel more comfortable with him. It's kind of annoying and homophobic, really.

Not all gay men get along any more than all straight people do.

I sat down across the table from her. She was right—the ceiling fan did feel good.

"So, someone killed Arlene Metoyer," I said. "In the same place her daughter's body was found almost twenty-five years ago. Kind of weird, don't you think?"

She narrowed her eyes for a moment before relaxing into a smile. "Oh, you talked to Ms. Castlemaine before you came out here, didn't you?" She shook her head. "God, but that woman is a drama queen. Have you known her long?"

"I met her for the first time last Friday. I was here. She had a housewarming party," I replied. "She's actually a friend of my sister's. That's how we got invited."

"She's perfect for that *Grande Dames* show she's going to be on." Venus rolled her eyes. "Lord. I wanted to tell her to save it for the cameras. She's going to be a natural once they started filming." She shook her head. "I guess we should be glad they weren't filming already. Last thing I need in a murder investigation is some damned reality show cameras around. It's going to be hard enough as it is."

"So, it's definitely a murder?"

"Unless she managed to club herself in the back of the head and fall facedown, it's definitely murder." Venus sighed. "Now, whose cell phone was that you were calling this morning? Blaine said you said Jesse?" She flipped open a new page in her notepad. "Would that be Jesse Metoyer, perhaps? Is he back in town?"

I bit my lip. Confidentiality to a client was very important—who would hire a private eye who spilled his client's business at the drop of a hat? But at the same time, a private eye wasn't a lawyer, and so there were no client confidentiality legal protections. I took a deep breath. It wasn't like they wouldn't be able to trace the phone, and it wouldn't hurt to cooperate. It might pay off in the long run. His phone being there wasn't proof of anything other than his phone was there. "Yes, Jesse Metoyer," I said slowly. "He hired Frank and me—and Colin—this past weekend."

"Hired you? To do what?"

"Well, for one thing, he wanted to find Arlene." I exhaled. "He also wants to find his actual mother. He also wanted us to look into his sister's death."

She raised an eyebrow. "Delilah Metoyer? Are you serious?"

"I—we—told him we couldn't promise anything," I replied. "Were you on the force back then?"

"How old do you think I am?"

"Oh, God, I'm sorry. I didn't mean—"

She shook her head with a low chuckle. "I'm giving you a

hard time, Scotty. Yes, I actually was on the force back then. I was only in my second year, and believe you me, I was glad I was nowhere near that case. It broke a lot of careers, I can tell you that. I was working the beat in the Seventh Ward back then. I felt sorry for poor old Rocky Champagne. He was a broken man after that case...and it pretty much ended his career." She gave me a look. "That was sympathy I would have felt for anyone in his place, you know. Rocky was a—" She shut her mouth, compressing her lips into a tight line. "I'll just say Rocky was old school, and leave it at that."

"A racist, you mean."

She cracked a small smile. "And maybe a sexist, but I didn't say it. Didn't think women belonged on the force, didn't think blacks—and he always said 'coloreds' when he thought he could get away with it, so you know what he said in private—had what it took to be on the force. He thought the force started going down when the coloreds were let on...and that's why crime was getting so bad in the city, you know. Because the colored cops would let the colored criminals go." A muscle in her jaw twitched, her eyes narrowed in memory. "So, you can imagine what he thought about black women wearing the blue. No, I felt bad for his luck in catching the case—and he'd been a good cop for a long time, no matter what kind of man he was. He didn't deserve to have his career end the way it did, scapegoated and driven into an early retirement." She shook her head. "He was an embarrassment they had to get rid of." She looked at me. "Why on earth would you think you could solve that case when no one else could?"

"I—we don't. We told him flat out it was a dead end and a waste of his money. Finding his stepmother, though—that was easy. Finding his mother...not so easy."

"They aren't in touch?"

"He hasn't seen or heard from his mother since the day she walked out on the family, before his father married Arlene." She was scribbling notes as I talked. "That trail is pretty cold, too. Arlene was easy to find, like I said. Serena had her phone number. I drove up to the North Shore yesterday to see her." I explained the cat situation.

She cracked a smile. "You bought a cat just so you could see her?"

I smiled back at her. "The kitten was adorable, and Frank's nephew was with me, too. There was no way we weren't getting that cat."

"And he wasn't in touch with Arlene?"

"The way I understood it, when Riley took the boys and left New Orleans, they never communicated again. He died several years ago—Jesse said it was cancer—and when Jesse's brother recently died, he wanted to reestablish contact with her...but she'd already sold the house." As I said it to a police detective, it sounded lame. "That's why he also wanted to find his mother, I guess. As for Delilah's murder...well, he just wanted us to really poke around a bit. See what we could find. I didn't get the impression he thought we'd be able to actually, you know, solve it."

She didn't say anything, though, just scribbled some more notes. "And when you saw Arlene, you mentioned that Jesse was looking for her?"

"I wasn't sure if I was going to, honestly." I shrugged. "But after I saw her...I couldn't not say something. I...I felt sorry for her."

"You did?"

I tried to find the right words. "All I could think when I saw her was, here was the woman who used to have it all. Wife, mother, house in the Garden District. She was a beauty queen. And then it was all gone, taken away from her. And there she was, living on the North Shore, drinking—I think she was drunk, it was the afternoon, and she was drinking in front of me. She looked bad, you know? Like she'd totally given up."

"There are those who think she killed Delilah." Venus kept scribbling. "And she got away with murder."

"Maybe." I took a deep breath. "Like I said, I felt sorry for her. She didn't seem to me like she was, I don't know, guilty. She seemed like she was still grieving, all these years later. Delilah's murder destroyed her life…and now all she has is the cats." I remembered how disorganized her house had been, how dusty and uncared for—but the barn had been pristine.

"At least she has the cats," Venus said without looking up. "Did you let her know Jesse was looking for her?"

I nodded. "I thought…well, wasn't it better she know ahead of time? I couldn't not tell her, and then have him show up on her doorstep. I mean, she might shoot him or something."

"Did you see any guns other than the shotgun?"

"No."

"Did you let him know you'd located her?"

"I left him messages on his phone."

This looked really bad for Jesse. But I couldn't lie to her. He hired us to find her. I told him where she was. And now she was dead. And his cell phone was at the crime scene.

Jesse needed a lawyer.

Storm always says to never tell the police anything they don't ask for; just answer their questions and don't say anything more. Never volunteer information, just give them the facts.

Which were, in this case, bad enough as they were.

"And he never called you back? Never responded to your messages?"

I shook my head. "No. That's why I called him again this morning."

"All right, thanks." Venus smiled at me. "You don't know where to reach him, do you? Besides by phone? Do you know where he's staying in town?"

I gave her his address on Touro Street. I couldn't think of a reason not to.

"You've been a real help, Scotty." She started to get up.

"Can I ask you something?"

She gave me an odd look and sat back down. "What?"

It was worth a shot, at any rate. The worst thing she could do was say no. "Do you think we could see the case file on Delilah Metoyer?"

She narrowed her eyes. It seemed like an eternity before she finally said, "You know, it's been twenty-five years." She said it slowly, like she was thinking about every word before she said it. "I can't let you see the file—you know that. The case is still open, even though no one is technically assigned to it. But I'll see if I can dig it up." She held up a hand. "This is a favor, and I am going to have to clear it with my captain, okay? But there's a chance—a slight chance—that these two cases may be related."

Jesse thought Arlene killed Delilah, Arlene thought he did.

"Which means I *can* have access to the file," she went on. "There may not be anything in there worth sharing. There may be things in there that are, but I am not going to let you see the file." She flashed her teeth at me in a mirthless smile. "What I will do is this: I'll give you the names of everyone Rocky and his team interviewed. That might help."

"Thanks, Venus." It was more than I could have hoped for—and I wasn't entirely sure she wasn't stretching the rules more than a little bit. "Can I ask you something else?"

She looked like she was counting to ten in her head. "Yes?"

"Can you check to see if a missing persons report was ever filed on Melanie Gallaudet Metoyer?"

"I can, when I have time," she said carefully. "But if she just walked out on the family, I doubt her husband ever filed one. He probably knew how to find her, just didn't tell the kids. I mean, if it were my kids and their father didn't want to see them, I don't know if I would tell them, you know?" She closed her eyes for a minute. "He divorced her, didn't he?"

"Yeah."

"Then there's a record of that. That's where I'd start looking for her."

"Thanks."

"I do have something to ask in return for this favor about the case file, though." Her voice was completely serious. "And you better understand I mean this."

"Yes?"

"Don't get involved in my case." She stood up, tucking the pen behind her ear. "Keep your nose out of the Arlene Metoyer investigation. Or I'll figure out some way to arrest you. And that's a guarantee."

CHAPTER TEN
QUEEN OF SWORDS, REVERSED
She is both sly and deceitful, a tendency to gossip

After I left Venus, I took the side path around the house to the front, lost in my thoughts while sweating out about five pounds of water.

Could it be a coincidence?

Frank hates coincidences, especially when it comes to a criminal investigation, and Colin agrees with him.

"There's no such thing as a coincidence when it comes to a criminal investigation. Whenever a coincidence would pop up on one of my cases when I was with the bureau," he'd say, "it set off every alarm bell in my head and I'd make a note to check into it further. And every single time I was right—it *wasn't* a coincidence. So, whenever you come across one in an investigation, you have to check it out and maybe even double-check...and trust me, without fail you will *always* find out that it was planned."

I never disagree or contradict Frank when it comes to stuff like this...but every time he says something absolute like that I always think, *but aren't there always exceptions to rules?*

Coincidences happen in life every single damned day—at least, they do in mine.

I mean, what were the odds that Jesse would show up at my mother's wanting to hire us to find his stepmother the very day after we learned where she was?

Jesse saw us outside the house after the party. He recognized me and that was why he came looking for us...and Mom told him we were private eyes. That gave him an excuse...

An excuse...an excuse for what, exactly? He didn't *need* an excuse to hire us to find his mother and stepmother. He didn't need an excuse to hire anyone. If he hadn't hired us, he would have just hired someone else.

He couldn't have known I'd be at Serena's party that night. He couldn't have known I was a private eye unless he'd looked me up ahead of time, which didn't seem likely unless for some reason he was stalking me.

Trying to find a pattern in his behavior was more work than just accepting it was all a coincidence, so sorry, Frank, whether you liked it or not—I believed all of that was a coincidence.

But I couldn't believe it was a coincidence Jesse's cell phone was found at the scene of Arlene's murder.

There was no doubt that things looked bad for Jesse. If I were a cop, he'd be my number one suspect. He'd hired us to find Arlene for him and we had. Now she was dead and his cell phone was at the crime scene.

Sure, it was all circumstantial—but juries had convicted on less evidence than this.

He needed a lawyer—if I were him the first thing I'd do was hire one, right away.

I had no way of reaching him. I could have gone to the place he was renting, but I imagine there were cops already on their way there.

I couldn't *not* tell Venus where she could find him, either. That would have been hindering her investigation, and I wasn't stupid enough to think she liked me enough to overlook that.

Isn't that what got Riley and Arlene in trouble? Calling a lawyer before they called the police?

Calm down, I told myself, *there's nothing you could have done to help Jesse. Just get to the car and then you can figure out what to do next.*

I walked through the front gate and nodded at the 'roidedout cop still pulling guard duty. His face was redder than it had been when I'd gone by the first time, and his uniform was wet with sweat. He looked like he was minutes away from having heatstroke.

The fire trucks were both gone, and the street was now open. The only official cars left on the street were Venus's SUV, a police car, and the Crime Lab van. A woman was standing in one of the windows of the house directly across the street, a teacup in one hand as she blatantly stared. I waved when she looked at me, and she disappeared behind her curtains again. I wiped sweat from my forehead and smiled grimly to myself as I headed down the street and around the corner to my car.

I unlocked the door and was greeted with a rush of hot air. I leaned in, put the keys in the ignition, and started the engine. Cold air blasted from the air-conditioner vents. I waited a few moments for the car to get cold and then slipped into the driver's seat. I pulled out my phone and tapped out a quick text message to Frank and Colin: *Arlene murdered at Serena's house. Jesse's cell phone at crime scene. Not looking good for him at the moment. Not sure what to do.*

I sat, waiting for them to respond, letting the cold air blow over me and dry my skin and my shirt. I was dehydrated and needed some water.

My mind was still racing.

And what was up with the carriage house? Serena said it was locked up the night of her party—but the door was open and the lights were on. I didn't imagine that. And I didn't imagine that music today, either.

I'd communicated with the spirit of a dead man once before. Was that happening again? Was Delilah trying to get through to me from the other side?

You're being crazy. Your imagination is out of control again. Besides, it's been years since you've had anything psychic happen. You can't even read the cards anymore. So why now?

I waited a few moments and checked my phone. No response from Frank or Colin.

I blew out a sigh. Maybe I was being ridiculous, but I felt guilty about telling the cops where to find Jesse.

After all, it was possible that Jesse hadn't killed Arlene. I started ticking off explanations for his cell phone being at the crime scene on my fingers.

First, he may have met Arlene there, left his cell phone behind, and someone else killed her.

Second, the killer may have stolen Jesse's phone and planted it to frame him.

Third, Jesse could have been there, left his phone behind, and never seen Arlene at all.

And why *was* Arlene there in the first place?

Storm likes to say he can turn anything into enough probable cause to get a jury to acquit. Jesse's phone being at the murder scene didn't prove anything other than he'd been there at some point—and the phone could have been there for hours before Arlene was killed. It proved nothing.

I'd been trying to reach Jesse since Sunday afternoon without any luck. Storm would run with that in court, especially if the messages had never been checked. *If Jesse never listened to my message, he wouldn't have known how to reach Arlene in the first place.*

Or was I just making excuses for Jesse? Just because he'd hired us…

I also couldn't rule out the possibility he'd hired us to find her precisely so he could kill her.

But why? And why now? If Jesse wanted to kill Arlene, he could have done so at any point in the last twenty-five years.

I didn't like the idea he may have used us to find his victim, but I couldn't rule it out. At least, not until I'd talked to him again.

I tapped my fingers on the steering wheel. There had to be something I could do…I picked up my phone and touched the icon for the notes app. Taylor had taught me how to use it—rolling his eyes at my lack of tech savvy the entire time—and it was amazing how much easier it made my life. I kept all of my lists there—grocery, to-do, etc.—and so I picked out the list I'd made of people I needed to talk to, and looked at it. Since I was in the Garden District already, I might as well get some of the necessary interviews out of the way.

Arlene's death hadn't solved Delilah's murder, and I was no closer to finding Melanie Metoyer. There was still work to be done.

I smiled to myself when I stopped scrolling on Lorita Godwin's name.

I actually knew her slightly, so it wouldn't be a cold call.

I'd met her a few times at parties at my Diderot grandparents' house, which was only a few blocks away from where I was sitting. Maman Diderot didn't like Lorita very much, dismissing her as vulgar, despite her old Louisiana pedigree as a Gallaudet. The Gallaudets had been old antebellum money—an important distinction in New Orleans society, for people who cared about that sort of thing. Lorita had been married multiple times, but still used her first husband's last name. There were rumors around town, whispered behind perfectly manicured hands at luncheons in fine restaurants, that Lorita didn't have much money left and her extravagant living and many husbands had drained her bank accounts dry. Jerry had said she was name-rich and house-poor in the book: the name meant something still around town, and she still had the big old house—but it was kept up for appearances only…which meant the first floor was elegant and stylish while the upstairs was falling apart, unfinished, and desperately in need of renovation.

I put the car in gear and drove around the block to head back up toward St. Charles Avenue. Her house, if I remembered correctly, was between Prytania and St. Charles. This wasn't the old Gallaudet house, which had been sold years ago. This was the place she'd bought with her first husband, and where she'd lived ever since. I pulled up in front and parked across the street, sitting in the cool while getting up my nerve to face the heat again.

The Godwin place was a three-story Victorian with several

towers with witch's hat–style roofs at each corner. There was a gallery across the front, but the upper floors had balconies rather than a gallery. It was painted fuchsia, with the shutters done in black. The shutters on the upper floor windows were sensibly shut against the sun. The yard looked well kept, the lawn the deep emerald green of St. Augustine grass. There were no fountains, but there were white marble statues, a little worse for age and wear, at various places. An enormous live oak shaded the house on the lake side, its enormous branches curving across the front of the house like arthritic claws.

I got out of the car and saw that Lorita herself was sitting in the shade of the front gallery beneath a ceiling fan rotating so fast it looked like a propeller. I crossed the street and opened the gate, walking up the cracked and bent sidewalk.

She was sipping absinthe from a small cut crystal glass and smiled at me as I climbed the front steps, which groaned and gave a little under my weight. The wood, despite being freshly painted, was soft—so maybe there was something to the story that she just kept the house up for appearances.

I hadn't seen Lorita in years, so I wasn't prepared for the changes in her appearance. The last time I'd seen her there had been evidence of a face lift—the skin being a bit tighter than it should be on a woman her age, the telltale signs of the eyes being a bit more sunken than they should be, the tightness in the cheeks. But it was subtle enough to not be noticeable unless you were looking. But she'd had more work done since then—and it wasn't as good as the original.

I hoped my face didn't show my dismay as I kept my friendly smile frozen in place.

It was hard to tell how old Lorita was just by looking at her, because of all the work she'd had done. So, at least in that respect, it could be called a success. Her lips were swollen into a permanent pout, her forehead frozen into immovability, and it looked like she'd had a little too much filler put in her cheeks to plump them up once the skin had been pulled tighter. The skin between her nose and her upper lip looked smooth and sunken, and there was a very sharp line running from each corner of her mouth up to her ears. You could tell she'd been a beautiful woman when she was young from the bone structure, but any traces of her original beauty had long been banished by her surgeon. Her hair was cut short into an asymmetrical bob, longer and curling up around her chin, and gradually shorter on its way back. It was dyed an almost garish yellowish-orange but I could see white roots at her pinkish scalp. Her almond-shaped dark eyes were hidden behind enormous false eyelashes so long they looked like tarantula legs with clumps of thick mascara clinging to them. She was wearing a pink T-shirt over extravagant breasts I doubted were real, and a matching pleated tennis skirt, her feet in sandals showing off a nice pedicure. A gold anklet circled her left ankle, and her feet were propped up on a chair. "Scotty, isn't it? You're Cecile's son, aren't you?" Her voice was high-pitched, almost squeaky, grotesquely girlish, a breathless parody. "I haven't seen you since you were a little boy."

"How are you, Ms. Godwin? Do you mind if I have a seat?" I asked, sitting down on the opposite side of the table from her. The fan was twirling furiously overhead, and it was remarkably cool underneath it.

"Lorita, please, darling. Call me Lorita." She grimaced at me again, and I realized she was more than slightly drunk. "Would you like some absinthe?" She fluttered her spidery eyelashes at me. "I was feeling decadent today, so I thought I'd sit out here and watch the cars go by while sipping absinthe." She shrugged her bony shoulders. "My mother always said people talk about people who drink alone, but I've never cared what people say about me. Let them talk, I say." She winked. "The truth is always much worse, I find, than anything someone can make up, don't you think?" She placed another sugar cube underneath the ice water tank and let it start dripping. She leaned back in her chair and crossed her arms around her impressive implants. "Jerry called and warned me you'd be coming by at some point," she said, her eyes blinking rapidly as she waited for the sugar to completely dissolve into the absinthe cup. "Do you really think you can find my sister after all this time?" She waved a hand airily.

"You never heard from her after she left?" I asked.

She laughed a little, her eyes never leaving the dissolving sugar cube. "Melanie and I were never close. We never liked each other, even when we were children. Does that surprise you?" She rolled her eyes. "Melanie was a born narcissist, you see. Had to always be the center of attention, and made things up. She was a natural born liar. I was very tired of it by the time I left for college." She waved her hand, the big diamond on her ring finger catching sunlight and flashing at me. "She was exhausting. What Riley ever saw in her, I don't know, nor do I care to know."

"Were they happily married?"

She snorted in a most unladylike manner. "Who knows what goes on behind closed doors? Riley was as big a narcissist as she was, of course, and he always cheated on her, even when they were in high school. I suppose you've read that ridiculous wedding announcement our mother planted in the paper?" When I nodded she laughed loudly. "It was all bullshit, of course. Melanie just wanted to get married and out of our parents' house, and Riley needed a wife because his parents were threatening to disinherit him and throw him out. He drank too much, whored too much, and was constantly having to be bailed out of situations…and that didn't stop after he got married, either." She shook her head. "I always suspected Melanie took lovers to entertain herself, as well…the image they projected and who they really were? Nothing alike. Nothing at all alike." She glanced at me shrewdly. "And you're looking into Delilah's murder, too, Jerry said. After all this time? It seems to me like Jesse is pissing away his money, if you ask me."

I shrugged. "Maybe people who knew things back then will be more willing to talk nowadays. Jerry hinted there was a lot of stuff that never came out in the investigation."

"Everyone gossiped about it, of course." She turned off

the water drip and raised the glass to her lips, taking a slight sip. "You're certain you don't want some? It's quite spectacular, really." She set it down again.

"Have you talked to your nephew?"

"Jesse?" She looked surprised. "Lord, no, I've not talked to Jesse or Dylan since Riley took the boys and disappeared into the night." She rolled her eyes. "I tried to be close to them when they were boys...I wasn't able to have children of my own—"

"I'm sorry." My mind was whirling. *She doesn't know Dylan's dead.*

"No need. I dealt with that years ago." She waved her hand again. "After I married Arthur—Arthur Godwin, my first husband—I tried to get closer to Melanie...and tried again after our brother died. We were the last of the Gallaudet line, and of course, our parents didn't like that we hated each other. But Melanie wasn't interested in friends, or family—she simply wanted an audience." She laughed. "I always thought when she left Riley, she expected him to come running after her...that was the kind of dramatic gesture she was always pulling. He finally got tired of her and said enough...of course, he was already sleeping with Arlene."

"Why did she leave? Was it because of Arlene?"

"No, I don't think so. I honestly don't know." She frowned. "Mom and Dad were dead by then, and of course our brother Dave was long in the grave...I honestly thought Melanie didn't mind Riley's women because it took pressure off her. I don't think Riley ever told me why she walked out on him. I think he just said it was more of her usual bullshit and he was done with it once and for all. If she wanted to leave, it was fine with him. I think he even had the locks changed." She laughed again. "And then after a year, he filed for divorce on grounds of desertion. She never even bothered to show up for the hearing."

"Where did she go?"

"I didn't know, and I didn't care," she replied. "And then Arlene moved in, and once the divorce was final, he married her. Not that he changed, mind you—once he married Arlene he still was chasing women. He even tried to get me in the sack!" She rolled her eyes.

"And you never spoke to her again?" It was weird. Storm gets on my nerves, but I couldn't imagine ever getting to the point where I wouldn't speak to him for thirty years.

She shrugged again. "She knew where I was. I didn't know where she was. She never called me." She wiped her hands. "I was done."

"And you were friends with Arlene?"

"I felt sorry for Arlene—it wasn't easy being married to Riley, and you know how these Garden District bitches can be. Melanie was crazy, but she was one of us, one of them...Arlene wasn't, and she was the second wife who'd been the mistress first." She clicked her teeth, shaking her head slightly. "Things are a little looser here now, but back then..." She shook her head again. The breeze from the ceiling fan was lifting little stray hairs into the air. "Back then there were rules, you know, and marrying a pageant girl from one of the Gulf parishes broke all of them. Especially if she'd been your mistress while you were married to your former wife. You didn't marry your mistress and expect society to accept her." She clicked her tongue. "That just wasn't done. I felt bad for her, like I said, so I went out of my way to be nice to her. I thought that since I was Melanie's sister... if they saw I didn't care, maybe they'd be nicer." She shrugged her bony shoulders slightly as she placed another ice cube on the slotted spoon. "I thought wrong. You sure you don't some of this? It's the real deal, from the Dominican Republic, made with wormwood...not like that phony stuff they peddle in the States now."

"No, thanks. So Riley cheated on her after they were married?"

She nodded. "Oh, yes. There was never anything serious, mind you—at least not until the nanny." She narrowed her eyes to slits. "Arlene was sure he was sleeping with the nanny."

That I'd never heard before. "Robin Strickland?"

"Whatever her name was, I guess. That sounds right." She

turned the little spigot so the ice water started dripping onto the sugar cube again. "There was something about that girl that wasn't right, you know. I always wondered…ah, it doesn't matter now."

"What? What did you wonder?"

"Nothing, It doesn't matter." She gave me a sly look. "You have a look about you of your mother. We went to school with her, you know. Melanie was in your mother's class at McGehee. Your mother was one of her bridesmaids."

Whoa. I tried not to compare my mother's natural aged beauty with the medically altered alternative in front of me but couldn't help it. It took me a second or two to realize that my mother had known Melanie Metoyer—had been in the same class with her, had been in her wedding.

Why didn't she mention it when we met with Jesse at her place? If she knew Melanie—who grew up with Riley Metoyer—Mom and Dad had to have known them both as well.

And why hadn't that occurred to me?

New Orleans was a very small town. Mom was from a Garden District family. I should have assumed she'd known the Metoyers.

Some detective I was.

I made a mental note to stop by Mom and Dad's.

"Melanie and Riley's marriage was doomed from the start," Lorita was saying as she took another sip of absinthe. She closed her eyes in bliss. "Everyone could see it, except Melanie. She was so determined to marry Riley she didn't care what she had to put up with. She wanted that house more than she wanted Riley… did I tell you he cheated on her with one of her bridesmaids? At the reception?" She laughed. "It's like something out of a bad movie, isn't it? But yes, while Melanie was talking to guests in her wedding dress and drinking champagne, Riley was in the house fucking one of her best friends." She glanced at me slyly. "I know that because I walked in on them. I never told Melanie…"

"But she left him eventually."

"Disappeared without a trace, just like that." Lorita snapped her fingers. "Our parents were dead by then, and of course they left her everything. Not a penny for me, may they burn in hell for all eternity...she'd sold the family home. No one cared, really...it never sat right with me, though, that she'd run off and leave those boys. I know she was a monster, she always was, and they weren't anything more than props to her...they were better off without her, even though those boys worshipped her." She scowled. "She always claimed the boys were everything to her and that was why she stayed with him...the marriage was long over, except on paper...after Dylan was born she stopped sleeping with Riley, they had separate bedrooms...she told him she didn't care whatever he did as long as he left her alone." She shook her head slightly, as though in sympathy, but I could see the malice in her eyes as she raised her glass to her lips again. "She didn't care if he slept with me."

"You slept with..."

"No, of course I didn't." She glanced at me slyly. "I was just saying Melanie didn't care." She lifted her shoulders slightly. "It wasn't some fairy-tale marriage, you know. It was a convenience marriage...Melanie needed a husband, wanted to get out of our parents' home, Riley could give that to her and Riley wasn't exactly a one-woman kind of man..." Her eyes glittered. "Our parents always made it seem like everything was just rosy in that home...but you know as well as I do that things in the Garden District are never what they seem on the surface."

"So Melanie didn't care if Riley had other women."

"No, she didn't. A lot of people thought she left him because he took up with Arlene, but it was stupid, she didn't care. I told you, she didn't care. She didn't care who he slept with, all she cared about was an audience to play to...she was upset about something and he didn't care, so she ran off so he'd come after her and he didn't do it so she never came back. She's probably sitting somewhere, carrying a grudge, still mad at Riley." She made a face, or rather, tried to—the way her lips pursed out and the rest of her face barely moved seemed a little obscene. "Although sometimes I've wondered...sometimes I've wondered if Riley got a little too tired of her games and that's why we never heard from her." She laughed again.

"Are you saying…"

"Maybe the reason Riley and Arlene were so uncooperative with the police was because they had something to hide… everyone else thought they were trying to hide the fact they'd killed their own daughter. Me, I thought it a lot more likely they were worried the cops would find out what really happened to Melanie."

"Did you tell this to the police at the time?"

"Of course not. For all I know, Melanie is living it up with a hot younger man on some Caribbean beach somewhere and has been for the last thirty years. Maybe she did really leave Riley." She made a face again as she squinted at me.

"Did you talk to her before she left him?"

"I had lunch with her about a month before she left. Riley was already fucking Arlene by that point. Everyone knew about it, but Melanie didn't care." She glanced at the dripping water, like she wanted it to hurry up. "I think we had lunch at Antoine's? We shared a cab there and back. No, Galatoire's. I remember, because Roberto was our waiter. It hasn't been the same there since he retired. Anyway, I asked her about it—someone called and told me about it, I don't remember, I'd been through a couple of husbands…I think I was married to Gilbert then…anyway, I asked her about Arlene and she just laughed it off. She didn't care. So when I called a month or so later to cancel our monthly lunch at Galatoire's because I was having surgery, you could have knocked me down with a feather when the nanny—what was her name?—the one who took care of the boys? Arlene fired her— anyway, she told me that Melanie had left. I called around to see if anyone knew anything and the story was the same." She shrugged again, the bones of her clavicle protruding through the overtanned skin. "Then he divorced her for desertion and married Arlene."

"And he also cheated on Arlene?"

"He wasn't a one-woman kind of man, I said that already, and Arlene was like Melanie, she didn't care. She wanted to be in the Garden District and now she was. Of course everyone cut her dead, no one invited her to anything, and I felt sorry for her. It wasn't until after Delilah was born that I started to wonder about whether Melanie had actually left or not."

"I've taken up enough of your time," I said, standing up. "But can I ask you one more thing?" It just came to me.

"Sure."

"Did you know the voodoo priestess Arlene went to? Jerry called her Madame Laroux in the book." I wanted to be sure he'd told me the truth.

She laughed. "Lord, that. Arlene was desperate, yes. Her name is Lurleen Tourvil. She lives in the Treme. Jerry had that all wrong, you know. He made it sound like Lurleen cast spells and curses." She shook her head. "She never does that sort of thing. She's more of a fortune teller than anything else."

"Thank you." *Of course he lied to me.*

"Tell your mother to call me, I'd love to catch up." She didn't stand, and her words were starting to slur a bit from the absinthe.

"I'll do that." I beat a hasty retreat back to my car and drove off as soon as I could.

It was interesting information, of course, but it didn't really give me any insight into Delilah's murder. So, Arlene and Riley may have killed Melanie to get rid of her. It was just speculation, idle gossip possibly invented by a bored woman who drank too much, one who hated her sister, even after all this time. And it certainly didn't provide any insight into Arlene's—

I braked at the corner at St. Charles.

If Arlene and Riley had killed Melanie...and Jesse knew about it...

But why would Jesse wait all this time to get even with Arlene? And there was no reason to believe Riley hadn't died of natural causes—but then, I only had Jesse's word for that.

I tapped on the steering wheel as I sat there. There wasn't

any traffic on St. Charles, but I didn't want to turn and keep driving yet.

There was something there.

I pulled out my phone.

I was out…and Treme was kind of on my way home.

Why not check out the voodoo queen before heading over to Mom and Dad's?

I did a quick search on my phone. Lurleen Tourvil's address was on Barracks Street, in the Treme.

I called Frank and once again got his voice mail.

I shook my head and turned onto St. Charles.

CHAPTER ELEVEN
THE LOVERS
Harmony of the inner and outer life

Sometimes it seems like the entire city of New Orleans is under construction.

The city has always been notorious for its potholes. There are no level sidewalks in Orleans Parish, and so it only stands to reason that the streets are just as bad. The water table isn't far underground, so the ground is constantly shifting. The city also isn't very good about responding to potholes. Some are enormous, and once they start, they grow like they're taking steroids. When the city begrudgingly puts an orange cone out to warn drivers, people who live in the area tend to start decorating the cones—especially at Christmas.

The bottom line is most of our streets need repair at all times. Since Katrina, a lot of buildings have come down, condos have gone up over what used to be parking lots, and still other buildings have been gutted and rebuilt. The city has also started making repairs to streets. Almost every major street running away from the river in Uptown—Napoleon, Louisiana, and Jefferson—has been under construction of one kind or another for what seems like years. The St. Charles streetcar line has also been impacted by all of this work.

It makes navigating the city a challenge.

Rampart Street is the border street that separates the French Quarter from Treme. In its infinite wisdom, the city has decided to put the Rampart streetcar line back in a mere sixty years after they tore it up back in the 1950s. The end result of this is that

Rampart Street has been under some sort of construction for several years now. Quarter traffic is a challenge under the best of circumstances, since every street in the Quarter itself is a narrow one-way lane. Rampart is a two-way street with two lanes on each side of a neutral ground, and is the best way for people driving across town to avoid the Quarter. With it being torn up and hard to navigate, those people now drive through the Quarter.

You can imagine how horrendous this made the traffic situation in the Quarter.

And of course, I was already across Canal Street and into the one-lane war zone nightmare of Rampart before I remembered I probably wouldn't be able to turn into the Treme anywhere close to where I'd need to—that was how it always worked. One day you'd be able to turn at Dumaine, the next day Dumaine would be blocked off. I don't know how people who had to drive it every day did it without becoming homicidal. The corner at Esplanade, where the signal was, had become a morass of stupidity and frustration. I gambled and hoped that I'd be able to turn at Barracks. If I wasn't able to, I'd have to loop back around to Esplanade through the Marigny and try to figure it out.

Fortunately, it was my lucky day. Barracks was open. I said a quick prayer of thanks to the Goddess and turned left, shooting across the bumpy, torn-up road as quickly as I could.

The Faubourg Treme used to be known in the old days as "back of town" because it was literally the back of town. The French Quarter was the original city, and Treme was the original suburb. The neighborhood was originally settled by freed slaves and free people of color, and it became more of a mixed neighborhood over the years. It was a thriving and busy community for years—the birthplace of jazz, Storyville was there, and back in the day its two border streets—Rampart and Claiborne—were the black business districts of the segregated post–Civil War city. The destruction of Claiborne as a business area with the building of I-10 along it also contributed to the economic collapse of the Treme. In the years before Katrina, it had declined into a high-crime neighborhood and was kind of sketchy—you always told tourists never to walk on the lake side of Rampart Street.

In the years since the levee failure, though, like so many other neighborhoods it was reborn and gentrified. While I didn't like the way the poor were being pushed out of Treme by rising property values, at the same time it was kind of nice seeing the gorgeous old neighborhood coming back to life again.

My main concern was that the change in the city's demographic makeup might somehow alter the essence of what made New Orleans special.

Madame Tourvil's address put her on Barracks Street between Treme and Marais Streets. The house itself was a cute double shotgun that looked like it had been converted into one dwelling. It looked like it had been painted recently, Caribbean coral with sky blue trim. A young live oak was growing between the curb and the sidewalk, and the two doors on opposite sides of the front both had brick stairs leading up to them. Three rolling garbage cans stood between the two sets of stairs—two of them the dark green for garbage, the other the black signifying recycling. The shutters on the big front windows were closed. I parked across the street and sat there, the engine running. It looked perfectly innocuous.

What were you expecting, a voodoo altar on the front steps? Skulls hanging from the overhang? Live chickens in the side yard? Get over yourself.

I locked the car and walked across the street.

There was a black iron gate on both sides of the house, guarding a paved sidewalk that probably led to the backyard. The next yard on the right was paved over and guarded by a tall iron fence. A rolling electric gate was at the far side; behind the fence I could see the motor equipment that ran the gate. The house on the other side of the paved lot was a single shotgun painted lime green and looked this side of derelict. On the left side of Madame Tourvil's house was a cedar wood fence on the other side of her gate. The yellow house on the corner lot was a style I didn't recognize; the second story seemed to be A-shaped with the roof meeting in a point.

When I reached the top step, the front door opened, and I got a blast of icy cold air in my face that felt amazing. A young woman holding a baby smiled tentatively at me. I moved out of her way so she could use the stairs. With her free hand she wiped tears away from her eyes and said "thank you" in a blubbery voice to the woman standing behind her in the doorway. As she went down the steps the woman in the doorway said, "You let me know how it goes, hear?"

The woman with the baby nodded and walked down the sidewalk in the direction of the Quarter.

I smiled and said, "Madame Tourvil?"

She was a beautiful woman of indeterminate age, wearing a loose-fitting sundress with a navy blue and bright orange pattern. Her feet were bare, and she was of about middle height. She was starting to spread out a little, her hips thick and her heavy breasts unsupported, but her figure had probably been spectacular when she was younger. Long braids ending in blue and orange beads hung at both sides of her face. She folded her arms over her ample bosom and leaned against the door frame, a crooked smile on her face. "I've been expecting you." One of her front teeth was made of gold.

"You have?" I tilted my head to one side. "How did you know I was coming? I didn't tell anyone."

I knew what her answer was going to be.

She laughed, deep and hearty. "Yes, man. I just *know* things." She cocked her head to one side and scrutinized my face. Her smile faded as she tilted her head back to the other side, her eyes never leaving my face. Her eyes narrowed as she investigated my face. "You just know things, too, don't you? You'd better come inside. You're letting all my cold air out, and I don't want to pay Entergy any more than I have to." She stood aside so I could enter. "Sit down and I will get you some iced tea." She walked through the room and vanished through a doorway on the other side.

I entered the dimly lit front room of the shotgun. The windows were all shuttered, and the only light was from candles, and they were everywhere. The walls were painted what appeared to be a somber brick-red. A ceiling fan spun lazily overhead, making the candles flicker. There was a low table in front of an overstuffed red leather sofa. I sat down and looked around the dim room. There was an altar on the other side of the room from me, decorated with feathers and masks and some bones. A red velvet cloth covered the altar, and stained clay jars and bowls scattered between the flickering white votive candles. It looked like the altar had been built around what used to be a fireplace. There was a beautiful yet somewhat crudely done painting of Our Lady of Charity of El Cobre resting on top of what used to be the mantelpiece, surrounded by candles inside glass jars with the faces of saints on them. I knew that Our Lady of Charity of El Cobre represented a voodoo goddess, but I didn't know which one. In the slave days, the Africans hadn't been allowed to follow their old faith and were forced to convert to Catholicism. They kept their old faith, but fooled the whites and their priests by associating their gods and goddesses with certain saints.

I was raised to be a pagan, despite being sent to Catholic schools. Mom and Dad's belief system wasn't that organized, and it wasn't like we went to worship ceremonies or anything. There were just certain things they believed that made a lot more sense to me than what the priests and nuns were trying to force down my throat: that the Great Power in the universe was feminine; that putting out positive energy brought positive energy back; sending out negativity brought it back threefold. You focused and meditated and communed with nature, with the universe, and tried to be the best person you could. And when I started seeing things, being able to read the cards and actually have visions, the power I always saw was feminine: the Goddess. I didn't know a lot about Santeria other than it was more commonly called voodoo—and voodoo was actually nothing like people believed. It didn't involve devil worship, for one, and there wasn't human sacrifice, either. Sometimes the voodoo priests and priestesses did sacrifice animals to their gods, but that was becoming rarer and rarer. They also believed in the power of the light and white magic—and black magic was taboo.

There was a lot more to it than what the shops in the Quarter sold to gullible tourists.

Just from looking around her front room, it looked like Madame Tourvil was a voodoo priestess, as Jerry had said in his book.

She came back into the room and handed me a sweating glass of sweet tea with a wedge of lemon floating across the top. I took a drink. It was delicious. She sat down in a chair across from me and started rocking slowly. She smiled at me again, her gold tooth flashing in the candlelight. She closed her eyes. "You are beloved of Oshun," she finally said when the silence was getting unnerving. "I can see it around your face, the glow that comes from the love of the goddess. But the glow is not as bright as it should be." She cocked her head again to one side and opened her eyes. "You were blessed by her, but you turned your back on her, no? So she no longer speaks to you the way she used to? You can no longer see the way you used to. Why did you turn your back on Oshun? She does not give her love to just anyone. She marked you from birth and blessed you."

I swallowed and set the glass down on a coaster on the wooden table. "I—I don't know what you mean."

"You can't lie to me, child." She reached over and took down one of the big candles, striking a long match and lighting the candle with it. "I am also beloved of Oshun, and she has blessed me, so I can see it in the others she also loves." She set the candle down on the table in front of me. "You may not know her as Oshun; she takes many forms when she comes to those she has marked as special to her. But for me, I have always known her as Oshun. I was raised in the faith by my mother as she was raised by her mother, and her mother before her, in a line going back to when my ancestors came here first as free people of color from Saint-Domingue, after the revolution." She smiled, lowering her eyelids down about halfway. "You don't know my religion, but I don't expect you to—we have been driven underground for so many centuries we do not know what it is like to be in the light anymore." Her voice was sad.

"No," I replied carefully, "but I respect all faiths, even those I don't know or understand. But that isn't why I am here."

"You turned away from her," she continued, ignoring what I said. "But she cries for you, you know. She feels great sorrow. Why did you turn your back on her? She cries for you, weeps. But she is a proud goddess, yes."

The hair on my arms was standing up.

"Like all her sister goddesses, she is proud," she went on, her eyes closed. "You need to ask her forgiveness, and she will embrace you again. Or are you, like she, too proud?"

"No, I am not too proud." I bit my lower lip. "Thank you," I said softly. "I may do that when I get home." As soon as I said the words, I felt something—an ecstatic, euphoric rush in my soul, as though it were screaming *YES! At last!*

And somehow, I felt better.

I didn't understand it, but I didn't need to.

"Have you missed your gift?" she asked, her voice still soft and silken, like the worn velvet cloth on the altar. She glanced at the painting on the altar. "I sometimes wonder what my life would be like, if I hadn't had it, or if I were to lose it. It isn't easy being beloved of the Goddess. But you already know that, don't you? That is why you turned your back to her, isn't it? She disappointed you? You became angry with her? Ah, yes, that is why she weeps so bitterly." She rubbed her arms as if she'd suddenly gotten cold. She turned her eyes back to me. "But you aren't here about Oshun, are you?"

I shook my head. "No, I talked to Jerry this morning—"

"Jerry Channing." Her voice got cold. "He sent you?"

"No, he didn't," I replied. "Lorita Godwin told me your real name and how to find you."

"My family, we've owned this house for generations." She waved a hand around the place. "And always, the oldest daughter was blessed by Oshun, and she inherits the house so that Oshun's priestess always has a roof over her head. We have been here since before the British tried to take the city. One of my ancestors told General Jackson he would beat the British, you know. Jerry—Jerry made me sound like a witch." She spat the words out. "My religion is just as valid as those of the white people. Jerry wrote about me like I had a bone in my nose and a bone necklace around my neck and danced topless around a cauldron when the moon is full and drank the blood of babies I sacrificed in her name. That isn't my religion. That isn't what I was about. He said those things to make Arlene sound crazy, desperate, and to sell copies of his book. I told him he couldn't name me, he couldn't let anyone know where I lived, or he would regret it." She raised her chin defiantly. "I would have risked the Rule of Three to curse him if he had. He hasn't come around me in years, and if he is smart he will never speak of me again."

"I didn't think so, and his book isn't why I'm here." I cleared my throat and reached for the glass of iced tea again. "Jesse Metoyer hired me."

"Delilah Metoyer," she said softly, settling back into her chair, her legs crossed at the ankles. She closed her eyes. "You want to find who killed her, after all this time. And you want to find Melanie, his mother." She shook her head. "I couldn't see who killed her then and I can't see him now. Maybe Oshun will show him to you."

"Is that why Arlene"—my voice caught on her name— "came to you?"

"Arlene." She smiled, her yellowing teeth bared at me. "Arlene Metoyer was an unhappy woman, and a foolish one, too. She didn't first come to me for Delilah's killer, you know. She came to me for a love potion, when she was just Arlene

Campbell." She laughed. "She wanted to make a man fall in love with her, a married man. So I made her a potion, even though I warned her that these things always come with a price—if you mess with the natural order of things, if you ask for the gods to intervene—there is always a price."

The hairs on the back of my neck stood up. "And that price?"

"She was his mistress." She shrugged. "So Oshun gave him to her—but she didn't change his heart and soul. As he cheated on the first wife, so he cheated on the second wife. I told her then that having a child wouldn't tie him to her any more than his first wife's children tied him to her. But she wouldn't listen, she need a potion so she could bear him a child…and so I made her another potion. And the price she paid for that was the child was murdered—the universe must always be in balance." She frowned. "There was a shadow on her, though, when she wanted that child. Most women who come to me to ask Oshun's help to have a child—they want that baby so bad I can feel it vibrating off them. Arlene wanted that baby, but not to have the baby. She had another reason. I told her that she should only want a baby because she wanted to be a mother. Women who have babies for other reasons—when a baby is born with that kind of darkness over them, it leads to tragedy…and I was right. The Goddess will always take her price…the universe must remain in balance. Arlene found out that out the hard way." She shrugged her shoulders. "But she did love that child. She brought her here once, for a prayer and a blessing, when she was getting into one of her pageants, a blessing, invoke Oshun's aid." She shook her head. "Arlene never understood that asking for blessings for selfish reasons…is not the best thing to do. Purity is important, to be pure of heart." She smiled. "I let her think she got what she came here for. But I wouldn't do that to her or her child. I liked her. And when—" She broke off.

Purity is important. The Goddess used to say that to me all the time when I'd have my visions, or when I was reading the cards. Hearing it from Madame Tourvil…

Maybe I should try when I get home. What harm will it do? All she can do is ignore me, and it's not like she's spoken to me in years anyway.

"Arlene had a lot of secrets," she went on. "Secrets she didn't want the police to find out about."

"Someone told me her husband—Riley Metoyer—was a womanizer," I said carefully.

She barked out a loud laugh and kept laughing, rocking back and forth in her chair, until the tears came to her eyes. I waited for her to get hold of herself again, which she eventually did. She wiped at her eyes. "That man couldn't keep his dick in his pants," she finally said, still chuckling a little as she spoke. "I told Arlene—a man who cheats will never stop cheating, and she was making her bed. Oh yes, she came here many times, crying, because of his other women." Her eyes glittered. "They kept all of that out of the news, didn't they? All those women kept their mouths shut. Today they would be all over the news, coming out of the woodwork…wanting a paycheck for spilling the dirt about that man. Back then, not so much."

That is *strange*, I thought. Even though the world had changed a lot in the twenty-five years since Delilah's murder, it was big news back then. It happened right around the same time as the O. J. trial, and everyone under the sun came out of the woodwork for that one. *Maybe there was a reason why Riley's women wanted that secret kept?*

"Do you know who any of them were?"

She shook her head. "Arlene never told me names. But there was one…the last one. Arlene was really worried about her. Oshun didn't see fit to open my eyes, to let me see into Arlene's mind to find out who those women were. But I sensed…I sensed with the last one that it really hurt Arlene. It was someone she felt close to." She nodded. "You're wondering how I know…a woman knows, Scott Bradley. A woman knows. Riley's last woman had her worried, and she was hurt. She came here for Oshun's help the week before that child died…she was worried about this other woman…" She shook her head again. "I don't know the woman's name…but there was something…I sensed something about her. I warned Arlene, of course, but she didn't listen to me. She was a danger to Arlene, a danger to all of them. She was inside their family circle. She had access."

"You think this other woman might have—might have harmed Delilah?"

"I don't know that. But she cast a shadow over that family. Arlene came to me later, afterward, wanted my help to find out what happened to her child." She looked me dead in the eye. "That woman was grieving, and that woman did not hurt her own child, no matter what mean-spirited people said about her. Her grief was real, and it was not about what she did. Her grief was about not saving her child, not protecting her. That woman suffered until she died."

I bit my lower lip.

She laughed. "Oh, I know she died last night. I was watching my television and I felt it…I felt something went wrong, and I prayed and Oshun showed me that Arlene had died. I hadn't seen her in years, and I couldn't see who hurt her, who killed her…but I knew she was dead." She crossed herself. "I hope she is finally at peace now."

"I hope so, too."

She tilted her head and flashed her crooked smile. "You knew her—not well, but you encountered her recently?" She narrowed her eyes. "A cat? You bought a cat from her."

If it wasn't for my own experience with the gift, I would have been seriously freaked out; regardless, the hair on the back of my neck stood right back up again.

"What Jerry wrote in his book about me, about me and Arlene, it was wrong, it was all made up," she said. "Everything about it was wrong. You have to know that."

"I do." I stood up. "Thank you for your time."

"Ask the Goddess for forgiveness," she called after me as I went down her front steps. "That woman—the woman who cast a shadow over Arlene and her family. I sense her again, you know? Ask the Goddess for forgiveness and maybe Oshun will show her to you, will open your inner eye so that you can see, so you can help Arlene to rest."

I paused on the bottom step. "Arlene isn't at rest?"

"Arlene knows the truth now," she said, closing her eyes and swaying a bit, "but she will never be at peace until someone pays for what they did to her child."

"You never met Melanie Metoyer?"

She smiled, opening her eyes. "No. I cast a spell to protect her from the effects of the love potion I made for Arlene. But something—something happened to her as well. I cannot see it. Oshun won't let me see it." Her face got sad. "You ask for her forgiveness. She wants to forgive you, you know. She wants to stop weeping for you." She closed the door softly, and I heard the deadbolt turn.

I crossed the street and got back into my car. As I started the engine, I thought, *it wouldn't hurt to try, would it?* I drove up to Marais and turned right and headed for Esplanade.

I had missed it, if I was going to be honest. I missed the feeling of the well-worn tarot deck in my hands, the sense of knowledge and power that reverberated from the cards into my hands as I prayed and asked the Goddess for enlightenment before spreading the cards out onto the table. I missed being able to look at the worn pictures on the faces of the cards and know their meanings instantly, or to get a slightly vague answer that I had to interpret.

I didn't miss the visions, which involved—I've been told—my eyes rolling back into my head and collapsing as my soul left my body to commune on another plane with the Goddess. I always came back drained, tired and…

I slammed on my brakes to avoid someone on a bicycle who suddenly and without warning swerved in front of me.

I muttered a curse under my breath and headed for Esplanade, where I turned right. The intersection at Rampart and Esplanade was a nightmare, as always. Traffic always backs up at least a block because the construction there has resulted in about a two-inch drop—which of course means everyone has to slow down to a complete crawl to go through the intersection, including pickup trucks and SUVs. I took a deep breath and tried to relax. There was no sense in getting annoyed or letting my blood pressure go up. It wouldn't change anything, nor would it make anyone drive faster. I resigned myself to having to wait a minimum of two light changes, and relaxed.

No sooner had I gone to my safe mental space than my phone started ringing. I touched the button on my steering wheel to Bluetooth the phone through the stereo speakers, which was probably the coolest thing ever. "Hello?"

"Scotty? This is Paige Tourneur."

"Paige! Nice to hear from you." Even as I said the words I wondered how she'd gotten my cell phone number.

"I hope you don't mind, but Serena gave me your number." Ah, mystery solved. "Is it true? Are you really working for Jesse Metoyer?"

I sighed. There wasn't any point in denying it, so I didn't. Obviously, she'd talked to Serena.

"Did he really hire you to find Arlene?" I could hear her fingers tapping on a keyboard. "And now she's dead?"

"Ye-es," I said cautiously.

"Scotty, I hate to put you into this position"—people always say that and then they do it anyway—"but will you promise me an exclusive interview? I can promise you *Crescent City* will be the most fair interview you get!"

"Why would you want to interview me?"

There was a pause. "Scotty, do you have any idea of what's going on?" Her voice sounded puzzled. "If you thought the Delilah Metoyer case was news back then, you have no idea what Arlene's murder is going to be like. I've been fielding calls from twenty-four-hour news networks and journalists all over the country as soon as the news about Arlene broke…and you're not going to be able to stay out of it. That's why I thought I'd try to reach you. If you say you've given me an exclusive, that's one way to keep the vultures off." Her voice was almost a purr as I finally made it through the intersection at Esplanade and

Rampart. "You're going to want to unplug your landline, if you have one. And once your cell number gets out…"

I felt my stomach starting to clench. "But I don't have any information anyone would want."

I reached the corner at Decatur and turned right. There was a crowd in front of our gate.

"Thanks, Paige, let me call you back." I disconnected the call.

As I drove past them, I noticed the news vans parked all down the street. They had video cameras, others were holding cameras, and there were several I recognized from local news reports.

Fuck fuck fuck, I thought as I turned right at the corner to head for our parking lot. They hadn't looked at me as I drove past, so they didn't know it was me in the SUV.

I had no idea of the nightmare that was just beginning.

CHAPTER TWELVE
THE TOWER, REVERSED
False accusations, oppression

I hit the button on the remote that opened the big door that led to our parking lot as I drove around the corner onto Barracks Street. My mind was racing and my heart was beating so fast I could hear it thudding in my ears. *How am I going to get through that crowd?* I wondered as I waited for a woman walking a chocolate Lab to cross the street. It didn't make any sense, but I felt somehow *violated. How do celebrities handle it, having photographers outside their door all the time, trying to take pictures, shouting insulting and rude questions at them…I guess this is what the Metoyers had to deal with for years after Delilah was killed.*

How…awful. I'd always felt sorry for them, having to deal with that awful media circus, but I'd never realized how bad it must have been. *Think what's out in front of the gate right now, times ten, times every day for at least two years.*

I felt like throwing up, to be honest. It was a wonder they hadn't all gone crazy.

Thank the Goddess Millie and Velma are still at the beach—they'd be furious, I thought as I made the right turn into the driveway across the sidewalk to our parking lot. The garage door always took a long time to open, but now it seemed like it was going slower than usual. *Of course, Velma's not above turning a hose on them to clear the sidewalk.* The image of my landlady opening the gate and spraying the reporters with water made me grin. *Maybe it's not a good thing they're out of town.*

Alas, the sidewalk was a public space, so there wasn't

anything we could do about getting them to leave unless they did so voluntarily.

I drummed my hands on the steering wheel as the garage door achingly, slowly continued to rise at its leisurely pace, occasionally glancing out the passenger window to make sure no reporters were coming at me from around the corner.

You're being ridiculous, I reminded myself. *They don't even know who you are.*

And just why were they out in front of our place anyway? We weren't a piece of their story, had nothing to tell them about Arlene. We were three nobodies, three private eyes Jesse had hired to do a job they couldn't possibly know anything about. We weren't their story—at most, we were a footnote to Arlene's murder. We certainly weren't important enough to warrant the mob out in front of our gate.

And how did they know about us in the first place? There hadn't been any news crews in front of Serena's place. So someone had tipped them off, told them we somehow had some information, something that their producers would think their audience would be interested in.

But who would have done such a thing?

It didn't make sense—but at the same time, I didn't want to go ask them.

It seemed to be taking the damned garage door an eternity to open. I was still glancing over to the right to see if they were coming around the corner. I repeated to myself that they didn't know our SUV, they hadn't known it was me when I drove past them...

And I couldn't think of a way to get them away from the gate, or off the sidewalk.

But...they could be avoided.

There was another way into our property that I never used—hell, I even forgot it existed most of the time. The back of our courtyard had a seven-foot-high brick wall enclosing it, with broken bottles embedded into the cement on top so even if someone could somehow manage to get into the parking lot and scale it, there was no way over the top without slicing their hands and arms open.

But there was also a door there that opened into the parking lot.

The reason I never used it was because it opened into what Millie and Velma referred to as the "tool shed." The shed was where Millie and Velma kept all their yard work tools and also contained the pump and motor that worked the fountain in our courtyard. There were no windows, which made it pitch black inside, but there was a single light bulb hanging from the ceiling with a pull string.

The trick was finding the pull string in the darkness without killing yourself in the process.

This was a bit more risk than I was usually willing to take.

Plus, there were spiders in there.

I am *not* a fan of spiders.

Finally, the garage door had opened far enough for me to drive inside. I hit the remote button to close it—it always closed faster than it opened. I pulled into one of our assigned spots and turned off the car. I checked my key ring to see if I had the key to the shed door, praying that it was there. It was, thank the Goddess. It was brass and looked brand new—like it had never been used. Come to think of it, I couldn't remember using it, even though it was a major shortcut from the parking lot.

Sometimes, when the back of the SUV was loaded down with grocery bags, I'd think about cutting through the tool shed rather than using what Frank called our "old lady cart." Then I'd remember the spiderwebs, the darkness, the scattered piles of discarded or rarely used things piled haphazardly inside and dismiss the thought with extreme prejudice. Millie and Velma weren't very organized when it came to their tools and gardening implements—it was always a mess in there, which was odd. Their apartment was always perfect. They were firm believers in the adage *everything has its place and everything in its place.*

Except, of course, for the shed. That rule clearly did not apply to the shed.

I'd never actually been inside the shed more than once or twice, now that I thought about it—I wasn't even sure the key would work.

I got out of the car as the big garage door finished closing. Our lot wasn't covered and was nothing more than a graveled vacant lot whose owner rented it out to locals for off-street parking. The big eight-foot-high brick wall along the sidewalk had razor wire stretched across the top to discourage break-ins, and there was a regular locking door out to the sidewalk right next to the electric door. I pressed the button on my key fob to lock the car and walked over to the shed door. I slipped the key into the lock. It didn't want to turn at first, and I was just starting to worry about the key breaking when it finally did turn, making a horrible screeching sound. *It needs some WD-40*, I thought as I removed my key and reached for the door handle. The door hinges also squealed as I pulled it open, some daylight filtering into the musty-smelling space. I was sad to see that my memory hadn't been exaggerating about the mess inside the shed, either. I couldn't see any open space on the floor other than right inside the other door from the courtyard, and barely enough for the door from the parking lot to open. Everywhere I looked was junk, piled in some places higher than my head, in others waist high. Huge bags of mulch and manure, a lawn mower, rakes and shovels tossed around like the place had been searched, boxes piled on top of other boxes, the bottom ones starting to sag so the entire pile was leaning dangerously to one side. Graceful cobwebs festooned the pump and engine for the fountain in a far corner, the metal works looking rusty and abandoned even as they hummed and worked. I found the string and pulled it, filling the space with weak yellow light. Some of the tools had cobwebs artfully draped over them, and there was so much dust—I started sneezing, my eyes watering and my nose itching, but it finally passed. And a sneezing fit was much better than having to run the gauntlet of vultures out front. I closed and locked the door behind me, stepped over the lawn mower, and opened the door to the courtyard, which was almost like entering another world.

I reached back to pull the light cord and stepped into the quiet calm of the courtyard. The fountain was splashing and it was so peaceful. I sat down in one of the chairs around the little table and took a deep breath to relax for a moment before heading upstairs.

Cleaning out the shed, I thought, would be a great job for Taylor, and a pleasant surprise for Millie and Velma.

I smiled. Sometimes having a teenager around can come in handy. And once it was cleaned and organized, we could start using it as a shortcut.

I was just getting up to head upstairs when I heard a loud commotion out front. Wondering what was going on, I stepped over to the dark passageway leading to the front gate just in time to hear Frank loudly snapping at people, "Let me pass! I just am trying to get home! Get out of my way! *Let me through, damn it!*"

I sprinted down the passageway and peered through the screen. What I call the "gate" is really a big reinforced steel door with a small screen at about eye level. It actually used to be a wrought iron gate, until someone broke in once to try to kill me (it's a long story). After that, Millie had the big door installed, and the top of the frame was, of course, decorated with razor wire. What I saw through the screen chilled me. Frank was in the middle of the mob of reporters, completely surrounded. They were shoving microphones in his face, while other voices shouted questions at him as he tried to get through the crowd without actually having to shove or hit anyone. His face was red with anger and frustration, and the scar on his cheek was bright purple. He looked like he was going to lose his temper in a matter of seconds.

That would not be good. He was, after all, a trained professional wrestler.

I waited until he was close and then flung the door open, shouting, "Frank!"

Frank shoved a couple of reporters out of his way and practically dove past me into the passageway. The mob turned and started yelling questions at me. I held up my hand for silence, and when the hubbub finally died down, said, "I'm sorry to disappoint you all, but you're wasting your time. We've already agreed to an exclusive with *Crescent City* magazine."

There was a disappointed murmur, but then someone from the back yelled, "Is it true you hunted the victim down for the murderer?"

Okay, if *that* was the story they were chasing...no wonder they were camped out on our sidewalk.

Fuck, fuck, fuckety fuck.

For an answer, I slammed the door as they all started shouting again. "Come on," I said, taking some of the bags from Frank. "Once they can't see us, they'll shut up." We hurried down the passageway. Sure enough, as soon as we went around the corner and out of their sight, the noise died down.

"What the holy hell is going on?" Frank asked. He was carrying plastic bags from the Rouses on Royal Street. "I mean, I just ran to the store to get some things, and when I came back there's a mob of reporters in front of the house. And what the hell did that guy mean with that last question? And why are we giving an exclusive to *Crescent City* magazine?"

I paused when we reached the back staircase. I stopped at the stairs and took a deep breath. "Frank, Arlene Metoyer's body was found this morning, in the carriage house at Serena's. And Jesse's cell phone just happened to be found at the crime scene."

"Holy shit." Frank started climbing the stairs beside me. "And you know this how? Or do I want to know?"

"I tried calling Jesse again when I left Jerry's—he was very helpful, and a lot nicer than I thought he would be, by the way—and Blaine Tujague answered. He was at the crime scene, wanted to know why I was calling a phone found at a crime scene. That's when I found out about Arlene." I filled him in on everything I'd done that morning, ending with Paige's phone call. "And now, apparently, someone's told the press that Jesse hired us to find Arlene so he could kill her."

By the time I was finished talking, we were in the kitchen

of our apartment. We set the bags down on the counter, and Frank started putting the groceries away. He whistled. "That doesn't look good for Jesse, does it? He needs a lawyer, pronto." A muscle in his jaw jumped, which always happens when he's thinking. "He never once answered any of your calls, did he?"

"I haven't spoken to him—" I leaned against the counter as he handed me a bottle of Pellegrino. "I haven't actually spoken to him since the day he hired us, actually." I opened the bottle and took a big swig. Colin had gotten me addicted to Pellegrino after his last job—he came back drinking it, and now I loved it. "All I ever got was his voice mail. I left him messages, but he never called me back." I tapped the bottle on the side of the counter. "I hope he's all right. Maybe we should be worried about him?"

"We'll cross that bridge when we come to it." Frank put the last of the groceries into a cabinet and stuffed the plastic bags inside another one. "Did you tell Blaine and Venus where they could find him?"

"I told them the address where he's staying, yes." I shook my head. "I didn't feel comfortable doing it, but I didn't really think I had a choice."

"No, you did the right thing," Frank said. "Anything else would be withholding evidence, or accessory after the fact, interfering with a police investigation, you name it." He leaned over and kissed me on the mouth. "We're all going to need shed keys, you know."

I nodded. "I'll send Taylor to Mary's Ace to get copies made."

"Where is Taylor? And Colin, for that matter?"

I glanced at the clock on the stove. "Taylor should be on duty at the Devil's Weed…and Colin—I don't know where he is. I haven't talked to him since this morning, have you?" I frowned. When they'd sent me out to interview Jerry that morning, Frank had said he was going to go do some research at the library, and Colin…Colin hadn't really said anything about what he was going to do. "Did you and Colin think of something for him to do?"

"He was going to go interview Rocky Champagne's son—I hate to think of either him or Taylor running into that crowd of vultures downstairs." Frank sighed. "Although I think he was going to the gym on his way back. Let me text him, give him a heads up, and I'll do the same for Taylor."

I nodded and walked into the living room, thinking about what Madame Tourvil had said. I could feel the pull of the cigar box holding my cards beneath the couch. I was just reaching for them when I heard the apartment door open. "Colin?" I walked back to glance down the hallway.

Frank poked his head out of the kitchen at the same time. Colin wasn't alone. "How on earth did you two get past the reporters?"

Colin made a face. "Reporters?"

Jesse groaned. "God, not reporters." He looked terrible as he walked past me and sat down in one of the easy chairs. He was wearing a pair of dirty-looking khaki shorts and a *I got Bourbon-faced on Shit Street* T-shirt. It, too, was dirty—there were a couple of what appeared to be grease stains on his chest and what looked like a ketchup spot on his stomach. He hadn't shaved, his hair looked greasy, and he reeked of stale sweat and sour alcohol. His eyes were bloodshot. "Anything but fucking reporters."

"No offense, but you look terrible. Do you need anything? Water?"

"Water would be great." He buried his face in his hands.

"I picked Jesse up on my way back here." Colin plopped down on the couch. "Rocky Champagne's son was a dead end, by the way. They got rid of all of Rocky's things after he died, other than some mementoes, and the son—Billy—wasn't too keen on talking about the case that 'ruined Dad's life.'" He made air quotes around the last three words. "All he would say was after he was taken off the case, Rocky was a broken man. He couldn't give me anything else, other than he always believed that Arlene killed Delilah." He made a face. "So Jesse and I came back here. We were upstairs, talking, when I heard you both come in. What is this about reporters?"

"Arlene's dead, Jesse." I sat down in the other easy chair as Frank came in and handed him a bottle of Pellegrino. "She was murdered last night, hit on the back of the head with a blunt instrument. In the carriage house at Serena's. The same place Delilah's body was found." I leaned back in my chair and folded my arms. "And your cell phone just happened to be there. Can you explain that? Because it looks pretty bad for you right now. You're going to want to get a lawyer, pronto."

"That's where I lost my phone?" He visibly sagged. "Great, that's just great."

"What were you doing there?" Frank pulled up one of the dining room chairs and straddled it backward. "You were trespassing, at the very least."

He took a deep breath. "I didn't tell you guys everything the other day."

Frank, Colin, and I exchanged a glance. I refrained from saying *no shit*. Instead, I said, "Go on."

He swallowed. "Yesterday I wanted to look up Robin Strickland."

"Delilah's nanny?" Colin asked. "Why?"

He looked down at his hands. "We were involved back then."

In the silence that followed, I blurted, "Wasn't she in her twenties?"

He raised his chin defiantly. "So what if she was?"

"It's a crime, for one thing," Frank replied. "You were, what, fifteen?"

"We loved each other." He insisted. "And then after Delilah was—was killed, there wasn't any real reason for her to keep living in the house. So Dad fired her, gave her a couple of months' severance pay, and she was gone. I wanted to keep seeing her, but we were under total lockdown. It just wasn't possible. And this was before cell phones and emails, so…it was just kind of over then." He got a dreamy look on his face. "I've never forgotten her. And since I was in town, I thought I'd look her up. What could it hurt?"

"But what were you doing at the carriage house?" Frank

asked, his tone clearly asking *why couldn't you meet her at a coffee shop or a bar like a normal human being?*

He shrugged. "That was where she wanted to meet me." He swallowed. "We never did anything in the house...we always met out there. It was...it was kind of like old times."

"But you were trespassing! How did you get on the property?" I stared at him. "And you didn't think that was weird?"

"Robin doesn't..." He took a deep breath and exhaled. "I lost track of her when we left, but I never stopped thinking about her. A couple of years ago I started looking for her online. I wanted to know how she was doing. I figured she was probably married, may have even left New Orleans...it wasn't easy on anyone who was involved in that investigation, we were all kind of notorious. A lot of negative things were said about Robin back then...so I wanted to check on her, make sure she was doing okay, you know?"

Robin Strickland *had* gotten a lot of flak back then. She was in charge of Delilah, and maybe had she not gone out that night...wait a minute. "Wasn't she supposedly out on a date the night Delilah was killed?"

Jesse bit his lower lip. "Yeah, well, it wasn't really a date-date. She knew Mike from one of her classes at Tulane. They went to a party together as friends. She—she kind of let people *think* it was a date. She didn't want anyone to know about me and her. It would have looked bad."

That was putting it mildly. She could have been charged. "You know that was a crime, right?"

"Of course I know that." He sighed. "As soon as Delilah's body was found...we both knew how much trouble she could be in if the cops found out. So...so we agreed to keep it a secret."

"That's what you were hiding." I shook my head.

He nodded. "Yeah. I talked to Jack—my parents' lawyer. He agreed not to tell my parents, but he advised me not to say anything. To protect her." He shook his head. "But I've always been a terrible liar. Everyone knew I was hiding something."

"And everyone thought it had something to do with Delilah."
This was Frank, and his voice was kind. "So you kept your mouth
shut."

"It drove me crazy!" He wiped at his eyes. "It drove me
crazy that Arlene thought—that people thought—I killed my
sister. But I couldn't say anything, I couldn't tell anyone the truth
because I didn't want Robin to get in trouble."

It was kind of noble, I thought. Stupid, incredibly stupid,
but still kind of noble. But I didn't say it out loud. "So you started
looking for her a couple of years ago?" I prompted.

He took a swig from the bottle of Pellegrino and wiped his
mouth with her arm. "Yeah. Someone had actually done—maybe
TMZ? One of those kinds of websites, anyway, they'd done one
of those 'where are they now' things about people who'd been
involved in notorious cases, even if they were just on the edges.
Kato Kaelin, people like that. And Robin was one of the people
they profiled. She wasn't going by Robin anymore, she used her
middle name, Kay, and she used her first husband's last name,
Hughes."

"Kay Hughes?" My head was buzzing. I seriously felt dizzy.
"The realtor?" Frank asked.

She'd been at Serena's party.

I'd never recognized her as Robin Strickland. Because
when she was Robin Strickland, she'd had long blond hair and
a very plump face and she'd been maybe ten, fifteen pounds
overweight. She'd been curvy, at any rate. Kay Hughes had short,
curly dark hair and was very thin. She'd changed a lot over the
years—probably deliberately. No one in town had recognized
Kay Hughes as the former Robin Strickland, because it would
have been talked about.

"She actually sold the house to Serena Castlemaine," Jesse
was saying.

"Arlene hired her to sell the house?" I shook my head.
That did not compute. According to both Lorita and Madame
Tourvil, Arlene thought Robin was sleeping with her husband.

She'd apparently been wrong—Robin had been sleeping with her eldest stepson—but why would she hire someone she'd thought had been her husband's mistress to sell the house for her? It wasn't like Kay Hughes was the only real estate agent in New Orleans.

My head was starting to hurt.

He smiled. "No, that would have been weird, even if Arlene didn't recognize her. She does look a lot different, but she's still the same old Robin. No, she was actually Serena's agent. So of course she had a set of keys to the house. So we thought—we thought it would be nice to meet there, you know, for old time's sake. She's currently in the middle of a divorce, so we thought..." He exhaled. "Never mind what we thought. So I met her there last night, around eight. Serena wasn't home. So we went in the front gate and around to the carriage house." He shivered a little bit. "It wasn't a smart idea. I mean, we did used to meet there and all, but Delilah—the place is too haunted for it to be romantic now. And that spark had died out a long time ago." He sighed. "So we just sat there and talked for about an hour or so. I must have put my phone down and forgotten it when we left. I didn't even notice I didn't have it until this morning. And someone—someone killed Arlene there?"

"Even better, the press seem to think the reason you hired us to find her was so you could kill her," I replied.

He buried his face in his hands. "This looks pretty damned bad for me, doesn't it?"

"You need a lawyer," Frank said grimly. "And that's why the reporters are hanging around our front gate. I would imagine there's a mob in front of where you're staying, too."

"Oh, Christ."

"You can hang out here," Colin said slowly, "at least until we can find you a lawyer. You're going to have to go down to the police station and talk to them—but you need to have a lawyer with you." He stood. "Give me the keys to your place. I'll go get you some clothes and your things." He shrugged. "The reporters won't bother me."

He said the last in a grim tone that made me pity the reporters. I also handed him the key to the shed door. "Go through the shed so you can avoid the ones out front."

He nodded. "I'll be back in a bit." He walked down the hall, and the front door shut behind him.

"I have some questions," I said. "I spoke to your aunt, Lorita—you remember her? She's your mother's twin?"

"Did she know anything?"

I shook my head. "No, but she was pretty certain Arlene thought your father was sleeping with Robin—or Kay, or whatever you want to call her. Was she sleeping with your father, too?"

He nodded. "I know Arlene thought so. She used to watch her like a hawk, trying to catch her and Dad doing something." He half smiled. "But Robin could always honestly deny sleeping with Dad, because she wasn't."

Or so you think. "You didn't think it was important to tell us about your relationship with her? Is there anything else you weren't honest about?"

"I hired a private eye myself a few years ago to try to find my mother," he admitted. "He couldn't find a trace of her, it was like she vanished from the face of the earth the day she walked out on us. He also told me that Dad had tried to have her declared legally dead when his own money started to run out, trying to get at her trust. Her will…Dad had her only will, and she left everything to the three of us—Dad, me, and Dylan—equally, and even though they'd gotten divorced, if she hadn't written another will, it would stand. But he couldn't get away with having her declared legally dead. As an ex-husband, he didn't have standing…and I guess he didn't want to involve Dylan and me."

I raised my eyebrows.

"Her money—it was all wrapped up in a trust. He'd divorced her in order to marry Arlene—I always thought he'd bribed the judge. She just disappeared…never tried to draw on her trust, didn't use her credit cards, nothing. She just vanished…but Dad did all of that without telling us."

"Did you ask him about it?" This was from Colin.

"By then he was dying, and I didn't…he always got really agitated when the subject came up, got really upset. I didn't want to bother him." He shook his head. "And I've kicked myself ever since Dad died. Why did he try to have her declared legally dead? What happened to her?"

"It's surprising none of that ever came up when Delilah was killed," Frank commented. "A first wife who just disappeared?"

"The tabloids had plenty of material already," Jesse said bitterly. "They didn't need to go digging into our past."

"There's still no sign of your mother anywhere," Frank said, standing up and starting to pace about. "I checked. No name change, no use of her Social Security number, no trace of her. It was a lot easier to disappear back when she did, of course, than it is now—but there should still be a record of her somewhere. If she were still alive." He pursed his lips. "But you don't think she's alive, do you?"

Jesse shook his head. "No, I'm pretty sure she's dead. And I think she didn't walk out on us, either. I think someone killed her, all those years ago, and hid her body well enough that nobody ever found it." He got up and walked over to the French doors that led out to the balcony. "What's even worse," he added miserably, "is that I think—I've started believing—that Arlene and my father may have killed her."

CHAPTER THIRTEEN
ACE OF CUPS
The first stirrings of joy and insight

Finally, I had the apartment to myself.

The last few hours had flown by, as we called around trying to find Jesse a good lawyer. Mom recommended Loren McKeithen, whom I knew slightly for his work with the local chapter of the Stonewall Democrats. We left a message with his service and hoped he'd get back to us fairly soon. I couldn't stop thinking about what Jesse had said about his mother. It made sense, in a very sad way. It also would explain why Riley and Arlene had been so reluctant to cooperate with the police—if they *had* killed Melanie, they had a lot to hide.

Everyone in that house had something to hide from the cops, apparently. Jesse, Robin/Kaye, Riley, and Arlene had all had secrets they didn't want to come out. I couldn't help but wonder if Dylan also was hiding something from the cops back then.

Rocky Champagne had never had a chance to solve Delilah's murder. He'd been stonewalled and blocked at every turn, mocked on national television, and his career had been destroyed. No wonder his son didn't want to talk to us about anything. It couldn't have been easy for Rocky's family to watch the case wreck him.

What other secrets had the Metoyers been hiding?

Melanie was almost certainly dead. She hadn't been heard from since she "left" Riley. She hadn't touched her own money.

No hits on her Social Security number. No one disappears that completely—not even in the days before the Internet.

The crowd of reporters had dispersed from our sidewalk. When Colin had returned with a bag of Jesse's stuff, he'd said there were no reporters over there, either. Jesse got himself cleaned up and changed his clothes. "I appreciate you letting me stay here more than you know," he said before heading upstairs.

I was itching to get my hands on my tarot cards, to see if Madame Tourvil had been right. So when Frank and Colin decided to go work out at the gym, I'd begged off. "You're the one who's worried about your weight gain," Frank said, his eyebrows raised and arms folded across his chest. "But you never want to go to the gym."

"I'm worn out," I replied, lying down on the couch and closing my eyes. "It's been a long and trying day." I didn't want to say anything to them about what I was going to try to do. They knew I didn't have the visions anymore and that the cards no longer spoke to me. We'd never talked about it in any great depth—what was there to say? They knew what was going on. Talking about it wouldn't change anything or bring my gift back. I appreciated their understanding. Rain and Storm weren't quite as understanding—I finally had to lose my temper with both of them to get them to drop the subject once and for all.

I got a bottle of Pellegrino out of the refrigerator and walked into the living room. Madame Tourvil had asked me if I missed it, and the truth was I had, very much. I didn't like to talk about it because it made me sad. For the last few years—where had the time gone?—I felt like I was missing an essential part of me, and I'd just been kind of floating through my life. *But she didn't warn me about what would happen with Katrina*, I thought as I took a swig from the plastic bottle, *how could she not warn me?*

I answered myself. *What could you have done? What would you have done differently had you known?*

I couldn't answer that.

I tried so hard not to think about that time anymore.

A flood of memories came rushing back as I stood there on

the edge of the living room. Of me and Frank packing up some clothes to head over to the Diderot house in the Garden District, where we were all going to ride out the storm. Marguerite was paranoid about hurricanes, so as soon as Katrina had crossed south Florida that Friday morning, she and Storm had packed and headed west to Houston. Frank and I nailed the shutters closed, turned off everything, and drove across town that Sunday. The on-ramps to the highway were backed up, and the city streets were deserted. It was eerie, the silence and the absence of life as we drove over to the Garden District. Maman and Papa Diderot had a natural gas–powered generator, so even if we lost power, we were going to be fine over there. We sat up that last Sunday night, in the quiet city, as outer bands began to come in, raining for about five minutes and then moving on. The news was bleak—the storm was enormous, it was powerful, and numerous times we all wondered if we should pack up and hit the road. "We survived Betsy and Camille," Papa Diderot insisted, "and New Orleans always endures. We will survive this."

And we had. Even though the city was filled with water, we were safe at the Diderot house. The generator still worked, but eventually the gas line was turned off somewhere and the power went out, I think on the Wednesday or Thursday after. It was hot, it was humid, and there were mosquitoes everywhere. Finally, on Friday, we packed up as much as we could and headed north.

We didn't come back for six weeks.

I took a deep breath and pushed those thoughts out of my head. I didn't want to be sad anymore. I didn't want to remember any of that. That time all seemed like a blur to me anyway, like it had all happened in another lifetime.

I'd changed, too. I wasn't ever the same again after the flood, and it wasn't just because I'd lost my gift. Something else was gone from me; another part of my soul had either shriveled up and died or had been walled off from the rest of me.

A tear rolled down my cheek, and I wiped it away angrily.

I will not ever cry about Katrina again.

The apartment was silent, empty.

I took a deep breath and tried to clear my mind of everything, of all distractions. I needed to focus if I was going to do this.

I turned off all the lights and lit long tapered white candles on the coffee table for purity.

I sat there, in front of the table, my legs crossed underneath me, holding the tarot deck inside its blue silk wrapping.

It had been years since I held them. They felt warm, electric, alive in my hands, like they wanted me to use them, like they were saying to me, *Finally, we've been waiting for you for so long.*

I didn't know—I couldn't remember—how to pray.

It had been a really long time.

I caressed the deck of cards again.

They'd been given to me when I was eight years old, after that dinner party.

I remember that dinner party almost as clearly as if it happened yesterday—it was for Mom and Dad's anniversary, and the house had been filled with some of their best friends. When I was a kid I could never remember all the people who were in and out of our apartment. Mom and Dad seemed to know everyone, to like everyone, and everyone seemed to like them. Our apartment was always full of people, talking and debating and discussing and laughing and smoking pot and drinking wine.

It's a wonder Children's Services never came and took us away.

Then again, Mom would have gone nuclear.

Madame Xena, though, is one of the few I remember distinctly.

She was hard to forget.

I sat next to her at the table that night. I don't remember exactly when she first started coming around, but that wasn't the first time I'd seen her. I'd never talked to her before, but she'd impressed me. She was very tall and immensely regal in her posture and bearing. She always smelled of either lilacs or lilies. That night she was wearing purple: a long purple velvet jacket that reached her knees, open and unbuttoned with a matching purple silk blouse beneath, and purple velvet slacks as well. Even her shoes were purple, flats with gold trim. She always wore a turban, and that night was no exception. Her purple turban covered all of her hair and was held together by an amethyst brooch in the front. She had gold bracelets with gold charms at both wrists, and a ring of some kind on every finger, including her thumbs. Her long earrings almost reached her shoulders— they were peacock feathers. I remember she had olive skin and enormous dark eyes and a very prominent nose, with a beauty mark just below the left corner of her mouth. Her nails were long and red. Earlier I'd seen her in the living room, sucking on a hookah pipe and blowing pot smoke toward the ceiling. There was always a sense of calm about her, like nothing ever bothered her.

Mom had told me was she was a psychic who had lots of wealthy clients all over the country, people would send private jets for her to come do a reading for them, and her name was Madame Xena. There was no other name: just Madame Xena. I had no idea how old she was, or where she was from. When she spoke she had a slight accent, maybe Eastern European, maybe Middle Eastern, I wasn't sure. Her voice was low and calm, and she always spoke assuredly and confidently whenever she was addressed.

I didn't know how my parents knew her or if they believed she was actually a psychic. But that night for some reason I was seated next to her at the dinner table—some kind of horrible meal with tofu as its base—and when I took my seat she had her back to me, talking animatedly to the person sitting on her other side.

But when I sat down beside her and pulled my chair up to the table, she froze and gasped audibly. She spun around in her chair and stared at me. She reached over and grabbed my chin with one hand and brought her face close to mine, staring into my eyes. Her eyes—I've never forgotten how intense her eyes were, so brown they were almost black and surrounded by gold rings. She had outlined her eyes with black pencil, and her long curling eyelashes were thick. After what seemed like an eternity, she let go of my chin and said, quite loudly, "But, Isabelle!" She clapped her hands, and the table fell silent. She always called my mother Isabelle, even though Mom preferred her middle name, Cecile. Madame Xena said Mom had the soul of an Isabelle, so she couldn't call her anything else. "He has the gift! Why have you never told me?"

Mom, a joint dangling from her lips as she set a steaming bowl of fried potatoes on the table, shrugged and passed the joint to someone after taking a massive hit. She blew out a stream of smoke. "I didn't know he had the gift, Xena. I've never seen any signs of it before."

"Well, he does have it, and it is very strong within him." She turned back to me with those huge, piercing eyes. "He is beloved of the Goddess. She has touched him, and she has plans for him." She touched my chin with her fingertips. "Don't ever forget that, Scotty. The Goddess has plans for you."

That was the end of the conversation, and she didn't speak to me again the rest of the evening.

Two days later a box arrived for me from Madame Xena. Inside the box was a deck of tarot cards, wrapped in blue silk, and a note, *Use the cards wisely and fairly, boy.*

There was also a book on how to read and interpret the cards.

The cards fascinated me. I used to shuffle them, look at the pictures, try to figure out what they were trying to tell me. Mom told me how to lay the cards out in patterns to divine their meaning, and sometimes I would look up the meaning of an individual card in the book—a lot of what they meant were beyond my child's understanding. But I would spread them out in my room and play with them. I kept them in an old cigar box Mom gave me, and the blue silk wrapper they were in now was the same one Madame Xena had sent them to me in.

I don't remember how old I was the first time the cards told me the future, but I do remember I was reading the cards for Rain. We were sitting in my room, just goofing off. I remember she was in high school already and she was wondering if a boy—I don't remember his name—would ask her to some dance. I had her hold the cards in her hands, focused, lit a candle, and spread them out in the tree of life. I closed my eyes and said a brief prayer to the Goddess—we were raised to worship the Divine Feminine in all of her manifestations, which was helpful since we were all sent to Catholic schools and could focus on the Virgin Mary without tipping off the priests and nuns that we were actual pagans. I opened my eyes, looked at the cards...

...and not only did they make sense to me, they told me a story.

"He won't ask you to the dance, he will ask Bethany Gable," I said as I frowned over the cards. "And you're better off without him. A better guy—I can't see his name, but he has dark hair and dark eyes—will ask you instead, and you will be with him several years. He won't be the boy you marry—you won't meet your husband until college—but he will make you very happy the rest of the time you're in high school. You will part friends in the end. But Bethany—something bad is going to happen to her. I can't see it clearly, and I don't know what it is...but something bad is going to happen to her if she goes to the dance with him."

Rain laughed, as she always did when I told her fortune, and went off to do her homework, leaving me frowning at the cards.

Two days later she came into my room, her eyes wide. "Barry did ask Bethany," she said in a hoarse whisper, "and Brandon asked me today. Should I tell Bethany not to go with him?"

"What are you going to say?" I asked. "My brother told my fortune with tarot cards and the cards told him something bad will happen if you go with Barry to the dance? She'd think you were crazy, she'd tell everyone, and people would make fun of us for the rest of our lives."

She nodded. Barry and Bethany were in a car accident the night of the dance—neither of them was seriously hurt, but my prediction coming true kind of unnerved both Rain and me. As a family, we decided that we wouldn't tell anyone outside of the immediate family; we didn't even tell either set of grandparents. And while the cards were helpful sometimes—and the more I used them, the better I became at understanding the messages they told me—they didn't *always* work. Sometimes I looked at them and they were just cards with interesting pictures on them, nothing more. I had no idea how to control it, how to make it work for me, and it wasn't like there was anyone who could teach me—Madame Xena had left New Orleans years ago, never to be seen or heard from again. Every once in a while Rain would ask me to do a reading for her, but most of the time I just read them for me, to get an answer when I wasn't sure of what I should do next, or just to give me some clarity.

They always helped me in that way.

Ironically, the weekend I met the boys was the very same weekend the gift changed for me. That weekend the Goddess actually came to me in a vision, and I spoke to her a couple of times in this weird, between-worlds kind of place where mist and warmth were the dominant sensations. I couldn't see her face, it was never clear to me, but I could hear her voice clearly and sense her presence. She helped me out of a couple of jams that weekend…but the gift was about to change again. A dead man's spirit reached through the worlds to me, because his son and his wife were in danger. It wasn't like he appeared to me or spoke to me, but I could sense him, and he directed me to solving the problem and finding the answer that saved his son's life and reunited his family. But…

…at Mardi Gras things changed. I got angry at the goddess—and that anger and disappointment got even stronger when Katrina roared into town, the levees failed, and the city was destroyed. I stopped using the cards. I stopped praying to her. I stopped everything. She came back to me one more time when I was in danger…but other than that, there had been nothing.

But now…now I was willing to try again.

I shuffled the cards and held them in my hands. I took a deep breath and closed my eyes.

"O Goddess, I pray to you for guidance, for assistance in reading these cards that I hold in my hands. I also humbly ask for your forgiveness and your pardon. Please forgive me for the anger I had with you, which is now gone. It is not for me to know your will, or your purpose, and I am but your humble servant. You are a goddess, and I a mere human. You are eternal, and I am but temporary. Please speak to me again, and accept my apology."

I opened my eyes and started spreading the cards out on the table.

I felt…*something*, some kind of power wrapping itself around me as I placed the last card on the table. The hair on my arms and the back of my neck was standing straight up.

I stared down at the images on the faces of the cards…the room started to get a bit fuzzy on the periphery of my vision. The cards spun in front of me…and everything started to get dark.

I was drifting, drifting through space.

I remembered this from before, and so wasn't frightened or worried or concerned, but merely at peace. She had heard me, she was ready to forgive me or at least let me talk to her again.

Love and peace, I felt as though I was wrapped in love and peace as I continued to drift, stars moving above my head in a dark blue velvet sky.

I felt warm as well as protected, surrounded by mist as I drifted downward, ever downward, leisurely and happily. The stars above me seemed close enough for me to reach out and touch, like I could pick them from the sky like diamonds scattered on a velvet cloth as I drifted, always drifting further and further down, and in the distance I could hear music I couldn't identify, but it was soothing to me.

I kept drifting. I never wanted to stop drifting, because here there were no worries and no cares, everything was peace and love, and understanding.

I never wanted to go back. I remembered feeling that before, that pull, that desire to stay here with Her, but She never allowed it, always sending me back because I had work to do.

I wasn't afraid because I had been here before. It had been a long time, to be sure, but this was that weird space between worlds or dimensions or universes where I always went when the Goddess wanted to speak to me. This was a good sign—she may not have forgiven me for my blasphemies, but I felt at peace. I knew this was something that I needed to resolve, something I had let go on for far too long. I'd been lucky, my entire life had been blessed by the Goddess, and I needed to be grateful.

The ground began to materialize below me and the mist began to fade away, ghostly tendrils disappearing as I looked at them. I could see the river rushing by, the currents and eddies, and the smell of the water. My body shifted in the air so that my feet were beneath me, and they came to rest on warm, velvety grass.

I smelled honeysuckle, magnolia, jasmine, and sweet olive.

And then I was aware of her.

I could never remember what she looked like from time to time; her face was always clear to me when I was with her, but afterward I could never remember what I'd seen. She was always different, that I did remember—sometimes she came to me in a form I recognized, Aphrodite or Isis or Kali. This time she was a woman of color, her hair braided into cornrows that ended in clicking beads of purple, gold, and green. She was wearing a blouse that barely contained her large breasts, open to the cleavage, her skin dark brown and glowing in the soft light of a sun much less harsh than an August Louisiana sun. Her face was hard to read, the diamond in her nose piercing glinting at me as she approached me. I tried not to be afraid, for although she could be quite fearsome, she was ultimately a goddess of love, the mother of all humans and the great mother of the earth and the night sky and the stars and the sun and the moon and all of creation.

She stopped several feet from me and held up her hand as I opened my mouth to speak. "I accept your apology," she said, her tone solemn but the words dancing into my ears like music. "Even though you turned your back on me, I never stopped watching over you."

"I thank you," I replied, bowing my head. "I thank you for your intervention, for your help. I am truly blessed, and I am sorry I forgot how much I owe to your generosity."

A ghost of a smile crossed her face and vanished so quickly I couldn't be certain I'd seen it. "Not everything comes from me, Scotty. I do watch over you and yours and do what I can." She shook her head, the beads clacking. "But you think I didn't warn you about the levees failing because I didn't care? That couldn't be further from the truth, Scotty. I didn't warn you because knowing would have made no difference. You and your family wouldn't have left. You couldn't have stopped the levees from failing, nor could you have convinced those who didn't leave the city that they should." She folded her arms across her breasts and tilted her head to one side as she looked at me. She reached out for my face with one of her hands, brushing the side with her fingertips. It felt like an electrical charge went through me. "I knew you and your family could survive. Had you been in danger, I would have come to you."

And as she spoke, I could feel the turmoil deep inside my soul cease. It was like there had been a knot there, a knot of bitterness and anger and rage that festered, formed as the power went out and we suffered through the horror of having no water and no food, no respite from the heat…those days of foraging for food, the unbearable heat, finally loading up everyone into SUVs and heading up the river road to Baton Rouge…the damage and destruction we saw on our way, the horrors we saw on hotel televisions as they replayed the film of what had happened in those horrible days we'd been holed up in the Diderot house, the anger at the loss that didn't have to happen, the rage…we'd come back as soon as the city was open again, and those months when nothing was open and the entire city was in ruins…the knot was untying inside me and letting go, and I gasped with the relief.

"Let it all go, and be free," she whispered. "Be free…be free…"

And the room swam back into focus in front of me. I wiped at my eyes.

I did feel free.

I hadn't even realized I was still carrying that knot inside me. For ten years. It had been there for ten years, festering.

I quickly said a thank-you prayer and shuffled the cards again, thinking, *Will we be able to find out who killed Delilah?*

I laid out the cards and slowly flipped them over.

A deceitful woman.

A difficult task ahead, but hard work will pay off.

An angry young man.

The light from above will show the way.

I looked at the cards again, watching them begin to take the form of a story in front of my eyes.

I grabbed a pad of paper and scribbled down some notes.

Then I got up and started pacing.

Melanie Metoyer had disappeared and had never been heard from again. Riley divorced her for desertion and married Arlene. He was having another affair when Delilah was murdered, Arlene was worried she was going to lose him—but the woman she thought was sleeping with her husband had actually been sleeping with her stepson.

And now Arlene was dead, Jesse was the number one suspect—and I wasn't really sure what to do next.

Maybe I could keep looking for Melanie until they got back. I wasn't very good at the Internet stuff—Colin was a whiz—but I wasn't completely useless at it.

Who knows? Maybe I'd get lucky and find her.

Three Metoyer women—okay, Delilah was a child, but she was a female—disappeared or dead. Two of them Riley's wives, the other his daughter.

I walked over to the computer and logged onto the Internet just as the front door slammed open, hitting the wall with a bang and sending me up toward the ceiling. "*Taylor!*" I shouted, knowing it had to be him. Colin and Frank wouldn't slam the door open.

"Sorry!" Taylor shouted back. He emerged from the hallway with a sheepish look on his face. He was drenched in sweat from head to toe. He disappeared into the kitchen and reemerged with a bottle of watermelon-flavored Gatorade, which he downed in two long gulps, followed by a belch. "Where is everyone?"

"Frank and Colin went to the gym." I pushed the chair back and pointed at the computer. "You're better at this web search thing than me, you think you can help me out here?"

He rolled his eyes and somehow folded his tall, lanky frame into the same chair I'd been sitting in. "What am I looking for?"

"Start with Melanie Metoyer, née Gallaudet." I spelled it for him. "She was Jesse Metoyer's mother, and she walked out on her family, never to be heard from again, before his father remarried Arlene."

"Never to be heard from again?" He arched an eyebrow. "That's weird."

"I don't like it," I replied, starting to pace. I walked over to the table and picked up the cards, wrapping them in the blue silk before replacing them in the cigar box, which I then slid back under the couch. "It just doesn't sit right with me, you know?"

He finished tapping at the keyboard, and frowned. "There's really nothing. Some old links to the *Times-Picayune*, a New Orleans history/genealogy site…how can she be completely off the Internet?"

"Jesse thinks she's dead." I glanced at my watch. "He thinks his dad and Arlene actually killed her and pretended that she'd left town."

"That would explain why they wanted their lawyer before they called the cops the night Delilah died," Taylor commented, scratching his head.

"Yeah, that's what I think, too." I filled him in on the situation with Jesse and Robin Strickland/Kay Hughes as well.

He whistled. "That's really sad. So that's what he was hiding from his parents? No wonder they thought he'd killed Delilah."

"And if they'd killed his mother…" I shook my head.

Just then my phone vibrated to let me know I'd gotten a text message. I clicked on the screen—it was from Venus: *I'm sending you the witness list from the Delilah Metoyer investigation. Tell Jesse Metoyer we need him to come in for an interview should he turn up.*

My phone buzzed again to let me know her email had come.

I sent it to the wireless printer.

"Yeah, sorry, Venus, he'll have a lawyer with him when he does come in," I muttered as I took the paper off the printer.

Finally, maybe we could get somewhere.

CHAPTER FOURTEEN
TEN OF SWORDS

Seeking meaning, closure, haunted by someone from the past

It was amazing how quickly Arlene Metoyer's murder went viral. Back when Delilah was killed, there was no social media and the World Wide Web didn't even exist. Yet the case was everywhere—the twenty-four-hour news channels, the tabloids, magazines—there wasn't any escaping the story back then.

But as soon as I sat down at the computer with the witness list Venus had sent me, Arlene's murder was the lead story on my web browser's home page. A quick glance at Facebook told me everyone was sharing the story and talking about it. Reporters and news agencies were, even as I started researching Venus's list online, digging through old files and reports and stories, looking for pictures of Delilah and Arlene, pageant videos, audition tapes.

It was going to be twenty-five years ago all over again—only much, much worse.

I wondered, as I started researching the first name on the list, if we'd be able to keep our names out of it...but given the mob outside the front gate, it seemed unlikely.

Periodically I would interrupt my research to go check the major news sites, terrified our names would show up—or a picture of our front gate.

Fortunately, no one knows Jesse is upstairs, I reminded myself as I closed the news site tab and opened another search engine.

As I worked through the witness list, I had to give Rocky Champagne credit. Despite all the abuse he got in the media and in Jerry's book, he'd been pretty damned thorough. He'd interviewed everyone with any connection to the family—the pool cleaner, the yard guys, the dry cleaner Arlene frequented, delivery guys, neighbors, agents, pageant judges. I crossed most of them off—I didn't think there was any need for us to talk to the vast majority of these witnesses. Most of them hadn't been around during Melanie's days at the Metoyer house…and we were fooling ourselves if we thought we were going to catch Delilah's killer after all this time.

Given Rocky's thoroughness, if he couldn't do it, there was no way we could.

In fact, if we were going to be looking for a killer, it should be Arlene's.

It's interesting about Kaye Hughes, though, I thought as I finally put the computer to sleep and leaned back in the chair. *Lorita was pretty sure she was having an affair with Riley. And Arlene was convinced he was having an affair with someone. If Riley wasn't sleeping with the nanny, who* was *he sleeping with?*

I got up and started pacing around the living room.

I was missing something, I just couldn't put my finger on it.

And who, besides Jesse, would want to kill Arlene? She'd been living under the radar for years. But why would Jesse wait so long, if he wanted to kill her? Why would he hire detectives to find her?

Something here wasn't right.

Finally I gave up thinking about and sat down on the couch. I picked up the remote control and turned on the television. It was getting late. And sure enough, the story was being covered on every news channel. CNN, MSNBC, Fox, HLN—I flipped from channel to channel. No live feeds from in front of our gate, thank the Goddess, but just to be on the safe side I kept flipping back and forth between the seemingly endless television reporters talking breathlessly into their microphones about the latest Metoyer murder. Even the local affiliates had interrupted their regularly scheduled programming for this breaking news story. I walked back over to the desk and picked up the printout of the witness list, carrying it back into the living room. I picked up the remote, bit my lower lip, and punched in the numbers for the International News Network, INN.

Sure enough, they too had interrupted their regularly scheduled programming for a special segment with the Queen of Tabloid Crime Reporting herself, Veronica Vance.

She'd become so ubiquitous over the years it was hard to remember a time when she wasn't polluting the airwaves.

The Metoyer case had been a godsend for Veronica Vance. Just before the body had been found, she'd resigned from her job as a prosecutor in Charlotte, North Carolina, to become a talking head on INN for their crime coverage. Her outrage over Delilah's murder—outrage that also extended to the apparently "bad parenting" of Riley and Arlene in pushing her into show business and beauty pageants—had made her a household name within a few days. Millions of viewers nationwide tuned into INN's coverage to hear what she would say next. Her outrage about every aspect of the Metoyers' lives made her a star. Soon, she had her own nightly crime show on INN.

I personally couldn't stand her. Her exaggerated Southern twang—which seemed to get thicker and faker every year—grated on my nerves. Her high-pitched shriek could shatter glass and make dogs howl when she went on one of her self-righteous harangues about how the criminal justice was stacked in favor of criminals over victims. She sometimes had a point, but it was all about ratings for her. She tapped into that dark place in the souls of humanity that used to lead to lynchings, with mobs of angry people howling for blood and vengeance. She played into the mentality that so many people have that the country had gone to hell and criminals were destroying everything and getting away with it because of those pesky constitutional rights we all have. Her entire show, her shtick, was predicated on the notion that simply because someone has been accused meant they must be guilty. On her shows, she served as prosecutor, judge, and jury—and refused to apologize to the people she maligned and slandered, even after they were proven innocent.

My brother Storm is a lawyer, and he considers her to be worse than a bottom-feeding ambulance chaser. "Innocent until proven guilty is the ideal our justice system is built on," he'll say, with a sad shake of his head, "and the burden of proof lies with the prosecutor to protect people from the abuse of the state. She should be fucking disbarred—and the school that gave her a degree should lose its credentials."

I hate it when Storm beats around the bush rather than expressing what he feels.

Frank and Colin came back in while I was flipping through the channels, sitting down on either side of me.

Much as I hate watching her, I couldn't stop watching her "special report" on Arlene's murder.

She was clearly sitting in a studio with a headset, in front of a blue screen on which an image of Jackson Square was being projected.

"Thanks, Brian," she said in that awful twang that set my teeth on edge. She shook her head slightly. "Twenty-five years ago a CHILD was brutally murdered in the Garden District of New Orleans, and her KILLER was never brought to justice. Many people—myself included—were not convinced of the innocence of poor Delilah Metoyer's immediate family. Now, almost twenty-five years to the day after her body was found in the carriage house behind her parents' impressive mansion"—at this point the picture behind her changed from Jackson Square to the front of Serena's house; I bit my lower lip and wondered how Serena would take to that—"and now, just today, her mother's body was found in almost the Exact. Same. Place." She paused for dramatic emphasis. "Only one member of the Metoyer family is now left alive, Delilah's older brother Jesse." Behind her now appeared what looked like a mug shot of a much younger Jesse, who'd clearly had a rough night.

"That's a terrible picture," Frank commented.

"Mug shot," Colin corrected him. "I wonder what he was arrested for? He looks like he's twelve in that picture."

"He looks about Taylor's age," I retorted. He kind of did.

"Is Jesse Metoyer the murderer?" she went on, her eyes narrowing for the cameras. "There were many people who theorized years ago that Jesse, the older brother young Delilah idolized and adored, was actually her killer. The police are now looking for him in connection with his mother's murder. I have it from reliable sources that Jesse Metoyer is back in New Orleans—he was seen this very weekend, and has rented a place in the Marigny neighborhood. I have also been told that he hired a private detective firm to look for his mother. Interestingly enough, he and his mother had not spoken in years. So on the same weekend he comes back to the scene of the crime and hires a detective to find his mother, she winds up dead. I didn't like coincidences when I was a prosecutor, and I don't like them now."

"I bet she misses abusing her prosecutorial power," Colin said, getting up. "I'll go check with Jesse and see what he was arrested for." A few moments later, I heard the front door open and close.

"And can it be a coincidence that almost all of the Metoyers have died under mysterious circumstances since little Delilah's murder? Dylan Metoyer, the middle son, committed suicide a couple of years ago—hung himself in his apartment. Was it a suicide? Or was it murder?"

"She's really reaching," Frank said with a shake of his head. "How does she get away with this bullshit?"

I picked up the remote and changed the channel to a repeat of *Grande Dames of Palm Beach*. "Public figures unfortunately are opened up to this sort of thing," I said, quoting Storm. "Nothing she is saying is libel or slander—she's just speculating out loud. It's horrible—I mean, she basically accused Jesse of killing Arlene, and Delilah, and will probably speculate about his dad, too…but it's not against the law. Speculation isn't actionable, and she can always use a 'public figure' defense were she to be sued. Most people don't bother bringing more attention to the shit she says by suing her. She says outrageous things some people like to hear, and she gets good ratings." I shrugged. "It's horrible, but unfortunately, there's not really a lot anyone can do about it other than hope she grows a conscience someday."

"That'll be the day," Frank said darkly. "You haven't seen anything tying us to this mess, have you?"

I shook my head. "So far, so good."

"DUI," Colin said as he sat back down a few minutes later. "While he was in college, he got pulled over and arrested for DUI. They must have really moved quick to get that mug shot."

"She's good at what she does," I replied. "I went through the witness list, guys. I don't think anyone on there is going to be worth talking to."

"We need to focus on clearing Jesse anyway," Frank replied, rubbing my leg. "He's got another appointment with Loren McKeithen tomorrow morning at ten, at his office."

"Terrific," I replied, resting my head on Colin's shoulder.

Needless to say, I didn't sleep well that night.

We all went to bed early—Taylor was out with some of his friends, so I hoped (*get off my lawn!*) he'd remember that Jesse was crashing in the spare room up there and wouldn't bring a trick home with him when he did finally come stumbling in. Frank and Colin both dropped right off to sleep while I lay there in between them, staring at the ceiling, unable for the life of me to doze off. I couldn't stop thinking about Melanie Metoyer.

She had to be dead. And how interesting it was that no one ever questioned the fact she'd just vanished from the face of the earth all those years ago. It was actually kind of scary—her sister didn't care, her parents were dead, and her only living child thought she'd abandoned him when he was a kid. If Jesse was right, and Riley and Arlene had killed her all those years ago, no one had ever suspected a thing.

How...awful.

My mother had known her. I could ask her. I looked over at the clock. It was only one in the morning—Mom and Dad were just getting going. They always stayed up all night. I slipped carefully out of bed and got dressed.

Neither Colin nor Frank stirred. I thought about leaving

them a note, but didn't see any point to it. They probably wouldn't wake up.

The Quarter was quiet as I slipped through the streets. I'd checked to make sure the gate was clear—the reporters had given up, but they'd probably be back at some point. I reminded myself to get more keys to the shed and the parking lot doors made. Although maybe they wouldn't bother us once Jesse turned himself in to the cops…I shook my head and kept walking.

All the lights were on at Mom and Dad's, as I knew they would be. I just hoped they didn't have a house full of people over, planning some protest or talking about politics. I was in luck—Mom and Dad were alone, watching the news on the BBC America channel. "Scotty!" Mom said with a smile as I walked into their living room. She was rolling a joint on a silver tray she was holding in her lap. Dad was stretched out on the couch, the remote control in his hand. "This is a pleasant surprise. Are the boys with you?"

"I couldn't sleep." I kissed her cheek and patted Dad's shoulder before plopping down into one of their easy chairs.

"How goes it with Jesse?" She licked the joint and passed it to me. I picked up a lighter and sparked it, taking a deep inhale and coughing the smoke out. By the time I finished coughing, my head felt like it was floating. It was excellent pot. "You don't think he killed Arlene, do you?"

"We don't know what to think," I replied. "Mom, why didn't you mention before that you went to school with Jesse's mother?"

She shrugged. "I thought you knew." She made a face. "We weren't friends, of course. I didn't really much care for Melanie or Lorita, to be honest." She rolled her eyes. "Vapid empty-headed girls who only really cared about clothes and boys weren't exactly the type of friends I've ever been interested in, you know."

"I know." I passed her the joint. "Jesse believes that his father and Arlene may have killed her. No one's seen her since the night she walked out on all of them. I've traced her Social Security number—nothing. Riley and Lorita tried to have her declared legally dead after seven years, but they couldn't."

"It wouldn't surprise me." She waved her hand. "Melanie...I never really understood that marriage—but you know the Garden District isn't something I've ever really understood. I mean, even in high school he was cheating on her. I guess she just wanted to be married to someone, and he was willing." She twisted her mouth. "Those girls were raised to find husbands and do charity work. Such a waste of potential. I remember when I heard that she'd left Riley. It didn't make sense to me." She raised her shoulders. "He'd always cheated. So why this time? What was so awful about Arlene Campbell sleeping with her husband that would make her leave him?" She closed her eyes. "It does make sense that they killed her and made up the story about her leaving." She smiled at me sadly. "Nothing Riley ever did would surprise me."

I didn't stay much longer. I don't know what time it was when I went home. But once I was in bed again, I finally was able to drift off into a horrible, restless sleep.

And I dreamed.

I was walking across the back lawn of the Metoyer place. There were no lights on in the house, and it was the middle of the night. The night was velvety dark, with stars winking and a crescent moon hanging almost on the horizon. There was no sound anywhere, but I was walking toward the pool. It was lit up, the water glowing with that eerie bluish green light that seems otherworldly. As I walked, a light in the carriage house came on, the sheer blue curtains on the window next to the door glowing like the pool through the night. I somehow knew that no one was supposed to be in there, that the light meant something was definitely wrong, something that shouldn't happen was happening. I didn't want to keep walking there, but I couldn't help myself, even as every alarm bell in my mind was going off, I couldn't stop walking. As I got closer I could hear music—the Carpenters again, only this time it was "Only Yesterday," which somehow seemed appropriate. My hackles were raised, and as I got closer and closer to the front door, it slowly began to creep open, barely moving an inch at a time, and I couldn't stop, no matter what I couldn't stop walking and I opened my mouth to scream but no sound came out...and then I was at the threshold, and there was—

I sat up in bed, sweating.

It was already daylight. My nightstand alarm clock said it was just past seven. I yawned and slipped out of the bed, pulling on a robe as I headed into the kitchen to make some coffee. I just wanted to go back to bed.

The coffee was brewing when my phone chirped with a text message. I looked at it. It was from Jesse: *We have a ten o'clock appointment at Loren McKeithen's office. Are you up?*

I am, but I'll have to get Frank and Colin up, I texted back. *Does he want to see us all?*

Yes.

Damn it.

I've never been comfortable around lawyers.

Unfortunately, I've had a lot of experience with them—but that's not as bad as it sounds.

Mom and Dad got arrested a lot when I was growing up, so their lawyers were around the house a lot. (Mom and Dad did manage to refrain from smoking pot in front of their lawyers, unless it was a social call.) A lot of their friends are lawyers. My dad's brother Skipper is not just the family alcoholic but is also a lawyer (the Bradley side of the family is right out of a Tennessee Williams play). My brother Storm is a lawyer. My landlady Millie is a lawyer. It seems like I've been surrounded by lawyers my entire life.

But that doesn't mean I'm comfortable around them.

I got Frank and Colin out of bed and cleaned up. Colin made us all breakfast—well, all of us except for Taylor; nothing was going to get him up and awake. We didn't talk as we ate our breakfast and drank coffee. Jesse looked, understandably, more than a little nervous. I couldn't blame him.

While they were getting ready, I made an appointment to meet Kay Hughes at her office.

The offices of Loren McKeithen's firm were in One Shell Square, an enormous marble memorial to Louisiana's sale of its soul in the 1980s to Big Oil. It's a beautiful building, but the sidewalks around it are also made of marble and slant downward toward the streets—as sidewalks are wont to do in New Orleans—so when they are wet it's very easy to slip.

It's a wonder more people don't wind up sprawled in the street and killed.

Loren's firm's office was on the twentieth floor. I'd never been inside One Shell Square before, but it was just as opulent as I thought it would be. The door to the offices of McKeithen, Lombard & Spencer was oak, and the reception area very plush, with expensive-looking overstuffed chairs, modern-looking tables of brass and glass, and every imaginable magazine spread out over them. The receptionist, a very pretty mixed-race woman probably around forty, offered us coffee once she checked us in. We all declined, and with a smile she told us to have a seat. "Mr. McKeithen will be with you shortly."

We sat down, paging through magazines. Jesse was fidgeting nervously, which made me nervous. I got up and walked over to one of the windows. The window faced the river, and there was a spectacular view of the city.

The phone at the front desk buzzed, and the receptionist looked up at us. "Mr. McKeithen will see you now." She stood, but put up a well-manicured hand. "Oh, not you, Mr. Metoyer—not just yet. He want you to wait for a moment." Jesse made a face and sat back down. She gestured to us to follow her. She led us down a long hallway to a corner office and knocked on the door lightly with her knuckles before opening the door for us.

Loren McKeithen was seated behind his desk as we entered, and jumped up to his feet. He was a short man, maybe five-five on a tall day, and his receding hairline went about halfway back on his skull. He had the coffee-colored skin of someone of mixed racial heritage—a look you see a lot in New Orleans—and large, almond-shaped brown eyes. He was sporting a thick waist, and the buttons on his vest were straining a bit. He was wearing large square-framed black plastic glasses. When he shook my hand, his was warm and sweaty, and the smile he had plastered on his face was almost crocodile-like.

Storm always said never trust a smiling lawyer.

"Sit down, guys, can I get you anything? Coffee, water, juice?" He sat on the edge of his desk, his hands resting on his legs, his eyebrows raised. When we all demurred, he went on, "All right, let's just get down to it. Jesse Metoyer has retained me to look after his interests, and we had a rather long session down at the police station yesterday with Venus Casanova and Blaine Tujague—you three are acquainted with them?"

We all nodded.

"Well, from now on, you three are working for me." He handed a contract to Frank, who he'd apparently decided was the leader of our group. "That means no talking to the cops about the Metoyer case without me present, right?" He smiled at me. "Scott—"

"Scotty."

"Scotty, I really wish you hadn't talked to them yesterday, but there's nothing we can do about that now, and I am not blaming you for anything." He held up his hand as all three of us started to talk at once. "I'm not. I encourage everyone to talk to the police, to cooperate whenever possible. And there was no way you could have known that Jesse was going to be suspect number one in his stepmother's murder, even despite his phone being there at the murder scene." He stood back up. "I'll let you look over that contract—it's standard—and I've got a retainer check for you as well. I am hiring you to help me investigate the Arlene Metoyer murder—and keep looking for Delilah's… this way, you're working for me, and we can claim privilege." He shook his head. "It may not hold up in court, but I can make a damned good argument for it. Look it over, talk it over, and I'll be back shortly." He paused at the door. "I hope we can work together on this, guys. I believe Jesse is not only innocent, but is being framed. There's some information I can share with you—but not until you sign that contract. I'm going to go talk to Jesse now, while you talk it over." The door shut behind him.

"It's pretty standard," Frank said as he finished reading it. "What do you guys think?"

"I think he's trying to dodge around the cops by hiring us," Colin replied with a shrug of his shoulders. "But I'm willing to sign the contract just to find out what he knows."

"There doesn't seem to be anything in it that could backfire and bite us in the ass later," Frank said, flipping through the pages. "And the retainer is nice—not that we need the money."

"We can put it in the Taylor car fund," Colin replied.

"Yeah, *I'm* the one spoiling him," I retorted.

"It only makes sense to get him a car." Frank went on, "We can't expect him to get to class on time if he's depending on the streetcar, and cabs would be expensive. Besides," he winked at Colin as he patted my leg, "you're the one who's going to be home every day. If he's running late, who's going to have to drive him to class? And he doesn't need a new car. Something used and dependable."

"The car is beside the point," I said. "The point is, do we want to take this job? It feels kind of hinky to me." I held up my hands to silence them both as each opened his mouth. "Come on, he's already said he didn't like me talking to the cops yesterday. He doesn't need to hire us—he's hiring us to keep our mouths shut. And that—I don't like that very much. We already have a client." *Who might be a murderer*, I added to myself.

"We have a client in common," Colin corrected me. "And really, it makes sense. This way, we have access to Jesse, for one thing—if we don't go through Loren, we won't really be able to talk much to our client anymore." He held up his hand to keep me from saying anything. "And yes, I know, you're thinking Jesse may be guilty after all. But we aren't going to find out one way or the other unless we talk to him...and with privilege..." He let his voice trail off.

"I would like to know why Jesse thinks he's being framed," I said begrudgingly. "But if any of this gets shady, I'm pulling the plug."

"That's fair," Frank said. He went to the door, and Loren returned. "We'll do it." We all took turns signing the contract, then Loren handed Frank a check.

"Why do you think Jesse is being framed?" Colin asked.

Loren sat on the edge of his desk. "Doesn't it strike you as incredibly convenient that Jesse's cell phone was at the crime scene?" He crossed his legs at the ankles, revealing black knit socks. "That sort of thing always gives me pause. What easier way to frame someone?"

"But who would have framed him?" I shook my head. "You'd need someone who'd want to kill Arlene, and who had access to his phone. That should narrow the possibilities down. Unless the killer just happened to find his phone."

"Coincidence?" Frank frowned. "I don't like coincidences."

"The more likely explanation is that Jesse's phone wasn't planted, but Jesse left it there." Colin winked at Frank. "And Arlene showed up later and was killed. His phone being there doesn't mean he was the killer. And yes, that would be an unfortunate coincidence." He looked at Loren. "What is Jesse's story?"

"Jesse went to his old house to meet his cousin, Alison." Loren folded his arms. "He met her at the carriage house."

"Alison Strauss?" I asked. "That's not the story he told us. He told us he met Kay Hughes, who used to be known as Robin Strickland, there. And how did they have keys?"

"Jesse has always had a set of keys, as did Alison," Loren replied. "Ms. Castlemaine didn't have the locks changed when she bought the place." He tilted his head slightly. "I suspect she will get that taken care of shortly." He glanced at his watch. "I have a meeting in a few moments, so I'm going to have to cut this off. Perhaps later this afternoon—say five—Jesse and I can come by your place and we can continue this discussion?"

We all rose, shook his hand, and headed for the elevators.

Once the doors closed behind us, I shook my head. "I have a bad feeling about this."

"As in—"

"No." I shook my head. "I don't like that Jesse's changing his story and expecting us to stand by it. Did he meet Alison or didn't he? I have a meeting with Kay Hughes...I'll head uptown."

I hoped we hadn't made a mistake signing that contract.

CHAPTER FIFTEEN
THE EMPRESS, REVERSED
A woman who is deceitful and cannot be trusted

I took the streetcar uptown.

The boys wanted to come with me, but I talked them out of it. Yes, it would be convenient to have a car, but on the other hand, having three of us show up at Kaye's office could be a bit overwhelming. I felt—and they agreed, after a bit of a discussion in the elevator—that if I posed as someone looking to buy a house in the Garden District or Uptown, I could probably get more information out of her than if we all three just showed up and started throwing questions at her. I said good-bye to them and walked out onto the marble plaza, pulling out my phone and intending to use my Uber app when I saw a streetcar was coming.

I don't get a chance to ride the streetcar very often, so whenever I do, I will.

It was crowded—more crowded than I would have liked, but I was able to get a seat in the very back. Despite all the people, it was cool once it was moving. All of the windows were down and the movement created a really nice, strong cool breeze for me in the back of the car as it lurched and rattled up St. Charles Avenue.

I don't want to work for someone who lies to us, I thought as the car stopped at Julia Street, letting some people off. *And he is lying. At least he is now. Why would he change his story?*

Maybe he just didn't want to get Kaye involved.

Which, I suppose, made sense. I wasn't sure what the statute of limitations on statutory rape was, but even if it had passed, it wouldn't exactly do her real estate career any good for it to come out she'd had an affair with a fifteen-year-old when she was in her early twenties. I hadn't recognized Kaye Hughes as Robin Strickland. Maybe she'd buried the past so successfully she didn't want that all coming out again. I couldn't blame her for that. Just glancing through my Facebook feed, at least every other post was something about Arlene's murder or a link to an old story about Delilah's.

The media was going to milk this story for everything it could.

Was Jesse guilty?

It made sense.

Everything I'd learned pointed to him. He hired us to find Arlene so he could kill her. He admitted he believed she'd killed his own mother. We'd found her, and later that night she was dead. He was at the crime scene. And he'd changed his story.

If he'd originally met Alison Strauss there instead of Kaye, why hadn't he told us that?

I got off the streetcar at Washington and crossed the street. Kaye's office was in a brick building on the corner of Washington and Prytania. I glanced at my phone one more time and realized I was an hour early. I stopped in and got an iced mocha at the coffee shop across the street from her office in the Rink shopping mall, but still had fifty minutes to kill.

Alison lived maybe four blocks from where I was.

Why not just ask her?

I was drenched in sweat by the time I reached her gate. The Strauss place, on Eighth Street between Prytania and St. Charles, was a raised center hall–style plantation house, painted yellow with white columns across the front veranda. There was a black wrought iron fence, maybe about waist high, separating the front lawn from the sidewalk. A big gate to the right opened into a brick driveway, with a black Lexus convertible parked in the shade of a live oak tree. The house was beautiful. The shutters along the gallery were open, so I could see into the front rooms on either side of the front door. A grand piano with a gold candelabra resting on top of it was clearly visible in the room on the right. The gate, when I tried it, was locked, so I pressed the buzzer.

"Yes?" a voice came through the speaker next to the buzzer.

"Alison? This is Scotty Bradley. We met at Serena's party?" I said, trying to sound as friendly as possible. "I was in the neighborhood and thought I'd take a chance and see if you were home. If this is a bad time—"

The gate buzzed and I opened it, walking up the brick walk. I wiped sweat from my forehead, hoping I looked a little bit presentable. As I climbed the white painted front steps to the gallery, the front door opened. Alison stood in the door. She was wearing a sleeveless yellow blouse that actually matched the paint of her house, and a black pleated tennis skirt. Her legs were bare, and she wasn't wearing much—if any—makeup. Her hair was pulled back into an extremely tight ponytail—so tight it looked like it hurt, and it gave her face a surprised look. My mom called this hairstyle the "Uptown facelift": hair pulled back so hard it smoothed out wrinkles in the forehead and pulled tight any loose skin.

"Come on in and get out of that heat!" she said with a broad, dazzling smile—her teeth had been recently bleached so white they glowed in her tan face. "Can I get you some iced tea or something cool?" She glanced at the plastic cup in my hand.

"Wouldn't that be a lot of trouble?" I smiled as I stepped inside.

She closed the door with a smile on her face. "Not at all. Come on."

I followed her down the center hallway. The kitchen was at the end of the hallway, an expansive room that had to have been an addition to the original house. She opened a refrigerator door and filled two glasses with tea, adding some ice to them from the dispenser on the front of the door. "Do you want to sit on the side porch?" she asked with the smile still on her face. "There's a fan, so we won't sweat to death."

"Okay." I followed her out onto the side gallery of the house, sitting down at a whitewashed iron table. She pulled a cord and the fan on the gallery ceiling began spinning. There was another building across the backyard from the main house, past a swimming pool and a hot tub.

"I'm glad you came by," she said, sipping her tea slowly and still smiling. "I had to turn off my cell phone and unplug the landline. No one remembers I'm a Metoyer until someone else dies." Her tone was bitter. "I can't believe this is all happening again. Wasn't it bad enough I had to live through this once already?"

"I can't even imagine."

The smile remained firmly frozen in place. "And of course all of my *friends* can't be bothered with me now. Just like before." She held up her hands, waving them. I noticed her perfect manicure from the party no longer existed—the red painted nails were ragged, chewed down to the quick. "You find out who your friends are when scandal strikes. No wonder Aunt Arlene was so fucking nuts. I thought this was all behind us." She shook her head, and I caught a whiff of alcohol and realized she was slightly drunk.

"Were you close to your aunt?"

She focused her eyes on me. "I was very close to Dylan and Jesse. I'm only a year older than them." She picked up her glass again, her hand slightly trembling. "After Delilah was killed, of course, we weren't around them very much. My mother was Uncle Riley's sister. They didn't get along. They were polite, and of course we saw a lot of each other, because we were family, but once Delilah was killed...not so much." She reached over and patted my hand. "I knew when I met you the other night you were a nice guy. Thank you so much for coming by to see how I am."

She is even drunker than I thought, and lonely. Terribly lonely.

"I had to take Gaspard to the vet this morning," she rambled on, "and of course, my bastard husband had to go to work because that's the most important thing in the world. God fucking forbid he take a day off when his wife might need him, when her aunt's been murdered and the world is going to fucking blow up in our faces at any goddamned minute." She gulped down the rest of the tea and covered her mouth with her hand to hide a delicate belch. "I don't even have my pig!"

"The way I understand it, you met Jesse at the old house last night?"

"Jesse." She barked out a hysterical laugh that morphed into a muted sob. "I haven't seen him in years and then he calls me out of the blue. I didn't even know he was in town!" She looked at me again. "After everything we were to each other I deserve better than that, don't I?"

"Everything you were to each other?"

"I know what you're thinking." She winked at me. She pushed herself up to her feet. "Wait here. I need another drink." She went back inside the house, leaving the door open.

I took a deep breath and leaned back in my chair. The ceiling fan, whirring madly overhead like a propeller, was combating the obnoxious heat and humidity beautifully. She elbowed her way through the door with a bottle of Hendrick's gin in her right hand. She slopped some into her empty glass. She smiled at me. "Fuck tea," she pronounced carefully, "I need gin. Don't judge me."

"No worries," I replied with what I hoped was a reassuring smile. "So, Jesse called you last night?"

She hiccupped. "How was I supposed to know he just wanted me to get him on the property?" She shrugged. "Arlene gave me keys when she moved out of town, in case, you know." She rolled her eyes. "She never asked for them back. I just figured they wouldn't work, but it was worth a try. I met him there…Serena wasn't home." She closed her eyes and took a deep breath. "I knew she wouldn't be. She was going out, she'd invited me, so I knew the place was empty and the coast was clear."

"But what reason did Jesse give you for wanting to meet there?"

Her eyes filled with tears. "You have to understand Jesse was the first love of my life, you know? I've missed him so much…"

My jaw dropped.

"We aren't really blood cousins, you know." She took another healthy swig of the gin. "That was another open secret in the family. Jesse wasn't Riley's son, so we weren't related at all."

My head was spinning. "What?"

"Everyone knew Riley and Melanie didn't love each other. They only got married to access their trust funds. They were friends, and he accepted the twins as his sons. But Delilah was his only real kid. So it was perfectly okay for us to be a couple. I wanted to marry him…he was my first love." She hiccupped again and wiped her mouth, smearing her lipstick in the process. "So, why not? He wanted to see me, finally, after all these years, and I knew Serena wouldn't be home…so I met him there. My bastard husband certainly wasn't at home. He never is…so why wouldn't I want to see Jesse? In our old place?" She laughed. "I would have gone even if Serena was home…when do you ever get a chance to relive your past? I've certainly aged better than Jesse."

"So you and Jesse…were involved when you were teenagers?"

She nodded. "And then someone killed Delilah and everything was different." She wiped at her eyes again.

"I thought…I thought Jesse was involved with Robin Strickland. The nanny." My head was spinning, and I was also really glad she was drunk. She probably wouldn't be sharing all this with me if she were sober.

"That *whore*." She spat the words at me. "Yes, she was trying to get in Jesse's pants. It was something to see, that's for sure. Uncle Riley was trying to get in her pants while she was trying to get into Jesse's. But Jesse loved *me*. He's always loved *me*." She was defiant. "It was so good seeing him there. And we left together when we were finished."

I didn't want to ask.

She gave me a beaming smile. "And so he promised me. He

promised me I could leave my husband and be with him. It's all I've ever wanted, you know, was to love Jesse and be with him." She lifted her glass. "But he went back and killed Arlene there, didn't he? That was why he wanted me to meet him there. So he'd have a reason for being there." She shook her head. "Just like when he killed Delilah."

"You think Jesse killed Delilah?"

"Who else?" She hiccupped again. "Delilah was a little monster. Everyone always acted like she was such a sweet little girl after she was dead, but she was a *sneak*, always spying on everyone, threatening to tell…she knew about me and Jesse. She threatened to tell our parents."

"But if you weren't blood relatives…"

"I thought it was stupid, I told him we had nothing to worry about. So my parents knew I wasn't a virgin anymore? Who the fuck cares. We were going to get married, so what difference did it make? Jesse freaked out, though. That very same day, the day she was killed, she caught us in the carriage house, told Jesse she was going to tell on us. He was mad, he was so angry…and he was angry because they were having to go to LA for an audition for her." She frowned. "I don't know…I don't remember why he was so mad about the trip. And then when he caught her spying on us, I went home. I told him to calm down, I knew I could convince the little bitch not to say anything but I needed time." She took another drink and moaned. "I—don't feel so good."

"Maybe you should lie down." I looked at my phone. It was close to time to meet Kaye Hughes. "Let me help you."

I let her lean on me and I walked her into the living room, helping her to lie down. She was asleep—or unconscious— almost as soon as she hit the couch. I hurried down the hallway and out the front door.

As I hurried down the street to Kaye's office, I couldn't stop thinking.

Jesse was furious with her when he caught her spying on us…he was angry because they had to fly out to LA for an audition…he wanted me to meet him at our old place…he was my first love…we were going

*to get married...we weren't really cousins...Riley wasn't his father...
Robin was a whore, she was trying to get into Jesse's pants while Riley
was trying to get into hers...*

I didn't want to believe Jesse had killed both Delilah and
Arlene, but it was looking that way.

*Arlene and Riley killed Melanie, Melanie was his mother but
Riley wasn't his father.*

I climbed the steps to the front door of the brick office
building where Kaye had her office. I went down the hallway
and found the office door. I went inside. No one was sitting at
the front desk where the receptionist should be. The door to the
next office was open. "Hello?" I called.

"Scotty?" A woman appeared in the door. It was Kaye
Hughes. I recognized her from her ads, and again I marveled
at how different she looked from the old images I remembered
of Robin Strickland. I would have never guessed they were the
same person.

She looked terrific, if a little thin. She was about my height,
maybe shorter, with thick dark hair parted in the center and
combed back from her angular face in waves. Her breasts were
big—maybe a bit too big for her slender, boyish frame. She wore
a khaki knee-length skirt and an ivory silk blouse, and a navy blue
blazer was draped over her desk chair. "Please, come in and have
a seat." She smiled at me. I could see the remains of a salad in the
trash can beside her desk. She saw me looking and she turned a
bit red. "I didn't have time for lunch today, so I grabbed a quick
salad." She held out her hand. "I'm Kaye Hughes."

I shook her hand before sitting. "It's nice to meet you, Kaye."

She opened a file folder on her desk and put on a pair
of reading glasses. "Now, you've lived in an apartment on
Decatur Street now for about fifteen years or so, with your two
companions. Are you looking for a particular neighborhood?
Any particular style of house?" She looked over her glasses at
me. "Your parents live in the Quarter, but the rest of your family
is either Garden District or Uptown. Are you looking to get out
of the Quarter? Prices there are too high right now, I think." She

made a bit of a face. "I am a little worried—I'll be honest with you—that the prices in the city right now in every neighborhood are high. I'm worried there may be a bubble coming." She put the folder down. "This may not be the right time to buy, is what I'm saying."

"Wow. You've done your homework."

She smiled. "You don't get to be successful without preparing, Scotty. I know you know that." She leaned back in her chair. "I'm not interested in making money from selling you a house you don't want at a time when the market is inflated. I want to be your realtor for the rest of your life, someone you can trust, someone you will send your friends and family to when they need a realtor without worry."

"I appreciate that." I took a deep breath. "And when I'm ready to buy, you definitely are who I'll go through."

Her eyebrows went up.

"I know you used to be…well, your name used to be…"

"Robin Strickland." Her voice was icy. "Yes, I used to go by that name. When I married I took my husband's name. Robin was my middle name, but my grandmother's name was Katherine, like mine was, so I went by Robin. I decided to use Katherine after I married…and Kaye instead of Kathy. I wasn't trying to hide my identity." This last was said defensively, and her face colored as she spoke.

"I didn't—"

She stood up, and her voice got a bit shrill. "That was a very dark time. But I've never denied who I am. Never."

"I didn't—"

"I was young." She got up and walked over to a filing cabinet. "Very young. And stupid. It wasn't my idea to kill her, you know." She opened the top drawer and reached inside. She turned and smiled at me.

My mouth went dry. She was holding a revolver, pointed directly at my chest. "Kaye—"

"I'm done," she said softly. "I'm done with it all. First Jesse comes back. I've moved on, Scotty. I have. I've moved on with my life. The Metoyers, Delilah, that is all in the past. I don't need this anymore. And I'm not going to let it ruin my life, take it over, another time, am I clear?" Her voice was strangely calm, even though her eyes were glinting wildly. "Delilah knew, of course, she always knew everything. She was a monster, that child. She knew about me and Riley. She knew about me and Jesse. That night I went to a party, yes, and then I came back to the house early. I went up to Jesse's room to be with him, the way we'd planned. How was I supposed to know she was going to catch us? She'd already told Arlene about Riley and me, I knew she had. Riley said she hadn't, he'd talked her out of it, but Arlene *knew*." Her voice was rising. "You can't tell me she didn't know, and then the little brat catches us again? I didn't mean to kill her. She was going to scream, you know, she was going to scream and so I grabbed her and put my hand over her mouth and we took her out to the carriage house to keep her quiet, talk to her, but she bit my hand once we were out there and jumped out of my hands and I grabbed her and she fell and she hit her head and then she was dead and our lives were ruined."

I could feel sweat trickling down the back of my neck.

"And Jesse, he was smart, he knew if they thought he did it they'd never say anything to anyone, they'd try to protect him, so he told me to go back to the house and pretend to come home again, write the ransom note, which I did, and it all went according to plan...you see, I knew they wouldn't want the police around even if they didn't think it was Jesse. I knew about Melanie."

"You know about Melanie?"

She laughed. "They buried her beneath the floor of the carriage house when they killed her. Riley killed her in front of Arlene. That was why he married her, why he stayed married to her—all she had to do was bring the police in and have them dig up the floor in the carriage house, so he stayed married to her. Delilah's death was the best thing that ever happened to Riley because it freed him from Arlene. Arlene couldn't talk about the body in the carriage house if she was a suspect in her own child's murder."

"Please put the gun away."

"And of course, *of course* Jesse went away, him and Riley both, they let me go because they didn't need me anymore, but they paid me off, oh yes, they paid me quite well." She smiled, her eyes glassy. "And then Jesse comes back, and threatens *me*, threatens *me* that he'll tell if I don't cover for him with Arlene's death."

"Were you there?" My voice was hoarse.

"I didn't kill her. Jesse did. Jesse killed her because she killed his mother, all those years ago, Oh, I was there. Of course I was there. He called me to be his alibi." She waved the gun around. "Calls me up, tells me to meet him there, and there she was, dead, just where Delilah was, telling me I'm going to cover for him, be his alibi or else he's going to tell everyone just what happened the night Delilah died." Her eyes filled with tears. "I can't do this anymore."

"Give me the gun, Kaye," I said softly, my heart thumping so hard I could hear it in my ears. "You don't want to do this."

She held the gun to her temple, her eyes filled with tears. "I can't. I can't go through this again. I rebuilt my entire life. Do you know what it was like for me? Everyone looking at me, staring and whispering? Judging me?"

"Kaye, put the gun down." I made my voice firm and couldn't believe it wasn't shaking.

"What does Jesse know?" A tear ran down the side of her cheek. "He tells me he'll keep me out of it, that he won't tell that I was there, that it was his cousin who let him in."

"When did he tell you that?"

"He called me this morning, to make sure I didn't say anything, that I didn't do anything, promising me he'll keep me out of it, and then you called." The gun didn't shake, even though her voice was. I couldn't not look at it.

It was pointed at me.

"Like I don't know who you are?" She licked her lips. "I

hoped…I hoped you just wanted to buy a house, that you were just another client. But I know who you are, I know what you do. You came here because you knew, didn't you?"

"Kaye, Jesse told the police you weren't there." I was sweating. I could feel the sweat running down the backs of my legs, down my sides from my armpits. It was ice cold in her office but I was sweating. Why hadn't I let Colin and Frank come with me? "Put the gun down, Kaye, and no one ever has to know."

"You'll tell." Her voice cracked.

"I won't—"

She put the gun to her head and pulled the trigger.

EPILOGUE

Melanie Metoyer's remains were found underneath the carriage house floor.

The hubbub and the furor took a couple of months to die down—you can imagine the headlines, and how much television time was devoted to the latest installment—and yes, my name popped up a lot.

I learned to ignore it.

Jesse is still waiting for trial.

It took me a while to get past Kaye's shooting herself in front of me. I dreamed about it a lot, waking up in the middle of the night drenched and sweat and trembling. I'm dealing with it.

I survived Katrina. I'll survive this.

And turning forty a few weeks later didn't seem quite as bad as it had before, really. When you've had a gun pointed at you... yeah, turning forty wasn't a big deal at all. I have my health, I have Colin and Frank and my friends and my family.

Scooter is growing by leaps and bounds, and I can't imagine how we ever lived without a cat, to be honest.

Maybe I do spoil Taylor a little bit.

There are worse things.

As for the Goddess and my gift...well, the cards are talking to me again when I focus and spread them out on the table in the proper ways. It's like she never went away, you know?

I really am blessed.

About the Author

Greg Herren is a New Orleans–based author and editor. He is a co-founder of the Saints and Sinners Literary Festival, which takes place in New Orleans every May. He is the author of twenty novels, including the Lambda Literary Award–winning *Murder in the Rue Chartres*, called by the *New Orleans Times-Picayune* "the most honest depiction of life in post-Katrina New Orleans published thus far." He co-edited *Love, Bourbon Street: Reflections on New Orleans*, which also won the Lambda Literary Award. His young adult novel *Sleeping Angel* won the Moonbeam Gold Medal for Excellence in Young Adult Mystery/Horror.

He has published over fifty short stories in markets as varied as *Ellery Queen's Mystery Magazine* to the critically acclaimed anthology *New Orleans Noir* to various websites, literary magazines, and anthologies. His erotica anthology *FRATSEX* is the all-time best-selling title for Insightoutbooks. He has worked as an editor for Bella Books, Harrington Park Press, and now Bold Strokes Books.

A longtime resident of New Orleans, Greg was a fitness columnist and book reviewer for Window Media for over four years, publishing in the LGBT newspapers *IMPACT News*, *Southern Voice*, and *Houston Voice*. He served a term on the Board of Directors for the National Stonewall Democrats, and served on the founding committee of the Louisiana Stonewall Democrats. He is currently employed as a public health researcher for the NO/AIDS Task Force and is serving a term on the board of the Mystery Writers of America.

Greg can be contacted at gregwrites@gmail.com
Blog: http://scottynola.livejournal.com/